THE Lovely DARK

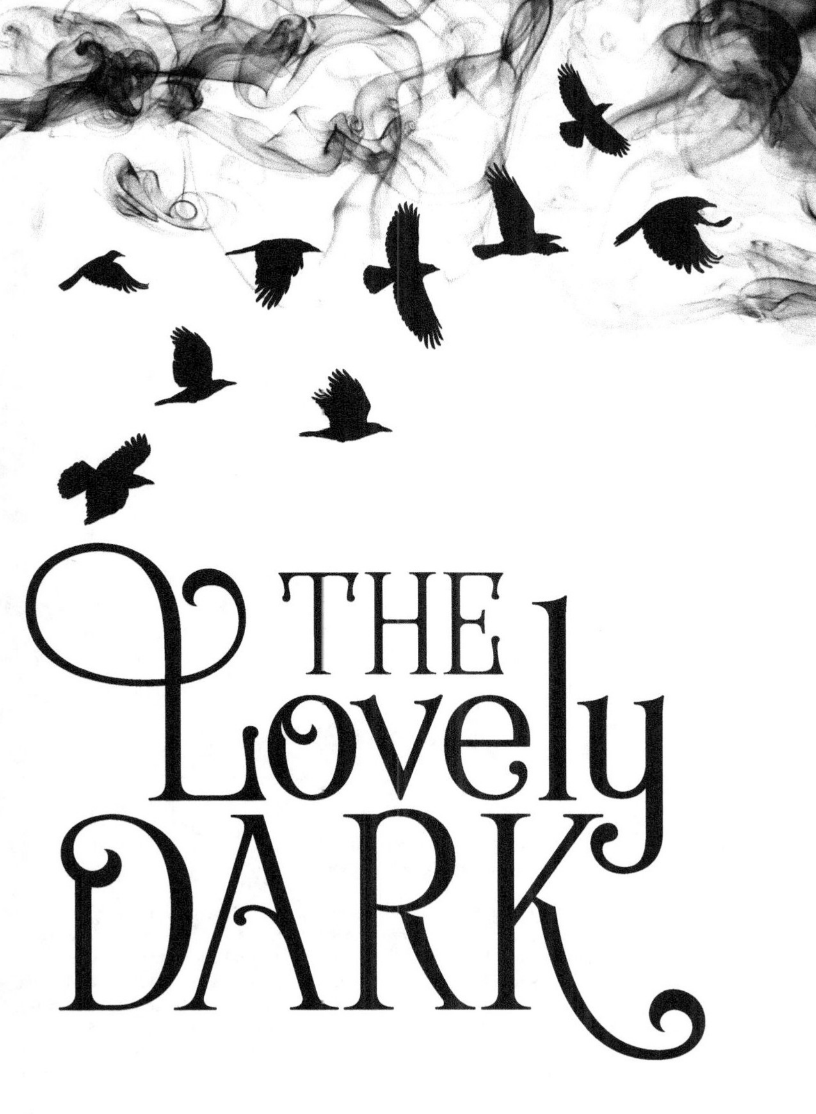

K. A. LAST

www.kalastbooks.com.au

For Selina. Without you, The Lovely Dark
would never have been imagined into existence.

And his eyes have all the seeming
of a demon's that is dreaming,
And the lamp-light o'er him streaming
throws his shadow on the floor;
And my soul from out that shadow
that lies floating on the floor
Shall be lifted — nevermore!

Edgar Allan Poe – *The Raven*

C amping. Not exactly my idea of fun. Fun for me usually includes my bedroom and Netflix until the early hours of the morning. I don't even have phone reception out here in the bush, which is pure torture, because all there is to listen to is the hum of annoying conversation about who's seeing who, and who wants to see who, and who's apparently doing who.

I focus on the sound of the chattering lorikeets and try not to listen to everyone else, because I'm not seeing or doing anyone. My best friend, Jack Marshall, would like to do someone, but he has no chance with ninety-nine percent of the girls in our year. The other one percent is my other best friend, Toni Garcia. But she doesn't count as a girl.

She's just Toni.

And right now, she's staring at us, shaking her head.

"You know you both fail miserably at being boys, don't you?" she says. "Look at this mess." She points to the pile of canvas at our feet.

"Giving *us* a tent and expecting us to know how to put it up is like expecting a fish to know how to ride a bike," I say. Then I laugh, because I'm thinking about fish riding bikes.

"It's not funny, Harvey," Toni says. "You have to have somewhere to sleep tonight."

I resist the urge to roll my eyes. Toni worries too much. We'll be fine. Half the time I enjoy stuffing things up just so I can see her reaction. In this case though, Jack and I really have no idea how to put up a tent. Unlike Toni, neither of us has been subjected to family camping trips. Especially me. My dad would never survive without his TV.

Toni pulls the tent from the corners and straightens it out. I watch with interest, rubbing my hands together to warm them in the crisp autumn air. I glance around the campground at the other students fussing about, erecting their tents. The teachers have arranged us so we're in two semi-circles around a central campfire with boys on one side, girls on the other. Most of the tents are up, but one or two are in as big a mess as ours, and I don't feel so bad. I look at the row of faculty accommodation and shake my head at how much nicer their tents are than ours.

"There." Toni puts her hands on her hips. "That pole goes there and that one there." She points to two small holes in the canvas. "Stand them up to make a pitch, then use the ropes to steady them and hold them in place."

"Shouldn't you be over there?" I point to the campfire

where those who have finished putting up their tents are gathered. "You know, with the other freaks of nature who enjoy this kind of stuff." I smirk.

Toni sticks her tongue out at me. "I'm done here. You're on your own now."

I shake my head as she struts across the campground, back to the girls' section.

"She thinks she knows everything," Jack says.

"She probably knows more than us." I pick up the canvas and step into the tent, dragging a pole behind me. "Come on. Let's try this again."

We manage to get our tent up, although it's a little lopsided. I don't care too much, as long as it doesn't fall on our heads in the middle of the night.

"You've done a better job than some of the others," a girl says from behind me. I spin around to see Lian Lin smiling at us. "Hi, Harvey." She leans her head to one side.

I freeze for a moment, holding the last rope with one hand and a tent peg with the other, wondering when the universe exploded without my noticing. Lian is one of the most popular girls in school. The kind who usually pretend people like Jack and I don't exist. The kind who make me nervous when they speak to us, because some catastrophic event is sure to follow.

"Hey," I say. *Act cool. Don't be an idiot.*

Jack trips over his own feet, and I almost have to shove his tongue back into his mouth. Way to go for us not looking stupid.

Lian doesn't stop smiling.

"Violette and I had to get help," Lian says. "We've never put a tent up before."

Jack chuckles. "Harvey and me, we're experts. Piece of cake."

I raise my eyebrows and shake my head. We are not experts at anything, unless you count reciting episodes of *Arrow*, or anything on Netflix from the Marvel and DC Comics universes, word for word. Somehow, I don't think our claim to nerd fame qualifies.

"Apparently, it won't be so lopsided if you get the ropes in the right spot," Lian says.

I stare at her, wondering how long it will be before she goes away. Maybe the universe is exploding slowly, and the fallout hasn't hit us yet.

Jack fusses around with our pile of stuff, adjusting our clothing bags so they're neat and will get the least amount of grass on them. He picks up his sleeping bag. Lian reaches for my hand, and her fingers brush mine. I let her take the rope, shoving my hands into my armpits to stop my fingers shaking. I glance around to see if anyone is watching us before staring at my shoes.

Dad insisted on buying me new hiking boots especially for this trip, even though I've never hiked anywhere before in my life, and now was not the time I wanted to start. I'd told him my sneakers would do, but he wouldn't have it. Apparently, I couldn't go on school camp unprepared for the rugged Australian bush conditions. He also wouldn't listen when I'd told him camp involved a clearing in the national park with full shower and toilet facilities. We aren't exactly roughing it, although it's close enough, with no phone reception.

I glance up and Lian loops the rope over the peg then bends down to push it into the ground. Her jeans tighten

around her arse, and Jack drops the sleeping bag he's unpacking. It spills out into a red puffy mass and he scrambles to pick it up off the grass. He hugs the bag to his chest and fumbles to push his glasses up his nose.

Lian stands up, smiling. "There." She twangs the rope. "Don't blame me if it falls over though."

"Hey, Lian," Gregory Watson calls from the tent next to us.

He steps over a rope and saunters towards us. I'm still waiting for the universe to do something, like kill me with a falling tree branch. I glance at the ground, willing it to open so I can jump right in.

Jack fumbles his mass of puffy sleeping bag into our tent and doesn't re-emerge. I imagine him sitting in there, wringing his hands. Mine are sweaty now and I pull them from my armpits. The air makes them cold so I pull my jumper sleeves down over my fingers.

Neither of us like Greg. Or rather, he doesn't like us.

"Hey, Greg," Lian says. I wonder if smiling so much is hurting her cheeks.

"What are you doing talking to these losers?" Greg asks.

I want to protest, and I actually open my mouth, but then I think better of it. There's no point wasting my breath. Greg is the kind of guy who hears what he wants to hear.

"Don't be mean, Greg," Lian says. "They looked like they could use a hand."

"I could use your hands." Greg raises his eyebrows and smirks.

I cringe and his expression changes. Maybe I should stop thinking with my face. I need to say something so these people will go away and leave us alone, but I forget how to speak English for a second, and my tongue feels heavy in my mouth.

"We're all good," I manage to say, but it's barely a whisper.

"What's that?" Greg takes a step towards me.

I don't want him to think I'm scared even though I'll probably have to change my underwear when he finally goes away, so I don't move. "We're … good," I say again, a bit louder this time.

Lian flicks her hair and looks at Greg. "I'd love a bottle of water."

He drags his gaze from me and stares at her. His mouth widens into a toothy smile. "Sure. I can get you one."

"Great. I'll meet you over at the campfire."

Greg gives me one final look before leaving, and I let out a breath. My chest is tight, and I rub my sternum to push the feeling away.

"You should go with your boyfriend," I say to Lian.

"He wishes," she says. "He's not my boyfriend."

I stare at her and my chest is still tight, but it's not from fear anymore. She tips her head to the side again, and I study her eyes. Deep brown, almost as dark as her black hair. I've never really looked at her this close before. I've never actually stood within touching distance of her before.

"How do you not have a boyfriend?" I ask, instantly regretting it.

"Who says I don't?"

"Is the coast clear?" Jack sticks his head out of the tent.

Lian giggles. "Greg is gone, if that's what you mean. You know, you shouldn't let him get to you so much."

"Yeah, well …" Jack comes out to join us. His shoulder

catches on the opening of the tent and he stumbles towards Lian but misses her. She giggles as he turns bright red.

"All right, listen up everyone," Mr Woodfield calls from the campfire. He's standing beside the camp instructor, Mr Kemp. "It's time to have some fun. Grab your backpacks and gather around."

A universal groan ripples through the forty or so students scattered throughout the campground.

"Talk to you later," Lian says. Her hair flicks around her shoulders as she turns to walk towards our gym teacher. Jack and I put our stuff into the tent, grab our backpacks and follow. The students stand loosely around Mr Woodfield, waiting to hear what he says.

"Those of you who haven't quite finished setting up can do so this afternoon." He glances around. "The first activity we're going to do is a bit of orienteering."

More groans.

"Settle down." Our geography teacher, Mrs Bryson, joins Mr Woodfield and Mr Kemp beside the campfire. "If you let yourselves, you might enjoy the week. But firstly, this exercise will take most of the day. There's a reason we had you up nice and early to get here this morning."

Mr Woodfield rocks back and forth on his heels, a clipboard in his hands. "We'll start by dividing you all into teams of four."

Everyone starts talking at once, and students move around to find the people they want to buddy with. Jack and I don't move but I search the faces for Toni. I don't want a fourth member. The three of us work together just fine. She spots us and comes over.

A whistle blares. "Stop!" Mrs Bryson yells. "These people go and stand together as I call your names."

More groans.

It seems today is the day for groaning.

Mrs Bryson calls out names, and one by one, those students move away from the pack. To my horror, Jack is put with Lian's friends, Violette Monroe, Madison O'Conner, and Noah Ward. Jack looks rather pale so I think he's in more shock than I am. When my name is called, I hold my breath. I ask the universe to be kind because, you know, it's totally had my back today already.

"Antonia Garcia." Toni's name is called next.

"Awesome, we're together," I say. "That's great. Maybe not so great we're not with Jack, but still great." Toni grimaces and I frown. "What's wrong?"

"Didn't you hear who we're with?" She stares at me.

"Um … I heard your name … I guess I wasn't listening to the rest."

Toni sighs. She grabs my arm and pulls me towards the other side of the campfire. Greg and Lian are walking towards us.

And the ground still has no cracks in it.

"This should be fun." Greg rubs his hands together and smiles at me.

It's times like this I wish I was taller. At least then I'd have something on him.

"Your definition of fun must be very different to mine." Toni folds her arms over her chest.

"I think it will be great," Lian says.

"Yeah … great," I say.

We're instructed to line up at a table near the teachers'

tents, and each group is given a map, a compass, a two-way radio, a small first aid kit, food and water, with instructions for us to decide who will carry what.

"The purpose of today is to work together as a team to achieve a common goal," Mr Woodfield says.

A murmur rolls through everyone.

"Quiet, please." Mrs Bryson waits for the voices to stop. "There are eight points on your map. Five of these points have flags, but to make it more fun, we're not going to tell you which ones they are. If you find a point without a flag, that's just bad luck." She pauses and smiles. "The team to collect the most flags and be back here by two o'clock will win. That gives you roughly four hours. But make sure you give yourselves enough time to get back, even if you haven't found all your flags."

"What do we win?" someone yells.

Mr Woodfield laughs. "The respect of your peers ... and maybe cake."

"Respect would be nice," I mumble.

Toni nudges my arm. "Cake would be better."

"You have a map and a compass to guide you," Mr Woodfield says. "You're to stay within a two-kilometre radius of camp. Mrs Bryson and I, along with camp instructor Mr Kemp, will be moving around to keep an eye on you. *If* you find yourselves in trouble, use your two-way radio, or your whistle to attract attention. We will also allow those of you who have phones to take them with you, although they probably won't work. Still, you might be lucky and get SOS reception."

"Your radios are not toys," Mrs Bryson adds. "They are all set to channel eighteen. Please do not use them to mess around. You have them to keep you safe, which means you need to keep the line open in case someone needs help. Don't clog it up with unnecessary chatter." Mrs Bryson stares at us, her gaze flicking around the students.

"All right, year eleven, let's go." Mr Woodfield blows his whistle, and everyone breaks into conversation.

I stare at the ground, wishing I was home in my room watching Netflix. Stupid me had forgotten to download anything before I left, which meant after today there'd be four TV-free days ahead of me. I'd have to settle for watching repeats of whatever was still on my phone.

"I'm going to start walking with Jack," Toni says, moving away from us and towards Jack's group.

"Suits me." Lian follows and falls into step beside Violette.

"Shouldn't we have a discussion and maybe a plan?" I ask, but Greg is the only one who hears.

"You need to get a life." He follows the girls.

"Harvey, come on." Toni looks back at me.

I adjust my backpack strap on my shoulder and catch up with them. Lian has the map out and is turning it around and around. I run a hand down my face and a sense of doom settles in my stomach. Toni glances over Lian's shoulder and then at the compass in her hand.

"How did the girls end up with all the good stuff?" Greg asks.

"This is going to suck," Jack says.

"You got that right." I laugh.

"Come on, Jack," Violette says. "We're going this way." She points into the bush. I don't see a path, and I hope we're not going to follow them.

"Good luck." I raise my eyebrows at Jack.

He shrugs but doesn't say anything, then follows Violette.

Lian and Toni stop.

"You need to have the map up the right way," Toni says.

"Are you calling me stupid?" Lian grips the edges of the paper.

"No one's calling anyone stupid," I say. I smile because Lian does have the map upside down. "See this here?" I point to a corner of the map. "You need to have the N facing the top. That's north."

"Oh," she says.

Toni clears her throat. "I think we should try and find point two. It looks like the closest one."

"I think we should aim for the farthest point then work our way back," Lian says.

I want to agree with Toni because she's my best friend, but Lian's idea makes sense.

"Can we get going?" Greg asks. "We're the only ones still here."

I glance around at the empty camp. All the other groups have moved off in various directions. I bite my lip, knowing what I'm about to say isn't going to go down too well with Toni.

"I vote for Lian's plan," I say.

"What?" Toni puts her hands on her hips. Her mouth opens and closes. She's too nice to say anything really mean while Lian can hear, but I know she doesn't like her. I'm not even sure if *I* like her, even though she's given me no reason not to.

Lian looks at the map. "Point eight is north-east." She turns on the spot. "This way."

"That's the wrong direction," Toni says.

Lian frowns. "Which way then?"

Toni holds the compass so we can all see. Lian nods then marches off, the map in front of her. Toni glares at me. I sigh and follow Lian. Toni will get over it. All I want is to get this done, and the only way to do that is to start somewhere.

We make our way through the bush. Now and then, I hear the voices of other students. We've picked a route that should lead us straight to point eight, but it doesn't cross paths with any of the other points. I begin to wonder if this plan was the best one, or if we're wasting time. What if the farthest point has no flag?

"Odds are they'd put a flag at the point that takes the longest to get to," Toni says.

"Are you a mind reader?" I ask. "Because I just thought about how possible it would be that it didn't."

"Have a flag?"

I turn to look at her. "No, a hippopotamus. Yes, a flag."

"You're acting really weird today." Toni studies the compass, and I wonder how she hasn't fallen over.

I stumble on a rock and mumble a swear word. "Weirder than I usually am? That's … weird."

Toni stops, and I almost bump into her. She looks at the compass and frowns. "The needle keeps jumping around." She glances up and scans the trees around us.

"Can you hear that?" Lian asks.

Greg moves away from us a bit, crunching sticks and leaves. "I can't hear anything."

"Stand still, you big oaf." Toni glares at him.

"Don't tell me what to do, nerd girl."

"Is that the best you've got?"

"What are we supposed to be listening to?" I ask.

The four of us stand here, silent, with our heads cocked to the side. If someone came across us we'd probably look pretty funny.

A low howl sounds through the trees. Goosebumps rise on my arms.

"What was that?" Lian turns towards the noise.

Before anyone can answer, a crow caws and takes flight, its feathers rustling.

"Crows," Greg says. "Don't be scared."

"I'm not." Lian clutches the map to her chest

I am. "Since when do crows howl?"

2

Leaves rustle behind us and I turn, my heart thumping. A few more crows take flight, and Lian jumps. Another crow caws, the flap of its wings making a horrible crackling noise, and lands on a branch above us. It stares at us with beady eyes.

"This is way too freaky," I say. "Where are the rest of the birds? You know, the pretty ones?"

Toni holds the compass in front of her. "Harvey's right. We should be able to hear the lorikeets. They're usually everywhere."

"I like lorikeets better," I say. "Crows are creepy."

Lian stares at the map, her hands shaking slightly.

Greg points into the bush. "Let's go this way. Walk in a straight line."

"You can never walk in a straight line," Toni says. "It's pretty much impossible unless you're following a path

or coordinates."

"What does the compass say?" I ask.

Toni frowns and looks at the device in her hand. "This way … I think." She leads, clambering over some sandstone rocks, and we all follow.

We walk for about ten minutes. The silence of the bush makes me nervous, and I try to listen for more familiar sounds. All I can hear are the usual leaves rustling in the breeze, and some more crows cawing. The eeriness is unsettling.

Toni is up front, picking her way through the trees. Lian is next, followed by Greg, then me. None of us talk as we move, and I fall into the rhythm of our feet crunching on the ground. We emerge onto a wider trail and follow it to a small cleared area. There's a wooden pole in the centre, coloured red on the top half. Attached to the pole with some twine is a plastic sleeve. Lian tucks the map under her arm and goes to the pole, grabbing the sleeve to read the piece of paper that's been slipped inside.

"Bad luck, keep looking," she says. "No flags here."

"So much for the farthest point should have a flag," Greg says.

"Why is one of the teachers not here?" Toni says. "You'd think this would be the point they'd watch the most." She glances around the surrounding area.

I shrug. "Three teachers. Eight points. Maybe they haven't walked out this far yet."

"Which way now?" Greg asks with a huff.

"Can I have the map?" Toni holds a hand out to Lian, who passes it over with a frown. Toni opens the map and lays it on the ground, placing the compass on it to hold it down. She crouches in front of the map. "If we're here …" she points to flagpole eight, "… then I think we should double back and try to find point five. It's not far off the path we took to get here."

Lian grabs the compass, gives it a gentle shake, then stares at the map. "Maybe we should go to point three. It looks closer distance-wise."

"Who cares?" Greg says. "Let's walk." He adjusts the straps of his backpack.

I take my pack off and sit on the ground, unzipping the front pocket to get my water bottle. "While you all decide, I'm taking a break."

"I'm cool with that." Greg plonks down next to me.

I stop with my water bottle halfway to my lips, eyeing him carefully, and waiting to see what will come out of his mouth next. He's usually mean to me every chance he gets.

"What?" Greg stares at me.

I shake my head. "Nothing." Taking a swig of water, I marvel at how strange everything is today. Never in my life did I think I would be spending time with the popular people. At least with my small group of friends I know exactly what to expect. With Greg and Lian, anything could happen.

"I don't agree with you," Toni says, standing from her crouched position.

"Aren't we supposed to be working as a team?" Lian puts her hands on her hips.

"My way is better."

"What's so great about your way?"

"Yours isn't as logical," Toni says.

"So you're saying I'm wrong?" Lian mimics Toni's stance.

"If you want to put the words in my mouth."

I sigh and run a hand through my hair. "Give me the map, please."

The girls look at me, scowls fixed on both of their faces. Still, I think Lian is pretty. When neither of them moves, I hold my hand out and gesture for them to pass me the map. Toni grits her teeth, grabs it from the ground, and brings it to me. I lay it out and stare at it, pretending I know what the hell I'm doing when really, I have no clue. I want to go back to camp, because I figure being at camp where I can hide inside my tent is the better of the two sucky options I have right now.

"I think Toni's idea to double back is good," I finally say.

"Ha." She folds her arms and smirks.

"But ... I think we should do what Lian says. Point three looks closer."

Lian smiles at Toni and raises her eyebrows. "Great choice."

"But you have to give the compass back to Toni." I look up from the map.

"Right, let's go." Greg jumps to his feet. "I don't care which way."

Toni holds her hand out for the compass. Lian gives it to her, but her mouth is pinched, and she frowns again. I fold the map and get to my feet, shouldering my backpack with a sigh.

"Lead the way." I look at Toni. "Point three is south -south-west."

She shakes the compass a few times, then heads back into the bush.

We walk, not talking much. Toni mumbles to herself

on and off and I tune out, concentrating on my steps. I'm not having fun. I'm not sure the others are either.

"Harvey?" Lian says.

"Huh?" I look up and she's beside me, her eyebrows raised.

"Do you go camping much?"

Oh. She's doing the small talk thing. Why do people have to do that? Next, she'll be commenting on the weather.

"He doesn't look the camping type," Greg says. "Do those boots go out much?"

"I don't camp," I say.

"What do you like to do?" Lian tucks her hair behind her ear.

I'm not sure what to do with my hands, so I slip my thumbs into the straps of my backpack and stare at my feet as they crunch on the ground.

"Why do you care?" I say, regretting it immediately.

"Yeah, Lian. Why *do* you care?" Greg says.

Toni stops, and I bump into her. She drops the compass and the glass cracks.

"Crap, Harvey." Toni picks it up and inspects it.

"Does it still work?" Lian asks.

"The needle is jumping all over the place again. We should have reached the next point by now." Toni glances around.

We're surrounded by bush and clumps of sandstone rock. The trees are thin enough for the autumn sun to shine through, and I'm glad we're not doing this in the middle of summer. There's an outcrop to our left that's high enough for a decent view. I walk to the closest crevice and clamber up to see if I can get an idea of where we are.

My feet slip on the rock, and I send little stones clattering towards the ground. When I look over my shoulder, the other three are peering up at me. I keep going until I reach the top. The sun is warm on my face and I realise for the first time how much cooler it is down in the bush. Spread out below me are trees, and more trees. There's a small clearing off to the left, and I wonder if that's where flag pole eight is and if we've been going around in circles. But it could also be the flag we're looking for.

"We should head that way." I point as I call down to the others.

"I don't think that's right." Toni stares up at me.

I shade my eyes with my hands and look out across the national park. I'm amazed that I can't see anyone else out there. The area on the map that we were told to stay in isn't any bigger than a couple of kilometres across. Maybe we've wandered outside the designated zone.

"I can see a clearing," I say. "I think we should head for that."

"Sounds good to me," Greg says.

I make my way back down the rock to the ground, taking my jumper off and stuffing it into my backpack.

Lian studies the map. "Which way did you say?"

I should have taken the compass to the top of the rock with me. I start walking anyway, with confidence I don't feel. Everything looks different on the ground. "This way, I think."

We keep moving, and Lian falls into step beside me. I watch her from the corner of my eye. She stares at our feet, her teeth pinching her bottom lip, her mouth moving

occasionally as if she's about to say something then doesn't. I'm unsure why she's trying to talk to me so much, or why she's being nice to me in the first place. It's never happened before. As a general rule, I don't get much attention from girls, and I don't mind.

Greg walks on the other side of me, every now and then having to move forward or drop back because we can't fit three across through the trees. Toni walks with her eyes fixed on the compass.

"What's our heading?" I ask, if only to break the silence.

Toni stops and throws her hands in the air, shaking the compass. "I don't know. The needle won't stay still. It was fine a minute ago, and now it's going crazy."

We crowd around and stare at the vibrating needle through the cracked glass. The little piece of metal bounces all over the place and won't settle.

"Stuff this." Greg walks away a few steps.

I take the compass from Toni and shake it.

"I've tried that," she says.

"Maybe we did break it." Lian stands close enough for her hair to tickle my arm.

"No." Toni shakes her head. "It was all stupid before we dropped it."

"Hey guys, over here." Greg stomps back into view. "I think I found the clearing you were talking about, Harvey."

We go to where Greg stands, climbing over some rocks to get there. There's a clearing below. Toni slips down the other side, falling hard on her arse. Lian picks her way down more carefully and goes to help Toni up.

"You okay?" she asks, holding out her hand.

"I'm fine." Toni stands on her own then brushes the

dirt and leaves from the back of her jeans. "But thanks."

Toni may not have taken Lian's hand, but it's the first time I've seen them smile at each other all day, if ever. They make their way down onto the grass.

"There's something weird about this place," I say to Greg. "It doesn't feel right."

"There's no flag here." Greg shades his eyes and stares down at the girls. "Where do you think we are on the map?"

I ignore his question and watch Lian and Toni, who are now in the clearing. The more I look around, the more uneasy I feel. The grass is unusually green for the bush, and several large rocks are scattered all over the place. There's something about them I don't like but I can't pinpoint exactly what it is.

"Do those rocks look weird to you?" I ask.

Greg shrugs. "They look like rocks."

He makes his way down towards the girls. I study Toni for a moment. She stands on the grass, her head tilted back and her thumbs looped through the straps of her backpack. She turns, taking in the clearing and the taller trees. Her chin lowers, and she looks at the rocks. I smile, because there's something I like about the moment. She seems content, but when she's turned enough for me to see her face my smile falls away. I can tell Toni feels as worried as I do.

I look again and draw a line between the rocks with my mind. There are five bigger ones and a whole bunch of smaller ones making a circle around the central part of the clearing, then one large rock in the middle. The smaller rocks are scattered, with a couple between two of the larger rocks, and then five or six between another two. In places the ground is lumpy as if to suggest there might be rocks underneath, but I can't tell from where I'm standing.

I take my backpack off and pull out a notebook and pen, drawing roughly where the rocks I can see are. I'm not sure why I want to make a note of them, but it seems important. Maybe I can figure out something about them later, because they definitely haven't been put there by nature.

I put my notebook and pen away, then walk down to the grass where Greg is looking at the map with Lian.

Toni wanders over. "Any idea where we are on the map?"

"This place is weird," I say. "It feels … weird."

Toni blinks a few times. "You've already said that."

"Well …" I shrug.

"It feels weird because it's a stone circle," Toni says with surety.

"As in magic … and stuff?" I've watched enough TV to know what a stone circle is.

"Yeah, and I don't think we should hang around for too long." She points to the compass in my hand. "That thing working yet?"

I shake my head, then I shake the compass again for good measure before putting it into my back pocket.

Lian spreads the map out on the ground and kneels on the grass, hunkering over the paper. "If point eight is here …" Lian points to the map, "… then we can't have gone too far in the wrong direction, if we even went in the wrong direction. See this little patch here?" She looks up and our gazes connect. "I think this is where we are."

I unshoulder my backpack and dump it on the ground, then go and kneel beside Lian. All I want to do is get

back to camp, but we can't do that unless we figure out exactly where we are.

Greg doesn't seem that interested in reading the map. He seems more interested in staring at Lian. Maybe he's bored, but I study the piece of paper because I want out of here.

"I think … you could be right," I say after a few minutes.

Lian smiles. "Then we should head back this way." She runs her finger along a contour line.

"That's a good theory," Toni says. "And I agree, we should go that way. But which way is it? The compass doesn't work properly."

"What about our phones?" I go to where I dumped my backpack and pull mine from the front pocket. "No service."

"Me either." Lian gets up, holds her phone out and turns around, as if that will help.

"I don't think any of us will have service out here," Toni says. "Most of us don't have any back at camp."

"So much for SOS only," I say, remembering that I got annoyed when we'd first gotten to camp and my phone didn't work. I feel like a bit of an idiot for suggesting we try them now.

Lian is still holding her phone in the air. "My compass app is going crazy, too."

"So we're stuffed." Greg plonks onto the grass and unzips his backpack. "I'm gonna eat. Seems as good a time as any."

The girls take their packs off and we all sit on the grass. We nibble on some crackers and have a piece of fruit each, agreeing to save our sandwiches for later. I take a few big swigs of water, and Toni warns me not to drink it too fast. I get the feeling she's more worried than she's letting on.

"I'm gonna look around," Toni says, placing her rubbish back into her bag. She wanders over to the larger rock in the centre of the clearing.

Lian has her head tilted to the side. I like the way she looks when she's thinking. I've never spent so much time with her before, or any girl other than Toni, and I feel strange around her. She seems nice, but I can't help wondering if it's an act or genuine. Maybe she has some ulterior motive that involves me and a very embarrassing situation.

"Maybe we should go check them out as well," Lian says.

Before I can agree, the ground tremors, and Toni screams. I jump to my feet and scan the clearing, but I can't see her anywhere.

"Toni?" I yell. "Where are you?"

"Harvey?"

Greg and Lian are on their feet, too, and the three of us fan out across the grass. Greg makes his way over to the trees on the left while Lian goes right. I still can't see my best friend. "Toni, say something. I can't see you."

"I'm over here," she says.

"That's not very helpful."

She screams again, and I run towards the large rock in the centre of the clearing.

"Don't fall in," Toni yells.

"Fall in what?" I ask, my feet pounding the ground.

"Harvey, stop." Lian stands on the top of one of the smaller rocks. "There's a big hole in the ground."

My feet skid on the grass. "What? Where?"

Lian points. The centre rock is not as high as it was, and it's tilted differently than before. Some smaller pieces have broken away and rolled across the grass. As I edge closer, the hole comes into view.

Lian jumps down from her perch and jogs over.

Greg comes closer from the other side. "Lian, move back. You don't want to fall in as well."

"I'll be fine." She makes her way towards me, moving closer to the edge of the large hole with every step. There's a crack in the ground that has zig-zagged from the base of the rocks, then opened up into a gaping wound in the earth.

"Harvey, where are you?" Toni asks.

"I can't see you." I move closer to the edge.

"Come around towards me," Lian says, dropping to her knees. "She's hanging onto the side."

"You can see her?"

Greg is beside me. "Get down and we'll crawl to the edge."

I look at him and raise my eyebrows. "What?"

"Less chance of us slipping."

"Oh. That makes sense."

"Hurry up." Toni says. "Get me out of here."

Greg and I get onto our hands and knees and move slowly towards the edge of the hole. I peer over and Toni is hanging onto the jagged dirt, her knuckles white. She's clinging to the side of the hole.

"Hey, you okay?" I smile. She's not okay. There's a massive drop below her and I don't want to freak her out.

"I'm … fine." Toni grits her teeth.

"Are you standing on anything?"

"Nope, just digging my toes in."

I stretch my arm into the hole. "Can you grab my hand?"

Toni glances down and adjusts her feet. I want to tell her not to look, but that would be a stupid thing to say to someone who's dangling over a two-storey drop. The side of the hole is sloped in her favour, making it easier for her to gain footing. If she does fall, hopefully she'll slide down rather than plummet to her death.

Stop thinking like an idiot.

Toni reaches up and our fingertips touch.

Lian crawls closer to the edge opposite us. "Almost. Just a bit farther."

Toni grunts. "I thought you had longer arms, Harvey."

Our fingers brush again. My arm aches.

"Let me try." Greg reaches down, grimacing.

Lian screams. A flash of colour goes past.

Rocks skittle into the hole, pounding the earth below. "Shit," Greg says.

Lian has fallen in.

3

A puff of air leaves my lungs, and my heart stops for a second when Lian hits the ground below, her body sprawled in the dirt.

"Lian?" Greg yells into the hole.

She doesn't respond.

Toni's fingertips lock onto mine, and I focus my attention on her. "Forget Lian for now. Help me with Toni first."

"What? No. Man, she just fell in."

"Shut up, you big oaf," Toni says. "If you don't help Harvey, I'm going to fall in, too." A tear rolls down Toni's cheek. It's the first time in a long time that I can remember seeing her cry.

"I've got you," I say, but sweat slicks my hands and our fingers slip.

Toni screams. Her feet scramble against the dirt wall.

Greg thrusts his arm down to try and grab Toni's

hand, but it's too late.

She screams again and slides down the rough dirt wall, landing on the ground below with a thud.

"Toni? Are you okay?" I call.

Quiet sobs echo around the cave below us. Greg looks at me, and I stare at him wide-eyed.

"Toni?" I say again. "Please tell me you're alive."

"You're a jerk, Harvey," she says.

"Why?" I get up on my knees and look down at her.

"You didn't grab my hand." Toni tries to get to her feet then cries out and falls over. "I think I've broken my foot. It hurts."

"What about Lian?" Greg says. "Is she okay?"

"Does anything else hurt? Are you bleeding?" I wish it were me down there and not her.

"What about Lian?" Greg yells.

"Would you shut up?" I glare at him. "One thing at a time."

"I'm cut up pretty bad, mainly my palms from trying to grab the wall, but nothing life-threatening," Toni says. "Lian is … I don't think she's awake."

"Can you crawl to her?" I ask.

"She's a few metres away, but I'll try." Toni rolls onto her hands and knees, holding her left leg in the air so her foot doesn't touch the ground. "Man, this hurts."

"What hurts?" I ask.

"My hands … they're bleeding, and I'm getting dirt in the cuts." She shuffles along the ground, and then she screams.

"Toni?" My chest tightens and I go cold.

"I'm fine."

"Why did you scream?"

"My foot, I bumped it … You wanted me to get to Lian. That's what I'm doing."

Greg leans forward. "Is she—?"

"She's breathing," Toni says. "I think she's bumped her head though."

I sit back on my haunches and think about what we should do next. I'm not cut out for this sort of thing. I hate camping, and bushwalking, and everything outdoorsy. If I'd had my way, I never would have been here in the first place.

I rub my face. "We have to get them out."

"Really? Because I thought we were going to leave them here." Greg stands and walks back towards where we came into the clearing. "There's rope in my backpack. Maybe we could tie it to a tree and drop it down to them."

I watch as he makes his way to where our packs are sitting on the grass. Greg loops his arm through all of them and lugs them back to where I am at the edge of the hole. He unzips his backpack and pulls out a coil of rope. It isn't very thick, and I don't think it would hold much weight.

"Maybe there's something else in here we can use," I say, and then I remember the whistle and two-way radio.

I scramble to find the radio in the packs, not remembering which one of us was carrying it. I open them all and dump everything onto the ground.

"We need to use this," I say, grabbing the radio from the pile. "Someone will come and help us."

Greg takes the radio from me and turns it over in his hands. He twists the knob on the top near the aerial and

static bursts from the speaker.

"How does it work?" I stare at it. I've never used one before.

Greg pushes a button on the side and the static goes away. He raises it to his mouth and talks. "Hello, anyone there?" He releases the button and waits, but we hear nothing other than white noise.

"Try again," I say.

Greg presses the button and talks into the radio. "Hello, anyone there? We need help."

When he releases the button, static blares out of the speaker. It scratches the silence and the noise makes the hair on my arms rise. A wail comes through the radio and Greg almost drops the handset. Fear claws at my chest, and Greg stares at me with wide eyes.

"That sounded … freaky," I say.

Greg's finger rests on the button of the radio. "Again? Someone has to hear us eventually." His voice shakes.

"Hopefully …" I lick my lips, scared because my best friend has fallen into a giant hole, and of whatever it was that wailed through the static.

Greg walks until he's standing in the open away from the rocks and the hole. He tries again to talk to someone, but I can't hear any answer, just the horrible screeching static. While he keeps trying, I unravel the rope to see how long it is. There's no hope of it reaching the closest tree. I consider tying it around one of the big rocks, but I can't be sure it won't move, or the ground won't fall away again.

A moan rises from the hole.

"Harvey, what are you doing? There's something down

here," Toni calls out. "I want to get out."

"I'm working on it," I say.

The moan intensifies, and a wind whips around the clearing, stirring up leaves and blowing them across the grass. Greg stares at me and moves his lips as if to yell out. A crow caws. He stops and stares into the bush before locking his gaze back on me. The moan drifts on the wind, turning into a howl before dissipating into the trees.

Greg comes back to where I'm standing beside the hole. His hands are shaking. He must be as scared as I am, but I don't say anything.

"It's not working." Greg throws the radio onto the pile of stuff from our packs. "I've tried ten times and no one's responding. Is the compass still broken?"

I grab it from my back pocket. "The needle's jumping all over the place like before."

"Harvey?" Toni's voice comes up from the cave. "Lian is awake, but she's groggy. We need to get her out of here. Her head is bleeding."

"And you've got a busted foot," I say. "I'm working on it, Toni."

"Any ideas?" Greg looks at the rope in my hand.

"One of us has to go down to get them out."

Greg is tall, and muscly, and athletic. I'm skinny, and very weed-like. He would be a lot stronger than me, and heavier, so there'd be no way I could lower him down without being pulled in myself. He'd be able to lower me into the hole, but I probably wouldn't be able to hold Lian or Toni's weight to get them out. They'd have to be well enough to use the rope to get themselves to safety.

And then there's the problem of me being afraid of the

dark. I'd much prefer not to have to go into the hole, but my best friend is down there. *What am I supposed to do?*

"Can we throw them the rope and pull them up?" Greg says.

It's a good idea, and one I hadn't thought of.

I kneel at the edge. "Toni, can you reach this rope?" I throw it down, holding one end firmly.

She crawls over to the wall and looks up. Digging her hands into the dirt, she pulls herself to her feet, favouring her right leg, and reaches for the end of the rope.

"No," Toni says. "It falls short by about a metre."

I pull the rope up and look at it. Seems my original idea of going down there isn't so stupid. "Any idea how to tie this around me so it doesn't come undone?"

Greg shrugs. "Sure. What's the plan?"

"You lower me in, and I try to help the girls climb out." I look down at Toni, who is standing with her hand on the wall. "It looks like we could get some decent footholds on the side."

I put the rope around my waist and try to tie a knot. Greg shakes his head and snatches it out of my hands. He's standing really close to me. I'm fascinated by how his hands move to twist the rope into a knot I would have no idea how to tie.

"You tell anyone I was this close to you, I'll—"

"Your secret's safe with me, Greg." I smile.

"That shouldn't come undone." He nudges me towards the edge.

"Where did you learn to do that?"

"Over ten years sailing with my dad. Now get in the hole."

I grip the rope and fear rises into my chest. "Toni, I'm

coming to get you."

I hear her sigh. "Finally. But promise you won't, you know, be you, and fall in or something."

"I could just leave you here." I lie on my stomach on the grass and wriggle until my feet hang into the gap in the ground. Slowly, I lower myself over the edge, and pray that the thin rope I have tied around my waist will hold my weight. I don't weigh much, so what's the worst that could happen?

I could have a panic attack and completely freak out.

Or I could look at Greg and focus on him lowering me down. I grip the grass with my hands. He stands with his legs apart. His knuckles have turned white from clutching the rope. I take a deep breath and go over the edge, digging the toes of my hiking boots into the soft earth. It gives way beneath my feet and I fall a metre or so, grunting.

"You okay?" Greg asks. The rope digs into the ground at the top, and I hear him straining.

"Just great." I dig my toes in again and grab the rope to steady myself. I'm more careful to test the wall of the cave before I put too much weight against my steps, and Greg does a good job of lowering me at the right speed.

"You nearly there, Harvey?" Greg asks.

"Almost," I say, in the hope that he won't give up. "Don't you dare let go." I worry he won't be able to hold me for much longer.

"I must admit," Greg calls down, "the thought has crossed my mind."

"Not much farther," Toni says.

I move a little more and Greg yells out to stop. "I don't

have any more rope. Are you near the ground yet?"

I steady myself with a hand against the wall and look down. "I'm going to have to untie myself. Hold on."

It won't be far to jump from the end of the rope, but maybe tying it around my waist was not the best idea. My weight pulling against the rope is too much for me to be able to undo the knot, and Greg has tied a really good one. I glance down at Toni, and she stares up at me, watching me fumble with the knot. I dig my toes into the dirt wall, but one foot slips.

"What are you doing?" Greg asks.

"He can't get the rope undone," Toni says.

"What's happening?" Lian's voice is groggy.

I regain my footing on the wall, then look over my shoulder. Lian is sitting up, rubbing the side of her head.

"You and Toni fell in a big hole," I say. "We're trying to rescue you."

Lian frowns, pulls her hand away from her temple and stares at her fingers. "I'm bleeding." She puts her hand on the ground and pushes herself to her knees, but falls sideways.

"Don't move," I say. "Just … stay still. Press your hand to your head."

"I'm bleeding. Why am I bleeding?" Lian tries to move again and manages to get to a sitting position. "What happened? Where am I? I'm bleeding."

"Calm down. Head wounds look worse than they really are," Toni says. "We can worry about patching you up once we get out of here."

Lian looks around and whimpers. She touches her head again. "It hurts."

"Tell me about it," Toni says.

The ground shakes, and Lian screams. Greg yells out above us. Toni falls over and yelps when her arse hits the ground. Another rumble shakes the ground, like an earthquake, dislodging my feet. Lian screams again, covering her face with her hands.

"What's going on?" Greg yells. "I can't hold on much longer."

"The ground is shaking," I yell back.

"Yeah, I noticed."

Lian pulls her knees to her chest, tears streaking her cheeks. She rocks on the spot, her gaze darting around, and a low whimper comes from her throat.

"Lian, look at me," I say. "Look at me." Her eyes finally stop moving, and she stares up at me. "We're going to be fine, okay?"

She nods and hugs her knees tighter.

I take a deep breath, then concentrate on getting the rope undone. I dig my toes in harder and grab a tree root that's jutting out. This time I'm able to hold myself up enough to take the weight off the rope, but I struggle with the knot using only one hand.

"Harvey?" Greg says.

"I'm almost done."

Then I slip again. My face hits the wall, and dirt falls into my eyes. I hit the ground with a jarring thud, knocking the wind out of me. The rope lands on my head and I throw my arms up, getting tangled in its mess. After struggling for a minute, I stop and fall back onto the ground. I'm not cut out for this kind of stuff.

Toni laughs. "You're so hopeless, Harvey."

I roll my head to the side and stare at her. A section of rope is lying across my nose, I push it away. "I don't see you trying to get yourself out of here."

"I can't walk."

"My head hurts," Lian says.

"Harvey, you okay? What's going on down there?" Greg peers over the edge and I can't see his face because the sun is behind his head. He looks like a black splodge against the blue sky.

"We now have three of us in a hole with no way to get out," I say. "That's what's going on down here."

"You pulled on the rope."

"You let go of the rope. You weren't supposed to let go."

"You're heavier than you look," Greg says.

"None of this is helping." Toni gets to her feet and hops a few steps before plonking down beside me.

She grabs the rope and unravels the mess I've made. I sit up to help her, but she bats my hands away so I lay them in my lap. My gaze flicks to Lian. She doesn't look so great. Our eyes meet. She opens her mouth to talk, then winces, closing her eyes and touching her temple again.

"My head *really* hurts," she says, her shoulders shaking.

"Don't worry. We'll fix it," I say.

Toni glares at me and I shrug. "What else am I supposed to say? We're stuck in a hole and we're all going to die?"

Lian runs the back of her hand under her nose. "I don't want to die."

Toni whacks my arm. "Don't listen to him, Lian. We're not going to die."

"But what do we do?" Lian asks.

"First." I grunt, getting to my feet. "I'm going to see if I've broken anything."

"You're fine, Harvey. *I'm* the one with the busted foot," Toni says.

"And I'm bleeding from my head." Lian holds her temple and squeezes her eyes shut.

"What is this? A competition to see who has the best injury?" I wriggle my feet and toes. Nothing seems broken, although I'm a bit stiff and my left arse cheek is sore. I'm guessing I'll have a large bruise on it tomorrow.

Blood seeps through Lian's fingers so I pull my hanky from my pocket and get her to press it to her head.

"What are you doing, Harvey?" Greg says.

I take a deep breath. "I *was* trying to help get us out of here."

"So *was* I. Would you hurry up and think of something? The first plan isn't working so well."

"You could think of something," I mumble.

I wanted to move to plan B just as much as Greg did, but we hadn't discussed plan B. We hadn't really discussed plan A; we'd just gone headlong into it. Now, we had to figure out a way to get the rope to the top of the hole again.

I look around and find a rock about the size of my palm. I gesture for Toni to pass me the rope she's coiled up neatly and I grab the end, tying it around the rock.

"I'm going to throw the rope up," I say to Greg. "Think you can grab it?"

"Think you can throw it high enough?" he asks.

I don't think I can, but I'm going to try. I wait for Toni to move over with Lian so both of them are out of the way. Then I pull my arm back and chuck the rock as hard as I can.

It doesn't even reach halfway up the dirt wall in front of me. There's a reason I'm not on the school cricket team, or the football team, or any team for that matter.

I try again with the same result. "This isn't working."

"What else can we do to get out of here?" Toni says. "We can't use the radio because that's not working. The rope is down here with us. What else do we have? Greg, what other stuff is in our packs? Can we use the whistle?"

Greg disappears, then pops his head back over the side of the hole. "I don't think there's much else that can help us."

"You'll have to go and find someone," Lian says. "Bring them to get us out."

"But what if I get lost on my own?" Greg says.

"Use the compass. There has to be something about this place that's messing with it," I say. "I think if you get far enough away it will work again."

We listen to Greg fumble around above. He swears a few times, then looks back down at us. "The compass isn't here."

"What do you mean, it isn't there?" Toni says.

I cringe because there's a reason my arse cheek is so sore. I know where the compass is, and I know what everyone is going to say when I tell them.

"Where is it?" Lian asks.

"Um … guys." I look at Toni, because I hope she'll be the nicest one to me. "It's in my pocket."

All three of them talk at once. Their voices raise, and I put my hands over my ears and close my eyes. This isn't happening. We're not stuck in a hole two storeys deep with no way out, and any minute now I'm going to wake up in my room with my TV remote in my hand, because this is all a bad dream.

"You idiot." Toni whacks me on the head.

"We're going to die." Lian starts rocking again.

"Okay, let's stop and think for a minute." Toni takes a deep breath. "Greg, mark on the map where you think we are so you can get back. Drop our packs down with our food and water, one of the emergency blankets, and the first aid kit. Lian needs some patching up."

"There's so much blood." Lian is looking around again, chewing on her lip. A rock skitters down the wall, and she jumps.

"Don't be scared. We can last at least three days without water," I say.

"Shut up, Harvey," Toni says. She stares up at Greg. "Walk out the way we came into the clearing. Maybe try and find something to leave a trail."

"Like Hansel and Gretel?" Greg asks.

"Something like that. Use rocks or break branches." Toni looks up at him. "Then go straight until you find something or someone. If you can get up high, do that. If the radio starts working, use that and wait for someone to come find you. You also have a whistle. Blow that sucker until someone hears it."

"I thought you couldn't walk in a straight line," Greg says, and I hear the smile in his voice.

"Has anyone tried their phone again?" I ask.

I pull mine from the front pocket of my jeans and swipe the screen. Still no service. Toni has no luck either. Lian doesn't even try to look at hers.

39

"I'm out," Greg says. "Hopefully it'll pick up something on my way back." There are rustling noises, and we wait for Greg to put the supplies we need into our backpacks. "Think one of you can catch these?" he asks. "I'd lower them down with a rope, but …"

"Ha ha, very funny," I say. "Just drop them, one at a time. Or maybe see if you can slide them down the wall."

He flings the first pack into the hole, then lets go. The backpack slides the first part of the way down, but then it hits a tree root and bounces into the air. I stand under it and hope it doesn't smack me in the face when I catch it. I manage to stop the bag from crashing to the ground, but its impact makes me stumble, and I fall onto my arse.

"Ouch!" I can't help crying out. Yep, I'll definitely have a bruise tomorrow, if not within the next five minutes.

Greg drops the other two packs in. "Don't die while I'm gone."

Toni scoffs. "You really have a way with words."

"Get us out of here," Lian says.

"Yeah." I don't know what else to say, so I go quiet. I'll thank him when we're out of this mess.

"I'll be back as soon as I can," Greg says.

We listen until his footsteps are gone and then I look at Toni and Lian, and back to Toni. I want to help Toni first, but Lian has blood seeping out of her head, so I make her the priority. She probably has a concussion.

"Want to help me patch Lian up then I'll look at your foot?" I say.

Toni nods, then hobbles over to a rock to sit on it. I dump all three packs at her feet and she searches through them to find the first aid supplies. Lian attempts to stand but can't so I take her arm, helping her to her feet. I walk her slowly over to Toni. She sits on the rock beside my friend, and I take my hanky away to have a look at her head. There's a small cut above her left temple. It's not very big, but it's let out a lot of blood.

"It doesn't look too serious," I say.

"Not life-threatening then?" Her gaze darts around, and I want to help her calm down but I'm not sure how.

I take her hand and squeeze because I don't know what else to do. "I think you'll live."

"It's creepy down here," Lian says. "I keep hearing noises."

"Just focus on me then."

Toni hands me a swab that she's doused in saline solution and I use it to clean as much blood and dirt from Lian's face as I can. Next, Toni hands me some iodine, and Lian winces when I dab it on.

"You've got a bit of a bump." I touch her head. She winces again, but her gaze holds mine. I want to look away because I'm embarrassed, and heat rises into my cheeks, but when Lian offers a small smile, I smile back.

Toni clears her throat. "Band-Aid?"

I tear my eyes away from Lian's face and nod, taking the small strip, opening it and letting the peel-off bits flutter to the ground. I stick the Band-Aid to Lian's skin so it covers the cut.

"You should drink some water." I hand Lian her backpack. "And have a bite to eat. Maybe take a look at what we have between us? It might keep you busy while I look at Toni's foot."

"Good idea," Toni says. "We don't know how long we're going to be down here. We should think about rationing."

41

Lian nods and stands. I have to steady her for a moment.

"I'm okay." She takes the backpacks and moves to sit on the ground near the rope. The sun shining through the hole above bounces off her black hair.

"She likes you," Toni whispers.

"Don't be stupid." I stare at my hands. "The universe will explode the day that happens."

"Oh, Harvey, you're … just Harvey."

I raise my eyebrows and look at Toni for a few moments, then shake my head. "Put your foot up. It's your turn."

"You hate camping and outdoorsy stuff, and yet you're an ace with first aid?"

"Who would've guessed?" I say, and Toni laughs.

I bend over and look at Toni's injury. She holds her left leg up by clasping her hands together over her shin, and she almost kicks me when I touch the skin above her shoe.

"It hurts, Harvey. Be nice."

"I'm always nice. When have I not been nice?" I stare at her foot, wondering what I should do. If we take the shoe off it could really swell up, but leaving it on wouldn't be the best thing either as the swelling could make the shoe tight. I think it should come off, but I don't know. I'm not a doctor or a nurse. Common sense tells me to put a Band-Aid on a cut, but it doesn't help me now.

"You should take her shoe and sock off," Lian says, tucking her hair behind her ear. "If it swells too much, you'll end up having to cut it off."

"Okay, shoe off then." I undo the laces for Toni and loosen them as carefully as I can. I hesitate, staring at her foot. "I don't want to hurt you. Can you take it off

yourself?" I look up and wait for an answer.

She presses her lips together. "It hurts like a bitch, Harvey."

"I know, but it'll feel better once your shoe is off."

Toni nods, grabs her shin and pulls her bad leg up to rest it over her right knee. She grimaces and peels the shoe of slowly, then lets it fall to the ground with a thump.

She grabs her leg and pulls it to her chest, resting her forehead on her knee. Carefully, I roll her sock down and then take it off. Already, her foot is puffy, and I think it may be broken. But I don't tell her that. Instead, I search the small first aid kit for a bandage and find one that would suit a sprain. I wrap it around Toni's foot and ankle and fasten it with a butterfly clip.

"That's the best I can do for now until someone can take a look at it," I say. "Maybe you should sit on the ground and elevate it. Doesn't that help with swelling?"

"I guess that sounds like a plan." Toni lets go of her leg and glances around the cave.

For the first time, I take a good look at where we are. The ground is hard packed, which makes me think we've fallen into a cave that has been covered up. On the right side of the space the ground is wet, which means hopefully there's water somewhere that we can access if we're here long enough and our supplies run out. I'm not sure how big the cave is because I can't see into the shadows, and the thought of walking away from our patch of sunlight makes me shudder. The rest of the cave is covered, and the roof is made mostly of dirt, but there seems to be a large section of rock in there as well. I don't think it's a good idea to sit underneath it.

"Maybe we should sit over with Lian," I say to Toni. "So nothing falls on us."

I help her up, and she hops over to sit down. Lian is going through the contents of our backpacks and has lined everything up on the ground in front of her. I find a rock so Toni can rest her leg on it to keep it elevated, rolling her jumper up so she has something soft underneath her skin. Once she's comfortable, I go and sit beside Lian.

We have the basics. A first aid kit, an emergency blanket, a hand torch, and two head torches.

"We can't light a fire to keep warm," I say. "No matches."

Lian shoves her hand into her pocket and fishes out a lighter. "I've got this."

I raise my eyebrows but don't ask why she carries a lighter in her pocket.

"There's nothing to make a fire with anyway," Toni says. "Rocks don't burn."

Between us we have three sandwiches, some muesli bars, a bag of chips, and about half a bottle of water each.

"I don't think this will last us very long," I say.

"It won't have to." Lian smiles. "Greg will be back, and we can get out of here."

"Are you feeling better?" I ask. At least she doesn't seem as jumpy as she was before.

Lian nods, then winces, raising a hand to her temple. "I'll be okay." She turns the lighter over in her fingers. "Think I was just a bit disoriented. I'm fine now."

I'm not completely convinced, but I let it go.

Lian grabs a head torch and wraps the strap around her wrist, then gets up and moves slowly around the cave. I sit back and rest my arms on my knees, staring at the meagre supplies we have while watching the girls from the corner of my eye. Lian trails her hand along the wall, taking a wide path around Toni when she reaches her. Toni watches her, but drops her gaze when Lian looks in her direction.

Lian walks into the shadows, and I shudder. Her torchlight flicks on and bounces around on the wall for a bit before disappearing.

"Lian, where did you go?" I ask.

"Harvey, come and have a look at this."

I glance at Toni and she raises her eyebrows. She knows I'm afraid of the dark. The sunlight fills the cave enough that it hasn't freaked me out too much, but where Lian went looks too spooky for my liking. Not knowing what's hiding in the shadows makes my skin crawl. The last thing I want to do is have a complete freak-out in front of the most popular girl at school.

Toni shakes her head. "You don't have to, Harvey. Call her back."

I get to my feet and take a few steps. "Lian, where are you?" I play with the hem of my T-shirt and stare into the darkness, unsure what to do.

"What are you doing, Harvey? Come on," Lian says.

"I don't want to leave Toni." I take another step towards the dark part of the cave.

Lian's light comes back into view and she emerges from the shadows, the head torch around her wrist illuminates a circle on the ground at her feet.

"There's an opening up here to the left," she says, her eyes wide. "Maybe it's a way out."

4

Lian glances between Toni and me, her head moving back and forth as if she's watching the tennis. "What are you waiting for, Harvey?"

Toni frowns. "What if you go in there and never come back?"

Toni's comment has me so scared I'm numb. I don't want to walk into the shadows, but if there's another way out then maybe we should try and look for it.

"Harvey?" Lian says again. "I think we should take a look."

"The first rule of getting lost is to stay where you are." Toni presses her lips together, and her frown deepens.

"But we could be here for a long time." Lian puts her hands on her hips. "I personally want to get out of here ... now."

"Well, *I* can't walk. And you should be careful. You

hit your head, remember?"

I rub my face with my hands. Leaving Toni on her own isn't a good idea, but I don't think Lian going off into a dark underground tunnel by herself is a good option either.

"None of us should go in there," I say. "It's ... dark."

"We have torches, Harvey." Lian raises her hand, and the light from her torch flashes in my eyes.

"We shouldn't leave Toni."

"Where's she going to go? You can stay here and I'll go by myself." Lian grabs some Band-Aids from our supplies, double checks she still has her lighter, shoves her phone in her back pocket, then ties her jumper around her waist.

"Be careful," Toni says.

Lian smiles with her lips closed. She turns and heads back towards the tunnel. Her torchlight bounces off the walls before disappearing around to the left.

Toni looks at the hole above us, and I follow her gaze. It's still daylight. My watch says five minutes to one. Hopefully someone will start looking for us when we don't turn up on time, if Greg doesn't raise the alarm before then.

Lian screams and I jump.

"I'm okay," she calls.

"Lian?" I listen, but she doesn't answer.

I take a few steps then stop to look back at Toni, wanting her to tell me what to do.

"You should go and see if she's all right," Toni says.

I bite my lip and grimace. "I don't know if I can go in there ... and I don't want to leave you."

"I'll be fine. Think about puppies and rainbows. Definitely

don't think about all the creepy things hiding in the shadows."

"That … is not helping." I grab the hand torch from our supply pile, press the button to turn it on, then shine it into the darkness. "I'll go find her and we'll come straight back."

"I'll be here," Toni says.

I hesitate once more before edging towards the dark patch at the back of the cave.

"Why am I doing this?" I mumble to myself. *Do I even like her?* I take a few more steps into the darkness. My torchlight bounces off the walls of the tunnel, and I use one hand on the wall to steady myself as I move along. My foot bumps something. "Shit." *Maybe I do like her enough to face my biggest fear.* I take a breath, my heart thumping, and train the torch beam at my feet so I don't fall over.

"Lian? Where are you?" I call.

"Over here."

"Why did you scream?"

"I slipped, but I'm okay. You have to come see this."

"In case you haven't noticed, it's dark." Something brushes my hand and I stifle a scream, my stomach rolling. I shine the torch around but can't see what it was. "Keep talking so I can follow you."

"What do you want me to say?"

I edge my way through the dark, feeling the wall and shuffling my feet. "I don't know. Anything."

"What's your favourite colour?" Lian asks.

"That's a stupid question. Why should I have one? If I said blue, then what happens if I like red the next day,

but the day after that I like orange? Why do I need to have a favourite?”

“It was just a question, Harvey.”

Lian goes quiet, and I edge a little farther along the tunnel. I shine my torch over the damp walls. A second later, I slip and land heavily on my arse, dropping the torch. It rolls away, its beam snuffed by the wall, plunging the tunnel into almost darkness. My shoulders shake as bile rises into my throat. I struggle to breathe. Sweat drips into my eyes. I hate what my fear of the dark does to me.

I crawl along the ground to retrieve the torch, and dirt sticks to my palms from the film of sweat that now covers them. When I grab the barrel of the torch I clutch it hard enough to make my fingers ache. My heart races inside my chest. Each beat is faster than the last. I try to take even breaths, but the panic has gripped me like a vice, and the air seems too thin. My stomach churns. I want to curl up into a ball.

“Come on, Harvey,” I mumble to myself. “Man up.”

I blink the sweat from my eyes and stumble to my feet, leaning against the wall. One after the other, I take deep breaths and stare at the circle of light from my torch that I’ve aimed at the ground in front of me. I want to call out Lian’s name, but I’m worried my voice will be so shaky I won’t be able to get the word out. I’m close to vomiting, the deep breathing only helping a little, when I see a light up ahead.

“Lian?” I call, walking slowly. “Is that you?”

The light moves. “Yep, it’s me. I’ll wait. I can see your light, just watch—”

“Ouch!” My head hits something really hard.

"—the rock hanging down."

I shine my light up. There's a section of the ceiling that's much lower. I don't think I've done too much damage, and I can't feel any blood. I take another deep breath before I keep going, making sure I have one hand on the wall to steady myself.

Lian's light moves back and forth and around, and I concentrate on it until I reach her.

I shine my light on her face. She's put her head torch on properly. "That's not hurting you?"

"I'm okay," she says. "What's wrong with you? You look terrified."

I scoff and try to hide the fact that I'm shaking. "How can you tell in this light?"

Lian leans in, her light shining straight in my eyes, and I squint at the brightness. She grabs my shoulders, and it's not until she's pressed against my chest that I realise she's fallen over. But I have no time to react, and we both tumble to the ground.

"Harvey. I'm so sorry," Lian says. "I tripped."

"It's okay." I'm on my back, holding my hands in the air because I don't know where to put them. Lian is lying on top of me and I want to tell her to get off because there's a rock digging into my back, but at the same time I don't want her to move.

She stares at me, and I try to look into her eyes, but her torch is really bright. I end up looking at her chest, which is probably not the best idea, so I turn my head.

"What's wrong?" Lian says.

"Your light is too bright," I say. "And there's a rock sticking into my back."

"Oh." She rolls off and gets to her feet, grabbing my hand and pulling me up. "Sorry. Come see what I found."

Lian doesn't let go of my hand, and I'm grateful. Touching someone else helps me not to focus on being in the dark. Instead, I concentrate on how her skin feels smooth, and how her hand is so small. Then I think about how sweaty my palms are and I worry that she'll notice, but I don't want to let go.

We walk over some rocks before squeezing through a smaller gap. We emerge into another much larger cavern, and my breath catches for a second. I stare in amazement at the millions of glow worms lining the cavern ceiling and parts of the walls. Fumbling through the dark, having a panic attack, freaking out and hitting my head, are all worth seeing what's in front of me.

"Wow," I say. "It's …"

"Beautiful?" Lian looks at me and smiles. She gives my hand a gentle squeeze.

The ceiling of the cavern is at least five storeys high. A path leads from where we're standing to the floor far below us. A small stream trickles along the left edge of the cavern before disappearing into a crevice in the far wall. Lian takes her phone from her pocket and snaps a few photos.

"Want to go down and take a look?" she asks.

I nod, a smile forming on my lips as well. I feel a bit better. My chest has loosened, and my heart rate has slowed. I take a deep breath to get myself together.

"Want me to go first, in case … you fall?"

Lian studies me for a moment, then laughs and moves away towards the path leading down. "I'll try not to trip this time." She clambers over a rock and jumps down to a patch of dirt. "You know, Harvey. If I knew you better, I'd say you were afraid of the dark." Lian glances over her shoulder, then keeps going.

I take a step and stumble. "What makes you say that?"

Lian stops and turns to look up at me. "You were terrified back there in the tunnel. In here, you're … different." She cocks her head to the side. "It's okay. I won't tell anyone."

She keeps walking, and I scramble to catch up. I stumble a few more times before we reach the bottom because I'm too busy looking at the glow worms. They're mostly on the ceiling, but there are some black sections where there's no light at all. I don't like the look of those patches, but I don't think much of it. I'm too caught up in how amazing it is that the worms can generate such an intense blue-green light.

The floor of the cavern is a combination of dirt and rock. It's damp in places, mostly near the edge of the stream, but other areas are dry and look as if they've been eroded away over many years. I glance at my feet and my boots leave prints in the dirt, which reminds me why we're here in the first place.

"Aren't we supposed to be looking for a way out?" I ask.

"That can wait, don't you think?" Lian smiles. She tilts her head back and looks around the enormous cavern, turning a circle on the spot. I watch her face and feel my own smile forming, but it drops away when Lian frowns.

"What's the matter?" I say.

Lian sucks her top lip between her teeth. "Something doesn't look right."

I move to her side and stare at the ceiling with her. "What are we looking at?"

"The dark patches ..."

Lian scouts around and finds a rock that fits into her palm. Before I can stop her, she pulls her arm back and throws the rock into the air. It doesn't reach the ceiling, but she has a pretty good arm. The rock falls into the stream, and a splash echoes through the cavern.

The ceiling falls on us in a deafening rush. I grab Lian, tucking her under my arm to protect her. The dark mass hurtles towards us, and I don't know which way to run or what to do, so I cover Lian as best I can and wait for it to hit us.

Lian shakes in my arms, but once the noise subsides I realise it's not because she's scared. She's laughing.

"What's so funny?" I say with my arms still around her.

"Bats." She grins.

"Bats?"

"You know? Small, leathery-winged creatures?"

"I know what bats are."

I look up at the last of the black bats hanging to roost. It's now that I understand why I thought the black sections of the ceiling were a bit odd. They're moving in small ripples as the creatures hang from their perches.

"You can let go of me now," Lian says.

I release her and step back. Heat rises up my neck, and I fix my gaze on my feet. "Let's look around," I say. "Hopefully there's a way out."

We move in different directions. Lian goes deeper into the cavern, and I double back towards where we came down. I negotiate my way across the stream, careful not to get my shoes wet, then find a section of the wall that has a high concentration of glow worms. There are a lot of jagged rocks around the edge of the cavern, so I pick my way over them carefully, looking for any gaps between them that may lead somewhere.

Lian calls my name. "Harvey, I've found something."

"Is it a way out?" I ask.

"No. I don't know what it is."

I sigh, knowing I should go and have a look. I pick my way back over the rocks, hop across the stream, and make my way over to Lian. She's standing on the far side of the cavern. Her head torch is back around her wrist, and she's shining it into a crevice.

"What is it?" I ask when I reach her.

"I'm not sure." Lian puts her face to the rock and looks through a large crack. The split is almost as tall as Lian, but not very wide.

"I don't think we'll fit in there," I say. "Unless you can squish yourself like an octopus."

Lian raises her eyebrows. "You're so weird, Harvey. I'm pretty sure I can squeeze through. There's something in there that's reflecting my torchlight."

"Let me guess—you want to know what it is?"

Lian pulls back and stares at me as if I've asked the dumbest question in the history of all questions.

"Of course I do," she says. "Don't you?"

5

Lian doesn't hesitate. She puts her left arm in, followed by her shoulder. For a second, I think she might be stuck. I wait as she slides in sideways, ducking her head, and a moment later she's on the other side of the wall.

I shine my torch in to see if she's okay. "What's in there?"

Lian's torchlight bounces around the dark space. There are no glow worms in the small cave, and I try to see if there's anything interesting, but it's too dark.

"There it is," Lian says.

Her feet scuff the ground as she moves away from me. I want to go in after her to make sure she's safe, but there's no way I'll fit through the crack. I also don't want to admit that I'm relieved, because it's darker in there. I resort to kneeling on the ground and looking through the widest part of the gap at the bottom.

I shine my light around again and see Lian over the

far side of the cave, about five metres away. The space is larger than I'd first thought.

"There are some candles," Lian says.

I move my light back on her. She takes the lighter from her pocket and strikes it, then holds the flame to a candle wick and it lights. She does the same to another two candles, and the small cave is filled with flickering light.

"There," Lian says. "Now we can see better."

The wall above the candles has a nook in it, but I can't quite see what's in there. Lian shines her light in and stares at it.

I swap my torch to my left hand. "Where's the shiny thing?"

Lian reaches into the nook. "I think this could be it." She pulls out a small book about the size of a novel. "It has a metal star on the front."

"Is there anything else in there?"

Lian shines her torch into the hole in the wall again. Then she sticks her hand in. Her arm goes in farther than I expected, and when Lian screams, I jump.

"What?" I say. "What is it?"

Lian pulls her arm out and screams again. A spider bigger than her hand sits on her wrist. She shakes her arm, but the spider runs up to her shoulder. She dances around the cave, dropping the book in the dirt, trying to fling the creature off.

I don't particularly like spiders, but I'm not scared of them. I laugh and Lian scowls. She watches the spider as it scurries across the floor and behind a rock.

Lian goes back to the nook and looks in again.

"You're going to stick your hand back in there?" I ask.

"I felt something. I want to know what it is."

"Another spider." I laugh again.

"I don't get you, Harvey." She puts her arm in the hole. "You're afraid of the dark, but you laugh at spiders."

"I was laughing at your reaction to the spider," I say. "And it's more a case of if I can see it, I'm okay."

"So spiders in the dark would freak you out?" She grimaces as she fumbles around inside the nook.

"Something like that."

Lian's arm emerges, and she clutches a box in her fingers. The box is roughly the same size as the book, and it also has a silver star inlaid on the lid. She picks up the book from where she'd dropped it and brings both items over to the crevice. She sits on the ground and puts the items between us.

"You don't want to come and look at them out here?" I ask. My knees are aching from kneeling on the hard ground. "Or maybe leave it alone. They look ... witchy."

"How do you know?" Lian stares at me.

"That's a pentacle." I point to the cover of the book. "It's a pagan symbol and often associated with witchcraft."

Lian tilts her head. "You're pretty fascinating, Harvey Anderson."

"I still think you should put those back where you found them." I grip my torch and get to my feet. I don't want to admit that everything I know about witches has come from watching too much TV.

Lian slides the book and the box out, then her leg and arm follow until she shimmies through the gap sideways to join me.

"Don't you want the candles?" I ask.

"We can get them in a minute." She picks the items up and tucks them under her arm, then goes and sits on a flat rock a few metres away.

Lian puts the box beside her and the book in her lap. She straps her head torch on again, careful not to have the strap sitting over her wound, then angles it so it points at the book.

The flames from the candles inside the crevice room cast a yellow flickering glow. I lean against the wall near the crevice and wait, folding my arms and gripping my torch. I'm not going to be able to talk her out of taking a closer look. I want to protest and tell her we've been away from Toni for too long, but there's something about the fascination on her face that makes me still. Her eyes are wide, taking everything in.

Lian turns the book over a few times, running her finger around the metal star that's inlaid into the leather. "I wonder how old it is," she says, and I know she's thinking out loud.

The book is tied shut with old string. Lian grabs one end and pulls to undo the bow.

I jump forward. "Don't do that."

"Why?" Lian stares at me.

"I … I don't know. I have a feeling."

"It's a book, Harvey. You're supposed to read them."

Lian opens it and her hair sways around her shoulders, as if it's being tossed by the wind. There's a rustling, and the candles go out. The globe in Lian's head torch pops, and she shrieks. The book hits the ground with a thump. The glow worms dim until their light is almost out. My heart races as the rustling sounds again.

The bats.

A crow caws.

What?

My heart hammers. "How did a bird get in here?" I shine my torch at Lian and then the book. It's lying open on the ground. A shadow darts across the pages. "What was that?"

"I don't know, but my torch is broken." Lian leans down to pick up the book, then pulls her torch off her head. "Can you take a look?" She holds it out to me.

I take it, shining my light on it, and try to look like I know what I'm doing when I really have no idea.

"Probably the globe," I say. Lian doesn't answer, and when I look up, she's angled the book towards my light so she can read the first page. "Anything interesting?" I return my attention to the head torch.

"There's a bunch of words I can't read. They look more like symbols. But one word is bigger than the rest. Nerezza," she says.

The pages of the book flutter, and Lian shrieks again. My torch pops, plunging us into darkness. The handle grows hot in my hand. I drop the torch and it lands on my foot. The cavern fills with a howling sound and the rustling returns, like feathers. My heart pounds like it's about to explode out of my chest. I move towards where I think Lian is because I would rather be near someone in the dark than on my own.

"I don't like this. Where's the book?" I can't see Lian properly.

"I don't know. I dropped it again," she says. "I can't see anything."

"Where's my torch?" I bend to search the floor for it and bump into Lian. She grabs my arm and I reach out to steady her.

"They can't have gone any farther than the ground in front of us," I say.

I kneel and run my hands through the dirt around me.

"Found it," Lian says.

I hear the snap when she closes the book, and a bright light startles me. I'm still holding Lian's head torch, and its beam is angled at my face.

I shake it. "That's odd."

"Yours is back on, too," Lian says.

I grab it from the ground and stand. "I think we should get out of here. Toni's probably worried. And you should put those back."

"No way." Lian fiddles with the old string on the book. It makes me nervous. "I want to take a closer look, and find out what's in the box."

"Well, I'm not staying here. Greg might've come back by now. And I don't like our chances of finding another way out." I don't wait for a reply and start heading across the cavern to where we'd climbed down to come in.

"We should get the candles," Lian says.

"What we should do is get out of here," I call over my shoulder.

The glow worms are slowly lighting up again, and by the time I reach the far side they're back to their full brightness. There's something they don't like about what we've found, and to be honest, I don't like it either. I think we should've left well enough alone, but one thing I've learnt today is that Lian can be as stubborn as she is beautiful.

Lian's footsteps sound behind me as we climb the rocks to the tunnel. I stop at the top and wait for her to catch up. I didn't like my first trek through the darkness, so I'm glad to have her with me this time.

"Want to hold my hand?" she asks when she reaches the top.

I do, but I'm not about to tell her that. "Um … okay. If you need me to. Let's hope there are no spiders on the way back or we'll both be a mess. You feeling all right? You know, with your head now?"

Lian smiles. "Much better, thank you."

She angles her head torch so it shines towards the ground, tucks the book and the box under her arm, and then grabs my hand and leads me into the tunnel. I concentrate on getting back to Toni, and not on the darkness that surrounds me. My chest tightens, and I can't help the panic that fills my stomach, making me sick.

"Harvey, ease up on the grip," Lian says.

I hadn't even realised I'd been squeezing her hand so tightly. Sweat slicks my skin and I want to stop, but I also want to get to Toni, so I focus on my breathing and the sound of our footsteps.

The journey back seems longer than when I came in to find Lian, even though this time I have her with me. When I see Toni, I've never been so happy. She's sitting where we'd left her, the bottle of water beside her almost empty. She has her head resting against the wall, and her eyes are closed.

"You've been gone a while," she says without opening her eyes.

"No one's come back?" I look through the hole above.

Toni sits forward and opens her eyes. "No one."

"We found a big cavern," Lian says. "With glow worms, and these." She holds up the book and the box.

Toni frowns. "Is that a pentacle?"

I take a deep breath. "Yep. I told her to leave it where it was."

"You should have listened to him," Toni says. "You don't want to mess with stuff like that."

"Why? It's a book." Lian repeats what she'd said to me. "You read them."

She sits on the ground in the patch of light from the hole and crosses her legs. Lian opens the book in her lap and hunches over. I wait for the howling and the rustling of feathers, but it doesn't come. I go over and sit with Toni against the wall.

"You all right?" she asks. "You look like you've … you know. Had an episode." She whispers the last part.

"I survived," I say.

Toni squeezes my hand, and we both look at Lian. She has the box open and is sifting through the various items inside. She holds up a dagger and inspects the jewel-encrusted handle. I think for the millionth time that she should have left it and the book where they were.

"I wouldn't play with that," Toni says. "It's an athame. Whoever owns it might get mad."

"Do you see anyone else here?" Lian says. "And it's covered in dust." She blows at the handle, then rubs the gemstones with her sleeve.

"What's an athame?" I ask. "Besides that it's obviously a big knife."

"That's exactly what it is. A knife used for spells and

rituals." Toni looks at me. "We shouldn't play with this stuff. It's making me nervous."

"What's there to be nervous about?" Lian lays the athame on the ground next to some black feathers, a couple of sheets of yellowed paper, and a small glass vial. "Oh, this is pretty." Lian holds up a pendant to show us.

Toni and I don't say anything, and I get the feeling Lian is the only one who is excited about her find. She undoes the clasp and puts the pendant around her neck. Toni stiffens beside me but doesn't say anything. The pendant is round with a swirly border and a smooth ruby-coloured stone in the centre. Lian continues to rifle through the box, bringing out some gemstones, little bottles of what look like dried herbs, and two other bottles, one the colour of blood, and one that contains a brown liquid.

"This is all really interesting," Lian says.

"Not as interesting as getting out of here," Toni says. "What's the time, Harvey?"

I glance at my watch, and I'm surprised at how long Lian and I were in the cavern. "It's after three."

"Hopefully they'll find us soon. They should be looking by now, even if Greg hasn't made it back."

I stand, because the ground is making my arse hurt, and stare at the dirt wall. Maybe I can climb out if I can get enough footholds, and Lian could, too. But how do we get Toni out? I look down at her bandaged foot. It's pretty swollen, so I'm guessing she won't be able to put any pressure on it.

Lian ruffles the pages of the book, drawing my attention back to her. I really wish she'd leave that stuff alone. Everything I know about witches and witchcraft I can

fit into the biggest button on my TV remote, but I don't think spells and all that sort of stuff is something we want to mess with.

"Can you read any of it?" Toni asks.

Lian looks up. "No, all the letters are … wrong. They keep moving around. But I'm … never mind." She blinks. "My eyes are kinda blurry, but I can read one word. I think it's a name. Nerezza."

The ground shakes and I stumble forward. Dirt rains down the wall where Toni is sitting, spraying into her hair. Rocks fall from the ceiling and Lian scrambles to her feet, sweeping the contents of the box into a pile.

A small rock hits her in the back of the head, and she puts her hand to it. Her fingers come away covered in blood. The ground shakes again and Lian lurches forward, landing on her hands and knees. She plants both hands on the ground in front of her to steady herself.

The ground stops shaking. I look around. The girls' eyes are wide, but they seem okay.

Lian sits back.

Her blood mars the dirt.

It glows red before seeping into the ground.

6

Toni takes her leg off the rock she's had it perched on and struggles to her feet. She hops over to Lian, a scowl on her face.

"You need to put all of that back in the box," Toni says.

Lian stares at her. "I'm all right, by the way." She touches the back of her head again and winces. Her fingers come away with more blood on them.

I grab the first aid kit and bring it over to her. Toni sits on the ground beside Lian and starts putting the items back in the box while I look at Lian's fresh wound.

"You're going to need a good check-up once we get out of here," I say. "Too many hits to the head for one day."

Lian turns and smiles at me, but her lips are closed. I pack up the first aid kit, put it back with the rest of our supplies, then join the girls on the ground. Toni inspects each item more carefully than I expected her to. She's about to put the athame into the box.

"Can I see that?" I ask.

She passes me the knife. The stone embedded into the intricate metal handle is the same colour as the one in the pendant around Lian's neck. Dark red, like blood.

I go to pass the athame back to Toni and fumble, grabbing for the knife and cutting the palm of my left hand.

"Harvey, what are you doing?" Toni takes the knife. "You cut yourself." She angles the blade so I can see my blood on the metal. "Things like this can get us into a lot of trouble."

"I know." I grit my teeth. I've seen enough TV shows to figure out blood and magic don't mix well. I go to the first aid kit, *again*, and fix my hand. The cut isn't deep but it's in an awkward spot, so I swab it and then wrap it in a bandage.

"I hope she's a good witch," Toni says after I sit down again.

"What makes you think she isn't?" Lian asks. She has the book in her lap, and the ruby stone around her neck reflects light from somewhere.

"I ... don't want to freak you out, but the ground shook when you said her name."

"Weird stuff happened when you did that in the big cavern, too," I say.

Lian waves her hand in the air. "Whatever. It's just coincidence."

Toni stares at the box in front of her. "Something about this place doesn't feel right." She slams the lid of the box closed and gets to her feet again, hopping over to the big rock. "You need to eat something, Harvey."

I glance at Lian, because she would be hungry, too, but she has her nose in the book again. It seems to have mesmerised her, as if she's reading a great story she doesn't want to put down. Her lips move in whispers, but I can't hear what she's saying. I get up and go over to Toni to rummage through our meagre supplies, finding two muesli bars and tossing one to Lian so it lands in front of her.

"We haven't eaten in a while," I say.

She reaches out and grabs it, peeling the wrapper off before going back to the book. I raise my eyebrows at Toni and shrug. She goes to sit in her spot again with her leg elevated.

"Is it hurting?" I ask.

Toni nods. "You know, I might know a little bit about witchcraft. I think that's a spell book."

Her ankle must be hurting a lot more than she's letting on—she's changed the subject. I make a note not to ask her about it again until we're out of here.

I want to ask her how she knows about witchcraft, so I decide to play along. "Where did you learn about witchcraft?"

"My grandmother."

"Nona taught you witchcraft?" I ask.

Toni shakes her head. "No, she was a witch. She didn't teach me anything; she wouldn't. But everything I know I learnt from watching her."

"You never told me."

"I've never told anyone."

Lian raises her head. "How can you tell it's a spell book? You haven't even looked in it."

"All the things in that box ... they're used for spells and incantations. Rituals and stuff."

Lian flips a few pages. "I can make out some words. But the rest is like reading Latin. And the symbols I've never seen before." She squeezes her eyes closed, then blinks a few times.

"Are you okay?" I ask.

"My eyes are just a bit blurry," she says. "Must be the light."

I stare at Lian. "Are you interested in witchcraft?"

"No." Her brow creases. "Why?"

I cross my legs at the ankles and fold my arms. "You haven't put the book down since we found it."

"I … there's nothing else to do down here."

I'm unsure why she's being defensive so I don't reply. If she wants to read the book, then I guess she can. To busy myself, I take a look around. There are more rocks scattered all over the place from the ground shaking. I look up at the hole. The light is fading fast now that it's late afternoon. If I want to try and get us out, then I'll have to work quickly before I lose all the light.

"What's going on in your head, Harvey?" Toni asks. "You have that look in your eyes."

"I'm going to build a pile of rocks," I say. "Maybe I can make it high enough so I can reach that bit up there that's jutting out, and climb the rest of the wall."

"It's a two-storey drop, Harvey. I don't like your chances of making a tall enough pile."

"I have to try something."

Toni sighs. "Okay. Want me to help?"

I raise my eyebrows. "No, you sit there and relax."

"I won't be able to climb it."

I take a deep breath. "I'll get you out. Leaving you

behind is not an option."

Toni puts her head against the wall and closes her eyes.

The girls are quiet while I collect as many of the fallen rocks as I can. The ones I can lift, anyway. I pile them against the wall, far enough away from Toni so they won't hurt her if they fall over. Every now and then, I glance at Lian, who hasn't looked up.

"Can I have a read?" Toni says.

I stop building my rock pile to listen.

Lian glances at Toni. "Did you say something?"

"I could reply with a really snide remark right about now, but I won't." She holds out her hand. "The book?"

Lian gets to her feet, but she has this weird look on her face. Confusion, maybe? I put another rock on my pile and watch as she hesitates before handing the book to Toni.

My best friend runs her fingers over the ancient leather cover, then carefully opens it. She scans the first page and leans closer. I move to her side to see what she's looking at. Toni quickly flicks through a few more pages before returning to the first.

"Lian, how many times have you said this name?" Toni holds the book up and points to the page. *Nerezza* is written in a calligraphic script and decorated with little swirls.

"Um … I don't know. Why?" Lian takes the book back and Toni lets her. "I think I have the pronunciation right."

"Don't say it again."

"Nerezza? It's just a name."

The book flies out of Lian's hands and lands open on the ground, its pages rifling back and forth. A dark shape darts from the paper and disappears into the shadows.

69

Lian screams and steps back. The ground shakes again, and some of the rocks from my pile tumble to the dirt floor.

The blackness re-emerges. I catch a glimpse of the shape of a crow surrounded by mist, but it dissipates as quickly as it formed. The mist rolls over the ground towards the book. I don't know why, but I lunge to pick it up. The blackness rises into the air like a cloud, and I edge my way over to Toni so I can stand between it and her. I don't want to be the brave one, but she can't run.

"What is it?" Toni whispers.

"I don't know, but it's getting bigger," I say. "I saw something down in the cavern, but I thought the shadows were playing tricks on me."

I stare at the black fog and a feeling of calm washes over me. The cloud grows, and I get lost in its black folds. It's the first time darkness hasn't filled me with fear.

"Harvey," Toni says, and I drag my gaze away from the mist to meet hers. "The book."

I'm glad when I hand it to her. My knuckles ache from clutching it so tightly. Lian hasn't said anything, and when I look at her she's staring at the cloud, watching it coiling in the air. The howling and rustling sounds I'd heard in the big cavern roll around us, and Lian takes a step forward. Toni flips through the book then mutters something, but I can't make out what she's saying.

The mist darts towards Lian and I run, tackling her to the ground. Dirt explodes above our heads where the black cloud hits the wall. I help Lian sit up. The mist circles around and comes at Lian again, this time hitting her in the chest. She flies onto her back. Toni's voice is a constant in the background, and I want to tell her to shut up. I help Lian get to her feet.

The black fog hovers above the box we left on the ground, swirling and rolling over itself, up and down in the air. I take three steps to the box, throw the lid open and grab the athame, slicing it through the cloud before stepping back. The mist recoils, and then it's gone, darting off towards the tunnel. The rustling sound disappears with it.

Toni snaps the book shut. "I think you should put it all back." She's breathing hard.

"Are you okay?" I stare at my best friend. "What were you mumbling while that thing attacked us?"

Her eyes are wide, and she pushes her hair roughly away from her face. "Three. The power of three. Have you said that name three times, Lian?"

"I don't know." She throws her hands in the air. "I might have."

"What's the power of three?" I ask.

"Whatever you do happens to you in return, three-fold," Toni says. "I don't know *exactly* what this says, but I think you've released an ancient witch. And from the looks of her, she isn't all that happy."

"What?" Lian and I say at the same time.

I stare at Toni, unable to believe what she's saying or even how she knows to say it in the first place.

"Can you read the book?" I ask.

"No ... yes. Some of it, but not much." Toni pushes herself up and struggles to her feet. "You have to go and put it all back." She shoves the book into my hands.

I don't want to touch it, so I step back, letting the book fall to the floor. I don't want to have anything to do with

it. That thing we saw was scarier than scary, and even more so when I thought it was lovely. Its darkness had some weird effect on me. But how does mist push someone to the ground? How is it hurt by a knife? Mist isn't solid, it's … misty.

"The only place I'm going is up and out of this hole," Lian says.

"Put. It. All. Back." Toni glares at Lian.

"I'm not following that thing in there," Lian says. "We should block the tunnel. So it can't come back out."

I agree with her. Blocking up the tunnel is an awesome idea.

"We can use the rocks," I say. "Stack them up to cover the entrance."

Toni watches as Lian and I frantically scramble around the cave, hauling rocks and stones into the shadows to the entrance of the tunnel. I'm scared we won't have enough to cover the gap. We struggle to move some of the bigger ones, and after about half an hour I have to stop to catch my breath. I'm not cut out to do heavy lifting.

"I don't think it's going to make a difference," Toni says. "She's mist. She can get through the smallest gap."

"We're not having this conversation." I go and stack another rock on top of the pile then come back to our cave. "It *will* keep her out. You saw that stuff hit the wall. It won't be able to get through solid rock."

Lian and I manage to finally block the tunnel entrance. Lucky for us, it isn't the full height or width of a normal door, and there are enough rocks to cover it. We go and sit with Toni, who has returned to her spot and turned the torches on. The light outside is pretty much gone, and I have lost hope of anyone coming to find us before full dark sets in. I'd been occupied stacking rocks, but now my stomach churns at the thought of being stuck underground in the dark of night.

"I wonder if Greg got back to camp," Lian says.

Toni and I don't answer. I, for one, do not want to speculate about what could or could not have happened to Greg. I think he's smarter than I have ever given him credit for, so I hope he found his way back.

"I think we should get comfortable," I say. "Looks like we're spending the night."

I get up and make sure the girls both have their jumpers on. I put mine on as well, then I pull out the emergency blanket just in case it gets cold later and we need it.

"We should sit closer together for warmth," Toni says.

Lian has moved away from us like she did when we'd first fallen into the cave. "I'm not snuggling with you." She stares at Toni.

"Harvey can sit in the middle." Toni smirks.

I sigh. It's going to be a long night. One thing I didn't miss while Lian and I were down in the cavern was her and Toni sparring with each other. Lian gets up and comes over, easing herself down beside me.

"We don't have to snuggle yet," I say. "It's still pretty warm."

Lian smiles. "Maybe I'm cold already." She draws her knees to her chest and rests her chin on them.

I feel myself blush in the fading light and hope that she can't tell.

"So, um, Toni," I say. "You didn't answer my question before. What were you muttering? You know, while the misty stuff got all agitated."

"A spell," she says.

"You cast spells now?" I raise my eyebrows and shine my torch in her face.

Toni squints. "A protection spell. One to keep us all safe. If you recite it in the presence of danger, then the danger will eventually go away."

"Did you know if it was going to work?" Lian asks.

"I had no idea." Toni looks around me at her. "But I think it helped … maybe."

I shine my torch around the cave until I find the book that's lying where it dropped before. "I don't get how you can read it."

"I can't really," Toni says. "It's more that I know roughly how this stuff works."

"Who are you?" I look at her under the glow of our torches. "And what have you done with my best friend?"

Toni laughs. "I'm still me."

"Yeah, but you can do … witchcraft. Why did you never tell me?"

"What? And out my Nona?" Toni shakes her head. "She was very secretive. Half the time she didn't acknowledge I was watching. I think it was the only thing she had that was truly hers. So I kept her secret."

Lian gets up and retrieves the book. She also grabs the box and brings it over to us. Toni takes a deep breath beside me, and I know she wants us to go and put everything back, but if she's right, and we've released whatever it is we've released, I can't see how putting the box and the book back will help.

Lian passes Toni the book, then sits beside me again.

THE Lovely DARK

Toni adjusts her head torch and opens the book to the first page, angling her light beam onto it, and holding it so we can all see.

"These are ancient letters, and there are a whole series of them that form the witches' alphabet. There are letters in here that we recognise, which is why Lian was able to read the name." Toni glances at her. "Don't say it again."

"It's just a name," Lian mumbles.

"No, it isn't. But I'll get to that in a minute." Toni runs her finger down the page. "Once you know what these symbols stand for, you can read the text."

"But I don't get how you know what they stand for," I say. "Did you learn this from Nona?"

"Sort of. I like to read, Harvey. You know that. It's something I've learnt over time when I had the chance to sneak a look at her books, and I don't know what every symbol stands for. Some of it I'm guessing using common sense."

"Okay, so where's this spell?" I say.

Toni flips through the book to a section closer to the back. "The book is divided up into parts. Each one focuses on a different kind of spell or ritual. This section holds protection spells, good luck blessings—all that kind of stuff. I picked the simplest one where I could read some of the words, and then I improvised with another spell of my Nona's."

"Seriously? What does it say?" I lean over to look at the page she has open, but the text is blurry. I'm not sure if it's my eyes or the writing, but it makes me feel ill.

Toni takes a breath. "It says: Great Goddess, I summon your power, here and now, at this hour. Use your will, your strength and might. Protect me, and all within sight. So mote it be."

"That's … it?" I ask.

"Spells are like poetry, Harvey," Toni says. "And they're also about believing in the words you're saying, and the action you want to happen. They don't need to be complicated." Toni closes the book and grips the spine with both hands.

"So you're a witch?" Lian asks.

Toni laughs. "No … maybe. I think magic is something anyone can perform, but you have to remember, the power of three always applies."

"That doesn't sound good," I say.

"It isn't … if you're not careful."

I take the book from Toni and flip through it. There are lines of text everywhere that I can't read, and entire pages that are blurry, so I take Toni's word for it that she knows what she's talking about. I'm tired anyway, so I don't ask any more questions. Lian remains quiet, too.

We sit in silence for a few minutes, and I try to decipher everything Toni has told me. How did I never notice she was interested in this kind of stuff? She's my best friend. I should have known. I make a mental note to spend more time with my friends *really* getting to know them. If we ever get out of this hole.

The sky is dark now, and I wish we could see the moon, but I guess it's in the wrong part of the sky. I don't even know what moon it is, if it's full or half full, or whatever. I suddenly really want to see the moon again.

"Is it a full moon tonight?" I ask, breaking the silence.

"Don't know. Why?" Lian runs her fingers through her hair.

"Crazy stuff always happens on a full moon."

"You watch way too much TV, Harvey," Toni says.

"What if we don't get out of here?" Lian picks at her fingernails.

"We can't think like that." I rest my head against the dirt wall and turn to look at her. "We'll get out. And if no one comes to get us tomorrow, then they'll come the next day. And besides, I'm going to have another try at climbing the wall in the morning. I might turn into Spider-Man in my sleep."

Toni chuckles. "You wish."

"I'm cold," Lian says, pulling her jumper sleeves over her hands.

I grab the emergency blanket and unfold it, draping it over all of us. Lian smiles, and her teeth flash white in the light of my torch. She's close enough for me to smell her florally scent, and it makes me a little dizzy. I do something I never thought I'd do with any girl, let alone her. I reach over and take her hand and give it a gentle squeeze. Lian squeezes my hand back, and her smile widens.

"We should get some rest," I say. "We've had a rough day."

Toni clears her throat beside me, and I roll my head the other way to look at her. Since I've already taken the plunge and I'm holding Lian's hand, I take Toni's as well. I guess she could use a little bit of comfort, too. Toni is tough, but there's only so much any of us can take.

Holding Toni's hand feels different, though. She's my best friend. I'm not attracted to her and I know she's not attracted to me, which is so great because nothing ever

gets complicated between us. I like it that way. I wish it were that way with all girls, because everything would be so much easier, and I wouldn't be having weird feelings while holding Lian's hand. I focus on her hand for a second, and my stomach does a flip-flop. I focus on Toni's hand and I settle again.

On one side of me, I have someone who is safe and familiar; on the other, someone who is scary and has the ability to shove me headfirst into the unknown. I fall asleep sitting up, thinking about girls and holding hands, and that finally, maybe there's someone I might *like*.

If only I didn't have to fall into a giant hole to figure it out.

7

My neck hurts, and I squeeze my eyes before opening them. Lian is resting against my shoulder so I try not to move. My mouth is dry and gummy. A toothbrush would be great about now. I hope I don't stink too much.

Dim light streams into the cave, which must mean it's morning. I didn't have the most restful sleep, but it wasn't too bad considering I'm sitting on a hard dirt floor. I want to know what time it is, but Toni is clutching my left hand, and I don't want to wake her either. I stay where I am for a moment, my head against Lian's, and let my eyes fully adjust to being awake.

Lian stirs and I straighten, my neck aching.

"Hey," she says. "Sleep okay?"

I nod, then glance at Toni. Lian doesn't say anything else. She gets to her feet and jiggles on her toes. I know what her problem is, but I'm too embarrassed to say

anything.

"I could do with a … you know," Lian says. "I could use the ladies room."

"Go behind the big rock. I think that's where Toni went while we were in the cavern."

"Promise you won't look?"

"Why would I want to watch you pee?" I ask.

Toni sits with a start, sucking spit into her mouth.

"Morning, sleepy head," I say. "You drooled on my shoulder."

She wipes her mouth with the back of her hand, then stretches. "Use the rock if you need to pee." She glances at Lian.

I look at my watch now that my hand is free. It's a quarter to seven, but the sun would've been up long enough for people to be searching for us. I assume they stopped when it got dark. I have high hopes that we'll be going home today, but I don't say anything because I really don't know for sure.

I get to my feet and wait for Lian to finish before I go into the shadows behind the rock and relieve myself, too. I use my hands to get some loose dirt from the cave wall and sprinkle it on the ground to reduce the smell. Then I sit back with the girls.

"We haven't had a proper meal for twenty-four hours," I say. "We need something in our stomachs."

We sit in a circle and I spread our meagre supplies on the ground between us. There's only enough water left for us to take two sips each. I consider unblocking the tunnel and going down to the stream in the cavern, but I don't suggest it because I don't like the idea. Maybe

I'll consider it later as a last resort.

None of us say anything about our diminished water supply, and we eat half a sandwich each in silence. That leaves the rest of our sandwiches and a bag of chips. Toni says the chips are pretty much out because they'll make us thirsty.

Light streams through the hole above us. *Has Greg been able to find help?* I hope someone is looking for us, but maybe they haven't managed to stumble on the clearing yet. I figure if they have equipment then they might have the same problems we had with the compass going haywire.

I get sick of sitting around and doing nothing, even though we've been awake for less than an hour, so I stand and stare at the dirt wall. There has to be a way that I can get us out of here. I go to the wall and poke the dirt with my finger. There are rocks in the dirt as well, some bigger in places than others, but a lot of the dirt comes away when I scratch at it.

"What are you planning, Harvey?" Toni looks up from her seat on the ground.

"Maybe I can dig some holes in the wall and use them as footholds," I say.

"I still don't know how you're going to get me out."

"Let's deal with that when we have to. How about I see if *I* can get out first?"

I don't want anything to come crashing down on Toni, so I get her to move to the middle of the cave. I also move the rock she's been resting her foot on so she can keep her leg elevated. Back at the wall, I use the end of my torch to dig at the dirt, creating an impression big enough to put the toe of my boot into. I stand back and estimate where the next hole should go and dig again.

Lian comes to stand near me. "You have long legs."

"Are they too far apart, do you think?" I step back and look at the wall.

"For you, they're probably okay, but I might have trouble reaching between them."

I forgot Lian could also climb out herself. "Okay. I'll put them closer together."

I work on the second hole, then the third. After that, I have to put my foot in the first hole to push myself up to get high enough to dig the next. I keep going like this for I'm not sure how long, but when I start work on the fifth indent, the one my right foot is sitting in collapses and I fall, getting a mouthful of dirt on the way down.

"Oh my God, Harvey," Toni says.

I land hard and my legs buckle beneath me, hurting in places I didn't hurt before. I spit the dirt from my mouth and grimace, thinking how gross that must have looked.

"Are you okay?" Lian helps me to my feet.

"I'm still alive, so I guess so." I wipe under my nose with the back of my hand, and it comes away bloody and streaked with dirt. There's still dirt in my mouth so I wipe it out as best I can with the sleeve of my jumper. I'm hot from working on the wall, so I pull my jumper off and toss it to the side.

I study the wall to see where I went wrong. "I think the holes need to be deeper."

The one that collapsed wasn't in far enough. I use the butt of my torch again and hollow it out some more, but it's hard digging with a torch handle, so I try using the

athame. It's not much better so I go back to the torch, preferring to have something that's not a ritual knife in my hand.

"Do you think you should try that spot again?" Lian asks. "Maybe above it a bit would be better."

"We'll find out in a minute, won't we?" I say.

I make the hole deep enough so my foot goes in until my shin hits the wall. Then I keep working on the fifth hole, the one I was digging before I fell.

The cave is quiet while I work, and the girls don't talk. Toni sits with her eyes closed, and Lian paces below me, biting the side of her lip. I wish she would stand still, but I don't say anything. Dirt flicks into my eyes, and I have to wipe it away before I can keep digging. I don't want to look down because I don't want to know how high I am. Firstly, in case I'm still too close to the ground, and secondly, in case I'm too far and freak out at the height.

The only sound I notice is the dirt falling to the cave floor as I dig, until I hear something else. I stop to listen, clinging to the wall via the holes I've made, and it takes me a few seconds to work out what I'm hearing.

"What's that?" Toni asks.

I glance down at her and her eyes are wide. I look up through the hole in the hope that I'll see what I think it is, so when I say it out loud it will be true. But I can't see anything other than blue sky with a whiff of cloud.

The sound comes again. *Whump, whump, whump.*

"Is that a helicopter?" Lian echoes my thoughts.

"I hope so," I say. "Because that means they're looking for us."

"It could be any helicopter flying past," Toni says.

I want to believe otherwise, and before I get the chance to tell her, I spot the red and white shape against the blue above.

"How can we get their attention?" Lian asks. "We have to let them know we're here."

I climb down the wall and stand with my head tilted back so I can see through the hole. There's no way they'd be able to see us from that high up.

"What do we do?" Lian says.

Toni struggles to her feet and hops over to our supplies. She grabs the athame from the box. "We shine this at them."

I press my lips together. "How, exactly?"

Toni takes a deep breath. "Reflection. From the sun? You're an idiot, Harvey."

She struggles to get back to the patch of sunlight, so I rush to help her. We stand with the knife raised, moving it around to try and get a glint of light off the blade.

"Move it this way." Toni leans on me and adjusts my arm.

Lian grabs the book and holds it up. "Maybe we can get the star to reflect as well."

"It's a pentacle," Toni says.

"Oh my God, does it matter?" Lian says.

Toni raises her eyebrows.

"Please don't fight," I say quickly before Toni can reply. I turn my face towards the hole again, angling the athame a few different ways. "Hey. Down here. We're down here."

"They won't hear us." Toni lets go of me and hobbles a few steps away before sitting and staring at the dot in the sky.

The whump of the helicopter is a constant sound, but all we can do is watch as it flies out of view. When I lose sight of it, I also lose a little bit of hope. But then it comes back into view and I think that maybe it has seen the clearing, or our attempts at making a light signal.

It's close to lunchtime and I'm hungry again, but our supplies are low, and there's no water. I stare at the wall. I should keep going with digging my footholds, but I'm not sure I have enough energy left.

"Keep trying to make a light flash," I say to Lian, handing her the athame.

"I'll try." She holds the knife and the book up to the sunlight.

I climb the wall and pick up where I'd left off. The whump of the helicopter continues, and the girls are quiet as I dig. I get about halfway up the wall with almost ten footholds dug when I hear voices. At first, I think I'm imagining them, and then I stop and listen.

"Can you hear that?" I look down at Toni, who is sitting with her leg up.

"Hear what?"

"I heard someone say something."

"What?" Lian asks. "What did they say?"

"I don't know. It was mumbled, but I think someone's up there," I say.

Lian tosses the book and the athame on the ground. She cups her hands around her mouth. "Help!"

Toni struggles to her feet and hops over to Lian's side. They both yell and scream and wave their hands, which I don't think will do much since we're in a hole and no one can see us. I keep digging so I can get higher on the wall while the girls keep calling out.

"Over here." Greg says.

"Greg?" I yell.

"Here's the hole in the ground. Harvey?"

"Hello?" someone else calls over the edge.

I push on my feet, grip the wall, and tilt my head to look up. Greg and another guy peer down at us. Lian starts to cry, and Toni falls silent.

"I told you the ground had collapsed," Greg said.

I'd never been so happy to hear his voice.

"Harvey, Lian, Toni, can you hear me?" a voice I don't know says.

"Yes," I say. "This is Harvey."

"My name is Brian Wells. I'm part of the SES, and we're going to get you out. Is everything okay? Are any of you hurt?"

"Toni has done something to her foot," I say. "We're not sure if it's broken."

"And Lian has hit her head a couple of times," Toni says. "But otherwise, it's scrapes and bruises."

"We're pretty hungry though," Lian says. "And thirsty."

"Okay, sit tight," Brian says. "We need to rig up some ropes, and then we'll come in to get you out."

I climb down the wall to the girls. Lian's face is streaked with tears, the moisture cutting through the dirt and blood on her skin. Toni isn't crying, but she looks as if she's about to. I put my arms out and draw both of them into a group hug. Toni leans on me, favouring her good leg. Lian puts her head on my shoulder and Toni pats her on the back. Something else I never thought I'd see.

"We'll be okay," I say. "I told you they'd find us."

We busy ourselves packing our stuff while they work above. I hear the drone of voices but I don't know how

many people there are.

Greg is at the top of the hole, and he calls down. "Lian, you okay?"

She nods. "I'll be better once we're out."

"What happened?" I look up at Greg. "What took so long?"

"I got a bit disoriented after I left the clearing. The radio wouldn't work for a while, and I blew my whistle until my mouth hurt. So I walked in the direction I thought I should go, and I left some markers along the way. Piles of rocks like Toni said. That kind of thing. Plus, I took some photos of this place and where I'd been so I could remember what it looked like. The radio started working and I ended up getting in touch with camp, because I got totally lost. They found me early this morning, and I led them here."

"You spent the night out here, alone?"

"Yeah," Greg says. "I'm good though."

"Well, I'm actually glad to see you," I say. "Thanks."

"No problem." He looks away, and for a moment I can't see Greg's face. "They're coming to get you now." He moves away from the hole.

Brian runs us through what's going to happen, and I listen carefully. Lian will go up first because she has a head wound, followed by Toni, then me. I'm okay with that. I want the girls out of here and safe.

Lian stuffs the book and box into her backpack.

"What are you doing?" I stare at her. "We should leave those here."

"I want to take them with us," she says, as if that's supposed to convince me it's a good idea.

"Harvey's right," Toni says. "We've messed with this stuff too much already."

Lian looks over her shoulder towards the tunnel we sealed up. "But what if we need it?" She turns back to me. "We might need it."

I don't have an answer for that, and I'm too tired to argue with her anymore. I've learnt that Lian is stubborn, and she usually gets what she wants.

"Whatever," I say. "Let's just get out of here."

The team above lowers a medic in on a rope, and he assesses all of us before getting the people above to winch down another rescue worker and a harness for Lian.

"I'm Tim," the medic says. "And this is Amanda. We're going to get you home safe and sound." He takes another quick look at Lian's wounds, then puts a helmet carefully on her head.

"You ready?" Tim asks.

Lian nods, and Tim helps her into the harness. Amanda gets Lian to stand in front of her and lean back so when they pull the rope from above, they go together nice and smoothly. Lian has the straps of her pack over her shoulders from the front so she hugs it, and Amanda holds her from behind. I watch as they go up, and Lian doesn't look back once.

"You can go via harness as well," Tim says to Toni. "The guys at the top will take a better look at your injuries."

A few minutes later, Amanda is lowered back into the hole, and they go through the same process of lifting Toni out. My best friend smiles at me on her way up, and I feel a weight lift from my shoulders when she reaches the top. She's going to be okay. We're all going to be okay.

"Your turn—Harvey, is it?" Tim says.

"Yep." I nod. "I guess we're doing it the same way?"

"You got it." Tim helps me into another harness, and then straps me to him to repeat the process one more time.

The crew above start winching us up. I hear the howling sound like the night before when the black mist had taken off along the tunnel. Rustling follows, and I tense. Sweat beads on my skin. I squeeze my eyes shut. *Not now. I'm almost out.* The last thing I want is that scary … *thing* coming back.

It looks as if no one is listening to my prayers, though, because when we reach the halfway mark, something below us explodes, and rock spews into the cave. I take a quick look. There are chunks and bits of stone everywhere.

"What was that?" Tim asks.

"Hurry up," I say, looking to the top. "You *do not* want to find out."

"Something exploded."

"I know. We have to get out. Now."

"You okay down there?" a voice comes through Tim's two-way radio. "The ground shook."

Tim puts his radio to his mouth. "Can we get a move on, please?"

"Roger that," the voice says.

I don't want to look down again, but I do anyway, and when I see the mist creeping out of the shadows and spilling into the cave, I think I'm going to scream. But the noise lodges in my throat, and all I can do is hope we reach the top in time.

The mist spreads below us as if it's waiting for something,

and I wonder why it hasn't moved closer. When we reach the top, hands grab me and pull me up. The time it takes Tim to unhook me seems like hours, and I struggle to get away from him. I drop to my knees to look over the edge. The black cloud writhes and swirls at the bottom of the cave, tendrils flicking in every direction.

"What is *that*?" Tim crouches beside me and looks down through the hole.

The mist parts.

Red splotches glow through the scuffed dirt.

Our blood?

The black cloud rises, rolling over itself as it meets the wall.

"That," I say, "is our cue to run."

8

The clearing is organised chaos. I jump to my feet, and the straps from the harness bump against my legs. Tim moves away from the edge of the hole. A dozen people are moving around, performing various tasks, but I can't make out who most of them are. I scan the open space, looking for my friends. Near the tree line, a paramedic is examining Toni's leg, and another is taking a look at Lian's head.

I look back into the hole, hoping I won't see the glowing blood I saw before, that I'd been seeing things because I was so tired, but it's not the case. The mist crawls up the wall and spills over the lip of the hole. I step back.

The mist rises into the air, its tendrils snaking out in every direction. It towers over me. Despite the cool autumn morning, sweat breaks out across my skin. I turn to run, but I don't get more than two steps before I'm slammed

into from behind, sending me face first to the ground.

Rustling and howling sound above me.

Someone screams.

I raise my head and the black cloud explodes into a flock of crows, ribbons of darkness linking the inky feathers together. The birds fly upwards before disintegrating into mist again. The black mass dives for the ground, and I scramble away on my hands and knees. It strikes the earth beside me. I sprawl onto my stomach again.

I search the clearing for Toni and Lian. Panic lines their faces. The paramedics attending them are staring in my direction, their mouths hanging open. Greg is near the girls but stops in his tracks as the mist creeps along the ground, rolling over and over in a wave of blackness. His eyes widen and he takes a step back, his mouth agape. Lian pushes away from the person helping her and scoops up the backpack that's sitting at her feet. The mist turns and heads towards her. She clutches the pack to her chest.

A stick pokes me in the stomach, and I shuffle forward a little before I make it to my feet. I'm running before I'm even upright. I want to yell something helpful, but what the right words are I don't know. *Run* doesn't seem to be enough.

The mist pools at Lian's feet, but she doesn't move away. Toni stands as best she can with her injured foot, staring at the mist in front of them. Greg has edged his way over to Lian, and I want to tell him to get away from the black cloud.

Lian slips her hand around the strap of the backpack and lets it fall to her side. Her face is blank as she takes a step towards the mist. *What is she doing?*

The mist rises into the air. Everyone stops to look. I force my feet to keep running. The clearing seems bigger than before, and my legs feel like lead. I'm almost at the treatment area set up at the tree line.

Lian takes another step.

Greg looks from Lian to the mist and back again.

The cloud is a few metres off the ground now, forming a tight ball, tendrils of blackness snaking out in every direction.

"Lian," I yell, my legs not moving fast enough.

The blackness darts at Lian, and Greg pushes her out of the way. She flies sideways, falling onto the grass. The cloud hits Greg in the chest, knocking him back, but it doesn't let him fall. Everyone screams. The mist goes around behind Greg, circling him and holding him upright as if it's embracing him.

A feeling of being mesmerised washes over me. The darkness looks lovely. Lian crawls towards Greg, reaching out her hand and brushing the edges of the mist. It recoils from her touch, rolling away from her, and Greg falls to the ground.

"What is that?" someone yells.

"Quick, help him," another voice says from across the clearing.

But Greg is already sitting up, and I let out a long breath.

The mist reaches three other people and singles out a female SES worker. It wraps its tendrils around her legs, arms, and torso. The other two people run, and the woman manages to scream before it forces its way into her mouth. She throws her head back, the blackness pouring into her. She rises into the air, carried by the black mist as its coils of darkness continue to pour into her mouth until the cloud is gone. The woman falls to the ground, landing on her knees. She lurches forward and vomits. A stream of blackness flows from her mouth and onto the grass. It coils around itself, then pools like thick oil slicking the surface of a lake.

Toni screams as I run the last few metres to her side. I don't want to let anything happen to her, but how will I stop the cloud of darkness if it attacks? The paramedic who helped Lian is checking Greg over. I hope he's okay.

"Lian." I step forward and take her arm to pull her back with Toni and me.

Toni looks at me as if to say, *"What the hell are you doing? She started this."*

Lian shakes her head and blinks. "What's happening?" She looks at Greg. "What happened?"

People run all over the clearing. Some run towards us and some run to help the SES worker who is now face-down on the grass.

The mist is hovering above the ground, back near the edge of the hole, but it doesn't look as if it will attack again. Maybe it's had enough of sucking face with people. But I've thought too soon. A second later, it darts across the clearing and attacks a man frantically packing up some equipment. It lifts him into the air, and more people scream as the darkness does to him what it did to the woman.

When I concentrate on the mist, that strange feeling of lovely calmness washes over me again, and I have to make the conscious effort to drag my gaze away from the blackness, using my peripheral vision instead. The man lands hard, and the mist rolls away from him. Another woman in an SES uniform runs to his side. The mist darts towards us again, and again I want to flee, but I wouldn't be fast enough to outrun it. And I won't leave my friends behind.

"What's it doing?" Toni says.

"Don't look at it," I say. "It's … don't look at the darkness."

"It's lovely, isn't it?" Lian says.

I shuffle around in front of her to block her view. "Lian." I shake her gently, and her eyes focus on me. "Don't look at it."

"I think it's angry," Toni says. "We've pissed it off."

"You think?" I stare at my best friend, my back to the evil cloud, which probably isn't the best idea.

"What should we do?" Lian asks.

No sooner is the question out of her mouth than the mist is at Lian's feet, curling around her ankles and writhing over the backpack that hangs from her hand.

"Does it want the book?" I ask.

"And probably the box," Toni says. "I told you to put it back, Lian."

I lunge at Lian and snatch the backpack from her hand, then run away from them towards the middle of the clearing. The mist follows, which is what I'd hoped it would do. I stop when I reach one of the bigger rocks. There are no people near it, so I hope my distraction will give everyone time to regroup.

The mist rolls across the grass.

"What are you doing, Harvey?" Toni yells.

"Just … stay away from it," I yell back.

I have no idea what I'm doing, but I hope whatever it

is will make this thing go away. I kneel on the ground and unzip the backpack, dumping everything in front of me.

I pick up the book. "Is this what you want?"

The mist stops and forms a sheet in front of me. I open the book and it recoils, parting in the middle and doubling back on itself to join together again a few metres away. It creeps forward slowly. I move closer with the book and it recoils again.

The mist doesn't like the book.

I smile, then the cloud of darkness hits me in the chest and I'm slammed backwards into the rock. My head makes a *thwack* sound as it connects with the stone, and my eyes go blurry. I slide to the grass and put my hand to the back of my head. My fingers come away bloody.

The mist curls around my feet and writhes over the backpack and the contents on the ground. I shield my eyes and try not to look directly at it. It slams into the box, moving it, but the box doesn't open. The cloud shoots into the air again, and when it comes down Lian is standing there. I didn't see her come across the clearing. The pendant around her neck glows.

"Lian, stay back." I wince because my head is pounding. I look around her and see that more people have come closer.

The mist slams into the box again, and this time the box pops open, spilling the contents onto the grass. The darkness rolls over all the items, sending out its tendrils. When it reaches the athame it pulls back, moving on to the next item. I don't move, partly because my head hurts and partly because I'm having trouble processing everything. The mist finds the vial of blood and coils around it. The glass makes a *tink* sound as the vial snaps and the blood drips out. Most of it seeps into the black cloud before it hits the ground, but a few drops splatter on the grass.

I grab the athame and swipe it at the mist, slicing through the darkness. It recoils. The ground shakes and Lian loses her balance, stumbling. Others in the clearing do the same, and the trembling continues. The mist spreads over the ground again, then ripples outwards, knocking everyone to the ground. It attacks three more of the SES workers, gushing in and out of each of their mouths before anyone has time to help. Crows caw and feathers rustle as the mist morphs back and forth from birds to clouds.

Lian runs towards the cloud and I move to get up to stop her, but my eyes blur again and I can't get to my feet. I kneel on the grass and watch as she confronts the darkness.

"Stop," she yells. The cloud hovers in front of her, the pendant around her neck pulsing red. "Go back." Lian points to the hole.

I rub my eyes, and search for Toni. She's sitting on the grass beside Greg. I blink a few times to clear my blurry vision. Her lips are moving, and I hope she's trying something to help us get rid of the darkness.

The mist slams into Lian's stomach, knocking her to the ground before darting across the grass and spilling over the lip of the hole. Another crow caws, but I can't see it.

Once the darkness is gone, the ground stops shaking, and I get my first chance to look closely at the destruction it has caused. Five people lie completely still, while everyone else is in various states of consciousness or struggling to get back on their feet. I get up on wobbly legs and find my way to Lian. Yesterday, I would never have thought I could care about someone I barely know.

I slip my arm under Lian's shoulders and pull her into my lap. The coppery aroma of blood mixed with flowers fills my nose.

She opens her eyes and stares at me. "Is it gone?"

I nod, unable to speak, because I don't want to say yes when I don't know if it's true.

9

The SES had set up base back at camp. The other teachers and students had packed up and gone home, but when we'd arrived, Toni, Lian, and I had been greeted by our frantic parents. The helicopter hadn't been able to land due to instrument malfunction, which didn't surprise me, so getting out of the clearing hadn't been easy. Our rescuers had come in on foot, but the mist's rampage had left five of them dead, and several others injured.

Toni, Lian, Greg, and I had spent the night in hospital. We'd had our cuts and bruises tended to, and were treated for exposure. Toni broke her foot but the doctor said it's not too serious. No cast due to the swelling, so she had it bandaged and has to wear a moonboot for a few weeks.

I flop onto my bed, feeling mostly okay. I stare at the map in my hands and the mark Greg had made on it. I can't remember how I ended up with it. I guess he'd

stuffed it into my backpack at some point when we were leaving the clearing. I run my fingers along the lines I've drawn, marking where I think we went. I have no idea why I did it. Too much time sitting at home because the doctors gave me a pass for a few days.

Time off school should be bliss, but not with a mum like mine. She hasn't left me alone since she laid eyes on me back at camp. I'm glad to be home, but coming to 'talk' to me every ten minutes is getting a bit much.

You'd think I almost died.

Jack has tried to call a few times as well, but I haven't answered. I don't feel like idle chit chat at the moment.

I put the map aside and pick up the TV remote, planning to find something on Netflix to numb my thoughts and switch my brain off, but before I can get to the Smart Hub menu, a news report flashes onscreen. Helicopter footage of the clearing fills the panel. When the reporter says five dead and several injured, I squeeze my eyes closed. I quickly hit the button on my remote and load my Netflix app before I hear any more. I already know what the reporters have been saying, blaming the 'incident' on a localised earthquake, and the deaths on an underground pocket of gas. Apparently, the girls and I are lucky to be alive. I don't disagree, but earthquakes and gas leaks have nothing to do with what happened.

A knock sounds on my door.

I love my mum, and it's nice to be loved back, but all I want right now is to be left alone. Those exact words are about to come out of my mouth when she knocks again before cracking the door and peering in. She opens the door wider, a plate of choc chip cookies in her hand,

and my words fall away to nothing.

"I baked." Mum smiles. "Want one?"

"Sure." I run a hand through my hair and get up from the bed.

Mum holds the plate out and I take a cookie, shoving it into my mouth so I don't have to talk to her. She's found about a hundred ways this morning to ask the same question.

"Are you feeling better?" Mum says. *Version one hundred and one.*

"I'm fine," I say, spraying cookie crumbs over her.

"Harvey, you shouldn't talk with your mouth full."

I raise my eyebrows and keep chewing, staring at her and hoping the look in my eyes says *please leave me alone.*

I swallow. "I'm going to call Toni."

"Okay." She presses her lips together, and I know she's sad because I won't tell her anything about the hole. "I'll be downstairs if you need me."

I put my hand on the knob and start to close the door, but she lingers. I don't want to shut the door in her face, but it's getting close to that. She eventually leaves the plate of cookies on top of my speaker and leaves.

The door closes with a click, and I press my forehead to it for a moment, closing my eyes. I don't *really* want to call Toni, because she'll make me talk about the clearing. But I do want to call her because I haven't spoken to her since we got home. I need to return Jack's calls, too. But what am I supposed to say to him? I spent the night in a hole with two girls? He'll focus more on that part than on being missing and injured, and thinking we were going to die.

Before I can pick it up, my phone rings. It vibrates as well, creeping across my desk. The buzz against the wood makes it sound louder. It's Toni, and I should answer it, but I don't move. My phone goes silent and I flop on my bed, turning my attention back to the TV. The phone rings again and I sigh, getting to my feet to retrieve it before it vibrates its way off my desk.

"Hello," I say.

"Harvey, it's me," Toni says.

"I know. Hello, Me."

"Don't be a goofball. Are you watching the Channel Ten news?"

"No."

"They're reporting on our rescue."

"So?"

Toni goes silent, and I hear her soft breathing on the other end of the phone. She wants me to watch the news, but she can't and she won't make me.

She sighs. "How are you?"

"Mum has found a hundred and one ways to ask me that exact question."

"And how many answers have you given her?"

"One," I say. "I'm. Fine."

"Well, I'm not," Toni says. "I'm going to be in this horrid moonboot for four weeks. Broken feet suck."

"Being dead would suck more," I say.

Toni laughs. "You really know how to put things into perspective."

"Have you spoken to Lian?" I ask, and then I immediately regret it. Of course she hasn't. They're not friends. Why would she talk to her?

"Actually, I have. She called and then came to see me last night."

"Why?" *What is happening?* "Where did she get your number?"

"She asked." Toni pauses. "She wanted to talk, and she knew it would be hard for me to get around with my new fashion accessory, so she came over."

I don't say anything for a few seconds. I'm mildly hurt that Lian didn't come to see me, but then I have two fully functioning legs, and I didn't make an effort to go and see her, either.

"How is she?" I finally ask.

"She's … shaken up." Toni pauses. "Harvey, what that … *thing* did—"

"Do we really want to talk about this?" I say.

"We have to do something. What if it comes back?"

I pull my desk drawer open and stare at the athame hiding inside. Toni made us split up the items we'd taken from the cavern. I got the thing that could actually kill someone. Lian was already wearing the pendant and she wouldn't part with the book, so Toni took the box. I didn't want any of it, but my best friend was stubborn.

I take a deep breath and close the drawer again. "Give me half an hour and I'll be at your place. Then we can talk. I don't want to do it over the phone."

"Okay, see you soon." Toni hangs up and her abruptness reminds me of the old Toni, the one from before we went on that stupid camping trip.

I toss my phone onto the bed, where it lands on the map, and sit on the edge. I don't want to go yet. Since I got home, I've tried to block out what we went through at camp. Being lost wasn't fun. Being lost, injured, hungry, tired, and tormented by a misty black cloud that morphed into crows was worse. My brain can't cope. I'm not generally superstitious, but I'm not a sceptic either. If I see something I pretty much believe in it. I don't know how many times I've wished something exciting and otherworldly would happen to me. But this? I don't want it.

Toni seems to know a lot more about witches than I realised she did. My mind runs through everything that's happened and everything we saw. The nook with the candles. The book. The glowing blood. The mist. The crows. The rocks … I jump to my feet. I drew the location of the rocks in my notebook. Where did I put it? My gaze darts around my room, landing on my desk and the pile of books beside my keyboard. The notebook is sitting on top. I grab it and flick to the last page I wrote on.

The mark in the middle of the circle was where we'd fallen into the cave above the cavern. The other marks are where the smaller rocks and the five bigger ones were. I'm looking at a rough representation of the stone circle, but there has to be something else I'm missing. I tilt my head and run an imaginary line around the outside, joining the dots together.

Then my brain clicks.

I rummage around in my desk drawer, pushing the athame to the back, until I find a ruler, then draw lines from one of the bigger outside marks to the two opposite it. I turn the notebook and do the same, then fill in the final line. I walk backwards until my legs hit the bed and I sit again.

I'm staring at a five-pointed star.

The bigger rocks in the clearing represent the points of a pentagram.

Crap.

I glance at my watch. I have fifteen minutes before Toni is expecting me. I need to get to her place. I rip the piece of paper from my notebook, fold it in half and try to think of a way to get out of the house without Mum getting all protective and stuff. Eating another cookie doesn't help with the ideas much, and then it does.

"Toni needs cookies," I say to myself, crumbs falling from my mouth. I stuff my wallet, the paper, and my phone into my pocket, then grab the plate of cookies before heading downstairs. Mum is scrubbing the kitchen sink, and I want to tell her she can already see her face in it, but I stop myself. She gets like this when she's upset. For some reason cleaning seems to calm her down, and I want her to be calm.

"Mum." I stand in the doorway.

She stops scrubbing and whirls around. "Yes, Harvey. Everything okay?"

I take a step into the kitchen, clutching the cookie plate with both hands. "I want to go and see Toni."

Mum stares at me for a few moments that feel like minutes. She blinks, then frowns, looking as if I've spoken to her in another language.

"You want to leave the house?"

"To go to Toni's," I say. "And take her some cookies. It's a five-minute drive. I promise not to fall in any holes along the way."

"Don't make jokes like that, Harvey." Mum blows her

105

hair out of her eyes. "Let me put those in a container for you."

She takes the plate from me and hunts through the Tupperware cupboard, coming out with the 1970s round, green container. It's always been perfect for Mum's cookies. She stacks them inside and presses the lid on, handing it to me with a tight-lipped smile.

"I'll be back for dinner," I say.

"Call me if you … Just be safe, okay?" She rubs my arm.

I kiss her on the cheek then head for the door, grabbing my car keys from the bowl on the hallway bookshelf as I pass. I want to get out of there before she changes her mind. I open the door of my car and a crow caws, sending a shiver up my spine. Rustling comes from the gumtree at the side of the driveway, and I spin around to see the black bird perched on a low branch. Its head twists, and it stares at me with one beady eye. It caws again, making me flinch.

I get in the car and slam the door. Toni's place isn't far from mine, and I spend the short drive trying to shake the creepy feeling that's made my stomach roll.

Toni's mum has the front door open before I've even had time to kill the engine. I climb out and she smiles warmly, eyeing the container in my hands.

"Let me guess," Mrs Garcia says. "Choc chip?"

I nod and return her smile, feeling a little better. "How's Toni?"

"She has a broken foot but, last time I checked, that's not life-threatening."

I really like Toni's mum. She's so down-to-earth and friendly. She's also the one Toni gets her wild curly hair from, and skin that tans when she looks at the sun. Toni hates her hair, and she's not into sunbathing. She's always complaining her traits are a waste on someone who doesn't want to use them to their advantage.

When I walk in, Toni is on the couch with a stable table on the cushion beside her. She has her foot resting on a footstool, the moonboot strapped to her leg. "Hey, Harvey."

"Hey," I say. "How's the foot?"

Toni shrugs. "I'm kinda peeved I don't have a cast. You could've written on it."

"How old are you?" I raise my eyebrows.

Mrs Garcia laughs. "I would've written on it."

"I wanted to as well." Louisa, Toni's little sister, bounces out of the kitchen. She brushes her wild curls away from her face.

I hand Toni the cookie container. "I'm not sure I'd be able to think of something worthy of setting in … plaster."

"I would write something on the back and not tell her what it said." Louisa grins. "Where she couldn't see it. That would be cool."

Toni and her mum laugh, then Mrs Garcia leaves us to our own devices.

"Are those cookies?" Louisa asks.

"Here." Toni pulls the lid off and holds the container out to her sister.

Louisa takes a cookie. "Can I hang out with you guys?"

"No," Toni and I say at the same time.

"Harvey and I have some things to talk about." Toni stares at Louisa.

"Fine." Louisa grabs another cookie. "I'm going to my room."

"We can hang out tomorrow," Toni yells as Louisa runs up the stairs.

Toni twists a finger into her unruly hair and looks at me. "Sit."

I move the stable table to the floor and do as I'm told, sinking into the couch. "Does it hurt?" I glance at her leg.

"It throbs, but it's not so bad. They said you did a pretty good job of first aid." She smiles. "You okay, Harvey?"

I fidget with the hem of my T-shirt, then pull the piece of paper out of my back pocket. "Remember when we first came into the clearing, you and Lian went down first and I stood at the top of that outcrop with Greg?" She nods. "Well, I thought something felt off, and then I noticed the rocks—"

"The stone circle."

"Yeah. But there was something weird … it didn't look like a normal stone circle … if a stone circle is … normal. So I drew the rock locations in my notebook." I unfold the paper and hand it to Toni.

"Oh … shit …" Toni looks at me, then back at the paper.

"That can't be good, right?"

"No, it isn't." Toni hands the paper back to me then gestures for me to grab her iPad from the stable table. She takes it and flips the cover open. "I've been doing some research, and there's a legend about a coven of witches who could be associated with the book and other stuff we found."

"Seriously? Witches and covens and legends?"

"Oh, my." Toni smiles.

"Stop it," I say. "What kind of legend? Wait, don't tell me. I don't want to know."

Toni waves her hand. "Yes, you do, Harvey. It's something I heard my Nona say once, but I'd forgotten about it. I've managed to cross-reference it with something I've found online. The details are sketchy because it's more than a thousand years old, but there was a group of witches who called themselves the Moonlight Coven."

She adjusts the screen of her iPad to show me what she's found.

"See. N ... was their High Priestess. She was accused of witchcraft and sentenced to burning at the stake, but she went a little crazy and worked dark magic to escape. She ended up massacring most of the town in Italy where she lived. The coven bound her so she couldn't kill anyone else." Toni hands me her iPad.

"The Moonlight Coven." I stare at the screen. "But it says here they're Italian."

Toni grimaces. "Yeah, I don't like that part, but fortunately for us, there's a small group of witches in Italy who still worship the Moonlight Coven, and they're now using the name. I guess the legend is a part of their history, which is why I was able to find some info on N."

"But how could your Nona have known anything about them being here?" I ask. "And the timeline is all wrong. Australia wasn't settled until the late 1700s."

"Keep reading," Toni says. "After the coven bound N, they left Italy to bury her far away from civilisation. But they never returned home. They were witches, Harvey. Who's to say they didn't end up here? Anything is possible." Toni takes the iPad from me and swipes the screen. "The legend says all the witches became lost with time."

"Except for the crazy one we woke up," I say. "How

did we do that anyway? You'd think if she was all scary and powerful they'd have done a better job to keep her locked up."

"Spells don't have to be complicated to be powerful."

"But that's just it. Letting her out was too easy. We have no idea about any of this stuff, and yet we managed to unleash a pretty pissed off witch."

"I don't think we should focus on *how* we let her out." Toni glares at me. "We need to figure out how to put her back. Before she kills someone else."

"Not that I'm disagreeing, but why is it our responsibility?" I ask. "Can't we just … hope she goes away?"

Toni puts her head back against the couch and closes her eyes. "I don't think she'll go away just because we ignore her."

"I still don't get how it was so easy to free her."

Toni sighs. "If you think about it, it wasn't that easy. We just didn't know what was happening."

"What do you mean?" I turn sideways and face her, pulling my leg up onto the couch.

"Three steps, Harvey. Remember the power of three? I'm betting the book was binding her. We set everything in motion by opening the book. Then her name was repeated three times, and the third." Toni stares at me. "Blood."

"Lian."

"All of us. You cut yourself with the athame, remember? But Lian bled the most, and since she was the one who opened the book, and repeated the witch's name, I guess everything worked in N's favour."

All this information is too much for my brain to handle and I stand up, running a hand through my hair. I'm way out of my comfort zone, and for a moment I consider leaving. It's not like Toni can chase me with a broken foot.

"What do we do?" I stare down at my best friend.

"We have to talk to Lian. I need to read the book."

Talk to Lian? I'm not ready to face her yet. We're back in the real world. With other people around. We should be returning to how everything was before, where I have my small group of not-so-popular friends, and she has her huge group of popular people hanging around her like a bad smell. We're from two completely different sides of the fence, chalk and cheese, black and white, coffee and tea, apples and oranges. Toni stares at me, her eyebrows raised.

"Why exactly do you want to read the book?" I ask.

"Because the internet is not the only place I found information about the Moonlight Coven."

I blink a few times. "Care to elaborate?"

Toni looks around as if she expects someone to burst into the room any second. "I found Nona's book."

"Another book ..."

"It's her Book of Shadows."

"This is too weird." I run a hand down my face. "I can't believe we're talking about thousand-year-old witches and your Nona. You can call Lian and tell her you want the book. You don't need me."

Toni looks at me with an expression on her face that I've come to know well. It's her, 'I know what you're doing, Harvey' face.

"You don't want to talk to her, do you?" she asks. "Well, toughen up because we have to. The three of us are in this together whether you like it or not."

"I don't like it," I say. "Why can't you figure it out, so I can go home and—"

"Do not say watch TV." Toni scowls. "We have to do this as a group, Harvey. The power of three."

"Stop it with the power of three. It sucks."

Toni sighs and presses her lips into a line. "I want the book so I can see if everything adds up. Nona has written some interesting stuff. And I think if *you* ask Lian, she's more likely to hand it over."

"I … okay, whatever." I play with the hem of my T-shirt. "I'll talk to Lian when we're back at school."

10

Mum was being her hovering, over-protective self, which meant I could spend the weekend in my room and not have to worry about anyone or anything.

I hurt in places I never knew could hurt, and it was a good excuse to be more of a hermit that I already was. Mum kept up the supply of choc chip cookies.

Jack called a couple of times, but I didn't answer. I texted him to say I'd pick him up Monday, and that Mum had put me under house arrest. I avoided Toni's phone calls as well. She resorted to sending me texts.

Toni: Call me. Want 2 talk.

Toni: Waiting.

Toni: Use ur finger 2 press green circle on screen.

Toni: Hello!!!

Toni: Harvey! Answer ur phone!!!

Me: Stop with the !!!

113

Toni: I want 2 talk.

Me: Don't make me come over there and move your phone where you can't reach it.

Toni: You wouldn't!

Me: I would!!!!!!!

Me: Talk @ school.

Now Monday is here, and I'm not in the mood to talk about anything. If Mum had her way I'd be staying home for a few more days, but the doctor has given me a clean bill of health.

I stop my crappy Holden Commodore outside Jack's house. He slides into the front seat and studies me for a moment before pulling his door closed.

"You look different," he says.

I put the stick in first and pull away from the kerb. "How so?"

"Like you spent the night in a hole with two girls." He smiles, and I want to punch him.

"One of them was Toni," I say. "She doesn't count."

"Are you going to give me the details of what happened?" Jack pushes his glasses up his nose. "You wouldn't answer my calls."

"No."

Jack sits back in his seat and crosses his arms. "You're no fun."

"You have no idea how much fun I can be." I smirk, guiding the car past the shops along the highway before turning off towards school.

I'm not looking forward to today. There's bound to be an endless barrage of stares and questions. Although, I'm mildly interested to hear what the rumour mill has in store for me and Toni. It wouldn't dare touch Lian.

I park in one of the empty spaces along the back driveway that leads into Saint Paul's High School. We don't even make it to the music block before people start to stare and whisper behind their hands.

"It's going to be a long day," I mumble as we reach Toni's locker.

She has her crutches tucked under her arms and is fighting with her biology textbook. I lunge to catch it as it falls from her grasp.

"They haven't assigned you a helper?" I slip the book into her locker.

"I don't *need* a helper, Harvey." Toni slams her locker closed, struggling to shoulder her bag and hold the crutches at the same time. I lift her bag strap onto her shoulder, and she smiles. "I've got you."

"Hey, Anderson," a voice says. I turn, and Noah Ward is heading towards us. "What'd you do to Lian?"

"Here we go," I mutter under my breath, facing him. "Nothing. We fell in a hole. Or didn't you hear?"

"Yeah, I heard." Noah stops an inch from me and I don't want to look away, but I can't help it.

"Leave him alone," Jack says.

"You, shut up." Noah pokes Jack in the chest.

"Get lost." Toni swats Noah's hand away. "You don't know anything about what happened."

"You better not have touched her, arsewipe." Noah leans forward, and I take a step back.

"What the hell? Why would Harvey do something like that?" Toni says.

Noah scowls and shoves me, and I bump Toni.

She stumbles backwards, and I can't stop her fall. One of her crutches twists around and hits me in the shin, and then she's on her arse, squeezing her eyes shut and grimacing.

"You're a dick, Noah," I say, before I can stop myself.

"What did you call him?" Logan O'Farrell shoves me from behind, and my shoulder hits the lockers. Crap. Where did he come from?

"Dick is a much better insult than arsewipe," Jack says.

"Leave them alone," Lian calls from down the hall.

I crouch beside Toni. "Want me to take you home?"

She shakes her head and takes a deep breath. "Just took me by surprise. I'm fine."

Jack and I help Toni up and back onto her crutches. My gaze meets Lian's and she smiles. I don't smile back. I don't like her friends. I never have. Lian's smile falters.

By now, we have a bit of an audience. Violette stands beside Lian, and their other friends, Madison, Nora, and Callie, are not too far away. Greg arrives on the scene as well, his eyebrows raised and his gaze fixed on me. He stands behind Lian but doesn't say anything.

I don't want to be the first to leave because I don't want them to think they've won, so I stand there holding Toni's arm, staring at the popular people and daring them with my eyes to say something else. But what I'm really trying to do is keep my legs from shaking and ignore the sudden urge to pee.

Eventually, Noah shoulders past me. He doesn't say anything, but he doesn't have to. Everyone knows this isn't over. One by one, they walk away, and everyone goes back to their own business. The homeroom bell sounds, and I'm grateful because it gives us a reason to move. Lian and Greg linger, and I turn to leave without talking to them. It's probably rude, but I've had enough of today already. Toni crutches along beside me and Jack walks on my other side.

"Harvey," Lian says. "Wait."

I stop and face her, but I don't speak. Right now, I don't like her much because I don't like her friends. I know it's not a good enough reason to write someone off, but it's the easiest one I can think of, because the truth is I don't want to like her. It's too complicated.

"You guys okay?" Greg asks from beside her.

"I'm sorry about Noah." Lian ignores Greg and fidgets with the edge of the folder she has clutched to her chest. "He can be—"

"A dick?" Jack says. "Yeah, Harvey already told him that."

I'm a little shocked to hear him talk like that to Lian. Jack doesn't usually have the guts to even breathe around someone like her. Greg has a confused frown on his face, and Lian doesn't respond. I turn away and keep walking to homeroom with Jack and Toni.

"Harvey," Toni says. "We didn't ask Lian about the book."

I glare at her, hoping she gets the message that I don't want to talk about it. I guess she does because her mouth snaps shut.

"What actually happened out there?" Jack asks outside the door to Toni's homeroom. "I mean, for those people to … die? And are you guys … you know?" He shrugs. "Are you all right?"

Toni rolls her eyes, and I press my lips together to

stop from smiling. Jack has never been one to show emotion of any kind. He's mostly deadpan.

"You read, don't you? And you have eyes?" Toni says. "I figured you'd get everything you needed from the news."

"An earthquake, aftershocks, and a freak gas leak … out in the bush?" Jack says. "I don't buy it."

"Will you be joining us today, Toni?" Mrs Emerson says, peering up from her desk. "And you boys are at the wrong classroom, which means you're late." She looks at her watch.

"Did you notice Lian's neck?" Toni moves awkwardly into the doorway.

"Can't say I was looking." I adjust the strap of my backpack on my shoulder. "I was too busy being angry."

"Ahem." Mrs Emerson clears her throat.

We wait until Toni is sitting at her desk, then we use her as an excuse for being late to our own homeroom.

The morning passes slowly. During recess, I avoid Jack and Toni because I don't want to talk about camp. By lunch, I'm sick of everyone looking at me, and I'm glad to head towards our usual spot and see my friends. Toni is sitting on the seat that lines the wall in the main yard. I dump my bag and flop down next to her. Today is feeling as if it's stretching on forever.

"You're a speed-demon on those crutches," I say.

"Science block is closer. Did you tell Jack anything?" Toni takes a bite of her sandwich.

"I haven't had the chance." I pull my lunch from my bag and unwrap it. "Do we need to go there?"

"Go where?" Jack chucks his bag on top of mine and sits next to me. "Where are we going?"

"I was asking Harvey if he's told you anything about our little camp mishap," Toni says.

"Nope." Jack pulls his own homemade lunch from his bag. "He's been avoiding eye contact with me all morning."

"I thought you said you haven't had the chance?" Toni elbows me.

I shrug and chew my food so I don't have to answer.

Jack puts his bottle of water to his lips and chugs it.

"We released a witch," Toni says.

Jack spits water, and the spray hits the asphalt in front of us.

"What?" He wipes his mouth with the back of his hand.

I take a deep breath and shove more food in my mouth because I do *not* want to talk about this. Toni and Jack talk across me and I tune them out, glancing around the yard at everyone and what they're doing. It's no different to any other day at school. Until someone screams.

We look towards the sound. Madison bursts out the door to the girls' bathroom on the far side of the yard. Lian follows. Her shoulders are shaking and her hands tremble as she plays with the pendant around her neck. I stand and take a step forward.

"She's dead," Madison yells, moving my attention to her. She's also crying.

Someone else screams as black mist flows out from the crack under the bathroom door. Howling and rustling fill the air as the darkness spreads over the ground. Those closest to it run back, screaming.

No one else moves.

"What do we do?" I ask.

Lian's brow is pinched. She covers her face with her

hands and screams into them. The pendant around her neck is glowing bright enough for me to see it from across the yard.

"Holy crap," Toni says.

The black cloud rises into the air and ripples out, exploding into a flock of crows. A few swoop and peck at the onlookers, and some students, including Madison, are knocked to the ground before the birds disperse into the sky. Madison sobs and Callie helps her to her feet, hugging her. Nora stands beside them.

Mrs Bryson runs over from the edge of the oval. She stops and talks to the girls, her head turning to the sky a couple of times, but I can't hear what she says. The birds are gone.

Greg goes to Lian but she pushes him away and runs in our direction, her gaze locked on the building behind us. She doesn't look at us or say anything. Lian passes with her head down and takes the ramp that leads to the library and front offices.

Greg reaches us and hesitates, then stops.

"What the hell happened?" I ask.

"I don't know." Greg looks back towards the bathroom. "And maybe we don't want to."

"We should follow her." Toni zips up her schoolbag, grabs her crutches from the seat beside her, and struggles to her feet.

"Already doing that." Greg goes after Lian.

"Shouldn't we see if we can help?" I point towards the commotion across the yard.

"There're enough people around already," Toni says. "And if someone's dead, we can't help them."

"That's … cold," I say.

Toni sighs. "It's the truth."

Jack fidgets with the wrapper from his sandwich and stays quiet, his brow pinched.

"Maybe we should leave Lian alone," I say. "She looked pretty upset."

"All the more reason to go and see if she's okay." Toni glares at me.

Jack jumps up. "I agree with Toni. I want to know more about what's going on."

"Well, she has Greg looking out for her. And I don't want to have anything to do with any of it." I shoulder my bag with every intention of walking in the opposite direction. "I want the supernatural stuff to stay *inside* the TV."

Toni adjusts her crutches under her arms. "I'm going to find Lian. She headed towards the library."

The crowd around Madison has grown. I'm not sure what to do, but when Jack follows Toni, so do I. Enough people are helping Madison and whoever she's talking about, and as much as I don't want to go and find Lian, I don't want to see another dead body either.

The library is quiet. A few students are browsing the books. Even though most of the kids in my grade would class me as a nerd, the library is not a place I frequent. Although the quiet is appealing.

We find Lian and Greg in the reference section. Lian is sitting at one of the tables with the witch's book open in front of her. She flicks through another book so fast I think she's going to rip the pages. Greg stares over her shoulder. He runs a hand down his face and sighs. It seems we've missed whatever it was they were arguing about.

"Hey, Lian," Toni says, easing herself into a chair on the other side of the table.

"I can't get her to make any sense," Greg says, folding his arms. "She keeps mumbling something about a spell."

Lian looks up, her eyes wide as if we've surprised her. They're red from crying. For a moment she seems confused, like she doesn't recognise us, but then she glances back at the books. "Toni, maybe you can help me. You can read this stuff, right?"

"Some of it." Toni stares at Lian.

"I need a spell for raising the dead."

Jack coughs, then sits in a chair at the end of the table.

No one speaks.

I grip the back of Toni's chair until my knuckles turn white.

She leans forward and clasps her hands together on the table. "Who died, Lian?"

Another tear rolls down Lian's cheek. She sits still, her hand resting on the open book. "Violette. That ... *thing*. It killed her."

"Oh boy," I say.

"We can't bring her back," Toni says. "That kind of magic is ... bad."

Lian slumps in her chair, her hand falling into her lap. She squeezes her eyes closed and her shoulders tremble. "She can't be dead."

Greg puts a hand on her arm.

"I think ... maybe we need to leave it alone and not mess with something we know nothing about," Toni says, her voice low.

I hold my breath and wait, because surely Lian is

going to disagree and the girls will start arguing again. Then we'll get kicked out for being too noisy. I tighten my hold on Toni's chair, and let out a slow breath.

Lian frowns. "I want Violette … I want to understand. That's all."

"So you can bring your best friend back from the dead?" I ask.

Lian glares at me. "You'd want to do the same."

"If this book belongs to who I think it belongs to, trust me," Toni says, leaning forward on the table, "you don't want to mess with it."

"Maybe we should go and see what's happening with Violette," Greg says.

"Nothing's happening with her. She's dead." Lian slams both books closed, tucks the witch's one under her arm, and gets up to return the reference book to the shelf.

"What Greg means is that you need to deal with what's happened." I look at Greg sideways. "Running away won't change anything."

"That's exactly what I meant," Greg says.

I frown and blink a few times, trying to understand how I'm living in a universe where Gregory Watson is agreeing with me.

Jack hasn't said anything since we came in, and I glance over at him. He has his head tilted to the side, watching Lian. I don't like the way he's looking at her, so I swat him on the arm and he jumps.

"Can I have the book?" Toni asks.

Lian turns and stares at my best friend, clutching the ancient tome to her chest. "Why?"

Toni clasps her hands together on the table. "I've been

123

doing some research. I'd like to … cross-reference it."

Lian looks down at the book in her hands, and a tear drips from her chin, staining the leather cover.

"I think Toni is right." Greg takes a step towards her. "We don't want to mess with this stuff. Give it to her, and we can forget any of this weird shit ever happened." He touches her arm again and I shift on the spot, frowning. "Let them deal with it."

"You should go be with your friends," Toni says. "I'll give it back to you when I'm done."

Lian comes around the table and stops beside Toni's chair, but she doesn't hand over the book. She smells florally, and I want to move away, but I also don't want to. Memories of holding her in the clearing come back to me, and my brain feels as if it's about to explode. Nothing makes any sense. I can't read her or Greg, and I have no idea what the hell is going on with them, or me, or my feelings, or the entire balance of the whole damn universe.

"I don't want to be with my friends right now," Lian says.

"What are we then?" I ask, then wish I didn't sound so mean.

Lian smiles. "There's a party at the lookout, up in the Heights, this weekend. You should come."

Yep. Nothing makes sense.

"I … um," I say. "Violette …"

Lian blinks. "We can make it a memorial party."

It's then I realise she's putting her 'popular' mask back into place. She's the one who always smiles, is nice to everyone, and who everyone loves in return. Now I understand why she ran to the library. It was to get away before anyone could see her break. And now she'll walk out there as if nothing happened. Pretend to be the perfect one again, and hold everyone else up with no one to hold her.

I want to be the one to hold her.

"We'll be there," Jack says, and I supress the urge to smack him on the arm.

"We'll think about it." I run a hand through my hair.

"Lian," Toni says, holding out her hand. "The book?"

Lian puts it on the table and rests her hand on top. "Will you come on Friday?"

"We'll come."

Greg takes a deep breath. "Come on, Lian. Let's get out of here."

"Yeah, you should. Before anything else catastrophic happens," I say.

Lian frowns but follows Greg. Toni twists in her seat to watch them walk away.

I sit at the table in the chair beside Toni and put my face in my hands. I don't want to go to a stupid party at the lookout. It will be all the popular kids getting drunk on cheap cask wine. Drunken popular people and sober nerdy people are not a good combination.

I splay my fingers across my face and stare through them at Toni. "We're going to this party, aren't we?"

"Yes." She pats me on the shoulder.

"Awesome," Jack says.

My forehead hits the table as the end-of-lunch bell rings.

11

When we get back to the main yard, police have taped off the area around the girls' bathroom, and ambulance officers are on the scene. We can't get near enough to see what's happening because Mr Woodfield is directing everyone to the hall. The headmistress, Mrs Johnston, tells us about Violette's death, and that Madison has been taken to hospital to be treated for shock. Lian, Callie, and Nora aren't in the hall, so I assume they've gone home or to the hospital with Madison. The main yard is now off-limits until the police are finished, and we are given information about grief counselling.

I don't want counselling, although I probably need it after everything that's happened. Violette wasn't my friend, but guilt fills my stomach to the point I feel like vomiting. She'd still be alive if we hadn't fallen in that hole.

I have trouble concentrating in last period not only

because I want to get away from school, but because Toni is messaging me, even though she's sitting right beside me. My phone buzzes in my pocket and I pull it out, keeping it hidden under my desk so Mrs Emmerson can't see.

Toni: U C Lian leave?

I glance up to make sure the teacher isn't watching before texting her back.

Me: No Y.

Toni: We shd make sure she's ok. Go C Madison 2.

Me: WTF 4?

Toni: Seriously???

Me: M isn't our friend.

Toni: We released the witch who killed her friend!!!

Me: Stop with the !!!

It's no use arguing with Toni. She usually gets her way, and I feel sick all over again. I can't go home and leave her to go by herself because she's practically disabled.

After the final bell, I help Toni into my car and we take the short drive across the railway line to the hospital. Jack has math tutoring, so he's pissed he can't come. Toni crutches it up the street because parking is limited, and by the time we make it to the front doors she isn't too happy.

We find reception and ask if we can see Madison White. The nurse behind the desk gives us directions and we set off, taking a few turns before finding Lian standing in the doorway to Madison's room. Toni and I stop behind her, and she glances over her shoulder at me.

"She's sleeping," she says. "Doctors say she went into shock."

"Where're Callie and Nora?" I ask, not *really* wanting

127

to know.

"Coffee," Lian says.

She goes into the room, and Toni follows. I hang back. I don't want to be here; I don't even know *why* I'm here, or why Toni wanted to come. My friend makes her way to the end of the bed and reads Madison's chart.

Toni frowns. "I have no idea what this says. The doctor's handwriting is bad."

"The nurse told me she'd be fine." Lian folds her arms around her middle.

"That's good … right?" I say.

"Yeah … as good as it can be after watching your friend die." Lian laughs, but nothing about the situation is funny.

"It was the witch?" I ask, even though it's the last thing I want to believe. "The black cloudy thing—did it go into her mouth?"

I wait for Lian to say something, but she stands there, staring at Madison. When she turns to face me, her cheeks are wet.

"I have to go." Lian moves towards me, and I step aside.

The pendant around her neck glimmers. I glance at Toni, who frowns and adjusts her crutches.

"Hey, Lian," I say. "Have you taken that off since you put it on in the cave?" She turns in the doorway, and I point to her neck.

Lian looks down and then back at me, her eyes glassy. "I don't want to take it off."

"Maybe you should." Toni glances at me sideways. "It could be … influencing you. And we don't know if it has any magical properties. If you let me have it I can find out."

"I have to go," Lian says again, and she walks out.

"Something's wrong," I say.

"Yeah," Toni says. "We have to get the necklace off her."

Loud voices echo along the corridor, and I rush to the door to see where they came from. Toni hobbles behind me. A couple of nurses are crouched on the ground beside a middle-aged man lying on his back. One nurse is doing CPR.

"He might have had a heart attack," she says. "Did anyone see what happened?"

"Get a bed," the other nurse yells at an orderly who's running towards them from the end of the hallway. Behind him, black mist rolls along the floor before disappearing around the corner at the end.

My heart pounds as the hospital staff get the man onto a gurney and rush him away, oblivious to the danger. I catch a glimpse of Lian turning at the end of the hall in the opposite direction from the one the mist went. I want to go after her, but I also want to get the hell out of here. The urge to flee wins.

"Let's go," I say. "Before the witch kills someone else … or us."

"We don't know if that man is dead," Toni says.

I raise my eyebrows. "Seriously? Mist in the area, and a guy who looks pretty damn dead. I think it's a safe guess."

We make our way back to the car and take the twenty-minute drive to Toni's house in silence. After helping her inside, I take her crutches, and she uses the banister to hop up the stairs to her bedroom. Her parents aren't home from work yet, and her sister is at gymnastics class, so we have a quiet house and freedom to talk about all the weird stuff that's been going on.

Toni sits in her desk chair and I take the end of the bed, grabbing the remote to flick the TV on. The early afternoon news is plastered with reports of what happened to Violette. They don't announce a cause of death, but there's an inquiry in progress because she died at school. Another woman who had been walking near the hospital around the time we'd left has also been found dead, and police are calling for witnesses to come forward because she'd been lying on the side of the road.

"What's happening?" I ask. "That's eight people dead since we fell in that stupid hole."

Toni switches her laptop on and waits for it to boot up. "Who knows? But we're not safe."

When her computer screen lights up, Toni opens Firefox and Googles the Moonlight Coven. She finds the web pages we looked at the other day, and I wait while she hunches over, scanning the rest of the search results on the screen.

Toni sighs and grabs the witch's book from her school bag, flipping through the pages. "I can't read enough of this to know ..." She gets up and hops over to the head of her bed, sticking her arm under the pillow and pulling out another book. "My Nona wrote about the Moonlight Coven, but I won't be able to see if what she's said is accurate without being able to read the longer passages in N's book." She hands me her Nona's book. "Can you see if anything stands out to you while I look at this again?" She holds up the witch's dusty, old tome.

I take her Nona's book and riffle through the pages while Toni returns to her desk. "What am I looking for?"

"Any reference to N. I haven't managed to get through it all, so maybe you'll see something I haven't. Start from where the bookmark is. Maybe stuff about a curse ..." Toni stops, and I look up. She's staring at a website with a black background and gold text. "It says here, if N were ever to be released, she would take souls until she had enough power to become corporeal."

I take a breath. "She's sucking souls?"

"Looks that way." Toni spins in her chair to face me.

I frown and keep flipping the pages of the book in my hands, not wanting to think about any of this, and not knowing what I'm supposed to be reading. Then the words *Nerezza* and *cursed* jump off the page and I stop, placing my finger on the paper.

Without thinking, I read, "Nerezza—"

"Don't say her name," Toni says.

"Sorry."

"Names have power, Harvey. If we say her name, she might ... appear."

"Okay—"

"Combined with the power of three, saying her name released her." Toni turns back to the computer. "And I do *not* want to try my chances with saying it again."

"Paranoid much?" I say.

"Um, yeah. Say that once the witch has sucked your soul."

"Can I read you this paragraph now?" I stare at Toni. She takes a deep breath. "Go on."

"Okay, this is what your Nona has written: *Through my research, I have discovered N was banished by the Moonlight Coven as punishment for the use of dark magic. However, her powers were immensely strong, and it took all twelve of the remaining coven members to bind their High Priestess into the coven's grimoire. I am yet to discover the nature of the spell that was used for the binding, but I would assume the grimoire is cursed."* I look up. "What's a grimoire?"

"This." Toni holds up the witch's book. "A grimoire is like a magical textbook. It seems the one we found belongs to the Moonlight Coven. The book you're holding is my Nona's Book of Shadows, which is more of a personal diary and spell book."

"Great. We found an ancient, cursed textbook, and unleashed a mad woman." I hold out Nona's book and look at Toni. "How did you miss this?"

Toni takes her Nona's Book of Shadows and studies the open pages before handing it back to me. "I haven't read that part yet." She opens the coven's grimoire to the first page. "Maybe the spell Nona's talking about is what's written here."

"Yeah, but how do we read it?"

"I don't know." She hunches over, studying the page in front of her.

I lie back on the bed and flick the channels on the TV. Afternoon shows are boring, and Toni doesn't have Netflix so I switch it off.

"Why hasn't she sucked our souls?" I ask, sitting back up. "She could've had a three-course meal in the cave, yet we're still here, walking around."

"It might have something to do with the spell I cast when she first attacked us," Toni says. "Or maybe because we released her, she can't kill us. But your guess is as good as mine." Toni struggles out of her desk chair and comes to sit beside me on the bed.

I run a hand down my face. "I should go. Mum will probably be wondering where I am."

Toni raises her eyebrows. "Really? You don't say."

"Okay, I'm going. I'll call you later." I close her Nona's book and toss it on the bed as I leave, taking the stairs two at a time on the way down to the front door.

I grumble on the way to my car and the entire drive home. How could we have released a witch? Witches aren't real. But a cloud killed people. Maybe it *was* gas. But I saw them die with my own eyes. How is any of this possible? By the time I open my front door, I'm in an exceptionally bad mood.

"Harvey, is that you?" Mum calls from the kitchen.

"Yeah." I kick the door closed with my foot. "I'll be in my room."

She sticks her head out of the doorway. "Dinner will be ready when your dad gets home. He'll be a bit late tonight. That okay?"

"Sure, Mum. Whatever." I make my way upstairs and close my bedroom door.

My keys clink when I throw them on the bed, and I dump my backpack next to my desk as I sit down to power up my laptop. I figure I'll do some of my own research to try and understand what the hell we're up against.

I spend the next hour Googling Nerezza and the Moonlight Coven. I don't find anything we don't already know. Then I think maybe I'm approaching it the wrong way. If we know we've let her out, and that we did it by saying her name, which I still don't buy because there has to be more to it, then we must be able to bind her again.

In a new window, I search for binding spells, and I get a million results. I sit back in my chair and rub my face because I have no idea where to start. I'm way out of my comfort zone with this. I grab my phone to text Toni.

Me: U there?

A few minutes pass before she replies.

Toni: Yep.

Me: Have idea 2 kill N.

Toni: U can't kill N. She's a cloud.

Me: Binding spell. Know one?

I stare at the phone, waiting.

Toni: Already searching. Leave with me.

Me: :)

I drop my phone on the bed, shut my laptop and go to my DVD cabinet. Netflix can wait tonight. I pull a special-edition boxset from the top of the shelf and run my hand over the cover to rub the dust off. Maybe Buffy has something to tell me about witchcraft that I don't remember, or that my brain hasn't filed away subconsciously for later use. I pull a random disc from the box and start watching from season five.

Mum calls me down for dinner around eight o'clock, and I eat with her and Dad before returning to my room. Mum has laid off a bit on the hovering, and I bunker down for a night of Buffy reruns. After a few episodes, I don't learn much, so I pull the booklet insert from the DVD box to scan the episode descriptions until I find something that might help.

Season six is where Willow goes nuts. I figure it might teach me something about bad-arse witches, and how *not* to get killed by them.

12

All day I've been dreading this moment, pulling into Toni's driveway, because it's the start of our spiral into humiliation. I must have said a thousand times over that I didn't want to go to this party, but here we are, going. Toni gets shotgun because I pick her up first, but she would have made Jack move anyway. She sits in the passenger seat, clutching the grimoire to her chest and staring out the front windscreen.

"Everything okay?" I ask.

Toni looks at me. "No, Harvey. Everything is not okay. It's like we've entered the twilight zone, and the universe is out of alignment." The corners of her mouth turn up slightly.

She's trying to make a joke, but I don't reply right away because I agree with her. We don't go to parties, especially when those parties are with Lian Lin and her friends. Parties for us involve pizza, a couch, and Jack's big-screen TV—which is exactly where I've told my mum I'll be tonight.

"Why did you bring the book?" I ask, pulling away from the kerb.

"Because ... when I got home today, some ... *thing* had tried to take it ... or read it."

"What happened?" I ask, pinching the bridge of my nose. "Why didn't you call me?"

"There's nothing you could've done." Her knuckles are white from gripping the book. "My room was a mess. I found the grimoire open in the middle of the floor. I'm too scared to leave it at home now. What if we lose it? It's pretty much all we have to go by."

"Did you mark the page that was open? It might be important later."

"Of course."

I take a deep breath because I'm tired of the weird stuff that's happened since school camp. I want Toni to leave it alone, but we're in too deep now.

"At the moment, I'm more worried about surviving this party," I say.

"That's not funny. People are dead, Harvey. We *have* to do something."

"What?" I say. "What are we supposed to do?"

"We bind the witch again." Toni blinks at me. "Remember?"

Yes, I remember. I also remember watching the horrifying moment when Willow stripped Warren of his skin. It was hard sleeping after that. I want to keep my skin.

"I think Lian needs to take that pendant off," Toni says.

I take a deep breath. "And you want me to get it from

her. Are you serious?" I turn the next corner. We're almost at Jack's house. "That's why we're going to this stupid party that doesn't involve any form of pizza or TV?" Toni smiles but doesn't reply.

I pull into Jack's driveway, and he's outside waiting. He walks to the car with a lopsided grin on his face. Already I want to go home, and we haven't even made it to the lookout. Jack climbs into the backseat and sits in the middle then puts the lap-sash on.

He leans forward. "Who's ready to party?"

I groan. "Don't be an idiot, please."

"What? Tonight is going to be awesome."

"The fact you used the word *awesome* proves how much of an idea you have," Toni says without turning around to look at him.

We pull out of Jack's street and head for the main road that leads to the Heights. At the roundabout, I take a left, and five minutes later I'm parking the car across from the lookout. There are several cars lining the street, and a few people walking about. When I open my door, I hear music distorted a little through the trees.

Jack helps Toni out, and we cross the road into the reserve that makes up the entrance to the lookout. Lamps light the area at regular intervals, and more trail along a path leading into the shadows. There's a kids' playground, and a couple of picnic tables. One has an esky on it with another three on the ground beside it. People from school are sitting on the swings and the slide, talking and drinking from cans and cups. Someone has strung up a banner between the swing upright and the fire pole on the play equipment. It says, "RIP VIOLETTE" in big letters.

"How tasteful," Toni says.

We stop on the edge of the so-called action, and I scan the scene, searching for Lian.

Jack jiggles from foot to foot beside me, and I want to whack him. He's getting on my nerves. Before I can say anything, I hear my name being called from the other side of the park.

"Harvey." Lian walks towards us, Greg at her side. "You made it."

Everyone near enough to hear stops talking and stares at us. Toni adjusts her crutches under her arms. Jack is still fidgeting.

"Hey," I say. "Nice turn-out." I glance around at the staring faces and swallow.

"You'd think none of them had seen us before," Toni says loud enough for most of them to hear.

"Guys, I invited them," Lian says, "Violette wouldn't mind." She swipes at her left eye as if she's wiping away a tear.

"Come on, Lian. Stop crying," Greg says. "We're here to have fun."

And just like that, everyone goes back to talking as if we weren't there.

I raise my eyebrows but don't say anything.

"Greg." Toni stares at him. "You look … well."

He chuckles. "Relax. I don't bite."

"That's nice to know." I shove my hands into the pockets of my jeans.

"I've decided to cut you guys some slack," Greg says. "You know, since you went through such a traumatic experience and all."

"That's ... so nice of you," I say.

"I'm sure we can all get along fine." Lian smiles. "I've told Greg all about how great you were, Harvey."

"That's ... So, um ... What do you do at these parties?" I ask. *Lame.*

Lian laughs. "You've never been to a party before?"

"Oh no, I've been to a party." I look around again. "Just ... not ... this."

"Harvey calls pizza and TV a party." Toni nudges my arm and laughs.

Lian frowns. Then she shocks me by taking my hand. "Come on. Let's go to the lookout."

She pulls me away from Toni, Jack, and Greg. I look back at them and shrug. Greg has a nasty frown on his face. Toni waves and smiles, then gestures to her neck mouthing 'pendant', obviously not angry at me for leaving her. Hopefully Jack will stay by her side. It's not like he's popular enough to go off on his own and survive.

Lian takes me along the path that winds through the bush and emerges at a platform with a chest-high railing. A single lamp at the side of the platform casts a puddle of light on the ground. We go to the railing and look over into the darkness below. I hear the rushing of the river, but I can't see it through the inky blackness. I turn away, unable to look over the edge for long. The darkness is disorienting.

There's a sandstone wall behind us with seats built into it. Surprisingly, no one else is here and we have the place to ourselves. It probably has something to do with the drink supply being up in the park.

"I like coming here," Lian says. "It's peaceful."

"I ... um." I grip the railing. "I don't go out much at night."

"You should get out more. It's not healthy sitting in your room all the time."

"Who would I go out with?" I ask before I can stop myself.

"Me."

I look at Lian properly for the first time since I arrived. Her hair is as black as the darkness in the bush below. I can't deny that she's nice to look at, and she's nice in all the other ways, too. But I'm not good with girls, even if I wanted to be. Toni is the only girl I can talk to without freaking out.

"Say something," Lian says. "You're staring at me."

I tear my gaze away from her face. "How are you? After ... Violette?"

Lian is quiet, and then she says, "It sucks. Everyone expects me to be so perfect all the time. I can't even cry in front of them."

"You can cry in front of me." I look at her again, and she's frowning. "Sorry. I ... I'm not very good at this."

"No, it's ... Want to go for a walk?" Lian squeezes my hand, smiling.

I look around. "Where?"

"There's a walking track that leads through the bush. We won't go far."

"I don't know." I shake my head. "It's a bit ... dark."

"I'll protect you." Lian tugs me to the far side of the lookout. She takes her phone from the back pocket of her jeans and flicks the torch app on.

We follow the track into the trees, and the farther we go the more anxious I get. My palms sweat, and I want to let go of Lian's hand, but I don't want to because I have no idea where I am. I don't do bushwalking very well, as I discovered on camp when we fell into a massive hole.

"Can we stop, please?" I ask.

Lian slows before finally stopping when I pull gently on her hand. She doesn't let go, and our arms are stretched out between us. The light from her phone makes a small circle on the ground.

"There's nothing to be afraid of, Harvey."

"Except maybe falling into giant holes in the ground, waking up ancient witches, and you know. Death." I stare at her face in the moonlight. Her skin has taken on an ashen colour, and the usual rosiness in her cheeks is gone in the dull light. "Isn't there something you're scared of?"

"Sure." Lian takes a step towards me but doesn't let go of my hand. "I'm afraid of losing people I love, but that's happened, and I'm still here. I'm afraid of not experiencing happiness. I'm afraid of never going on an adventure … I'm afraid of never having the chance to kiss you." She takes another step, and we're close enough to do that word she just said.

"Me …" I swallow. "You—"

And then her lips are on mine.

I don't know what to do. I've never kissed anyone before.

Lian pulls back and smiles. It happened so quickly. It wasn't a movie kiss. There was no open mouth or tongue, but she's smiling.

I don't know what to do.

Lian's fingers are locked with mine, and she pulls my arm around her waist, then kisses me again. This time,

I think *what the hell?* What's the worst that could happen? She could hate the taste of my spit and run away, telling everyone how awful I am at kissing. *Oh crap. Do I have bad breath?*

Lian gently parts my lips with her tongue, and before I can stop myself I'm pressing my hands into her back and pulling her closer. This is more like a movie kiss, and when she pulls away I take a big gulp of air.

"That was nice," Lian says. "And now I'm afraid of one less thing."

"If only it were that easy to cure me of being scared of the dark," I say.

Then I realise in this moment, standing here with Lian Lin, I'm not scared, because I'm with her.

I want to kiss her again.

I lean down but stop when I hear voices.

"Probably someone at the lookout." Lian puts her hand on my cheek and closes the small gap between us. Her lips brush mine again.

A scream pierces the night.

Lian jumps. "What was that?"

So much for not being scared.

"More like who?" I put my arm around Lian's shoulder.

She clutches me and shines her phone torch along the darkness of the path. "Maybe we should go back?"

Another scream comes from the direction of the lookout, and Lian tenses in my arms. I'm not sure I want to find out what's going on.

"Crap," I say, remembering Toni and Jack.

I tug Lian along the path. When we reach the lookout platform there are people gathered around the railing.

Lian and I run to the nearest gap in the crowd.

"What's going on?" Lian asks.

"They're down there," Callie says, her face streaked with tears.

"Who?" I ask. "What do you mean?" I look around again and see more people crying. Some are on their phones, and others are sitting on the sandstone seats in shock. I can't see Toni or Jack. Greg is running towards us, but I focus back on Callie. "What happened?"

"They went over," Callie says.

"Oh my God," Lian yells before I can ask who Callie is talking about.

"Don't look," Greg says. He tries to pull Lian back but she's gripping the railing and staring below us. I push to her side and look over the edge.

Bile rises into my throat.

Noah is sprawled on the rocks about five metres down, his face turned to the sky. There's someone else, a girl, but I can't see who it is. She's tangled amongst his legs, her arms hanging over the rock edge.

"Who was with him?" I ask, turning away from the sight. "Callie, who was with Noah?"

Callie shakes her head, her hands covering her mouth.

"What happened, Callie?" Lian screams, pushing away from the railing. "Did they jump?" She turns in a frantic circle, her fingers in her hair pulling. Greg reaches out to her but she swats his hand away. "Where's Madison? Callie, where's Madison?"

"They fell. Noah, he ..." Callie sobs and lets out a wail. "He tried to help her."

"Has someone called an ambulance ... the police?" I

go back to the railing and grip it so tightly my hands ache, staring into the darkness.

"I'll call." Greg moves away from the crowd.

"What happened to you, Noah?" I say to myself.

"Callie, is that Madison?" Lian yells.

Callie nods, and Lian's knees buckle. I lunge to catch her and she grips my forearms, her eyes wide.

"What have we done?" Lian asks.

"Come and sit down," I say, putting an arm around her and leading her to the stone seats. A guy jumps up so Lian can take his place. I glance around, and almost everyone is staring over the railing.

Greg pockets his phone and jogs over. "The police are on their way."

"Can you sit with Lian?" I ask.

Greg nods, and I go back to the railing to pull Callie away. She's staring down at Noah's upturned face, sniffling and wiping at her eyes. "Madison was goofing around. She sat up on the railing …"

"Come on." I take her elbow. "Come away from the edge."

"There was a crow, and … You're not going to believe me." Callie puts her hands over her face and takes a deep breath but lets me lead her over to Lian and Greg.

"Try me."

"It … it was … dark." Callie stops and shakes her head, looking at Lian. "I've had too much to drink. It was the shadows from the trees." She takes a breath. "I'm not crazy."

"I never said you were," I say. "Did anyone else see what happened?"

"No one else was around. Just the three of us …"

144

"You said there were crows?"

A second after the words leave my mouth, a crow caws, and Callie jumps. She grabs my arm, pressing against my side.

"The crow … it turned into more crows." Callie's gaze searches the darkness. "There was this awful rustling sound, and Madison gagged, and then Noah grabbed her, but she went over. He caught her hand, and I clung to her through the railing so Noah could climb over, but … they both fell."

"Was there mist?" Lian asks. She's staring into space and I want to comfort her, but Greg has his arm around her shoulders already.

"What?" Callie frowns.

"Mist," I say. "Was there a cloud of black mist?"

"It's dark, and I'm drunk." Tears roll down her cheeks.

"This isn't good." Lian's voice is flat.

Another scream. The crowd at the lookout railing disperses and a cloud of blackness spills over the edge from below, creeping across the ground. The flap of wings sounds above us and a crow flutters to the railing. It caws, and my muscles tense. People run in all directions. The mist rises towards the crow.

I grab Lian's hand and pull her to her feet. "We need to find Toni and Jack."

We run towards the park, Callie and Greg hot on our heels, when another loud scream pierces the din of the commotion. I look over my shoulder to see where the mist is, but it's not behind us at the lookout. The crow launches into the air and blends with the shadows.

Ahead of us on the path is a group of four girls, their

legs surrounded by a black cloud. Lian is at my side, clutching my hand. The girls keep screaming, and they run in the direction of the park. The darkness rolls towards us. My palm goes sweaty in Lian's hand. I glance at her and then stare at her neck. The pendant is pulsing again, like it did in the clearing when the witch attacked her.

"We have to get out of here." I tug Lian's hand. "Everyone, move. Up to the road."

I don't wait for a response. I tighten my grip on Lian's hand and run. The only way out is through the mist. I brace myself for when we meet it, focusing on anything but what it's going to feel like when I touch it. The black cloud is low on the ground, and its edges flick out in snaky tendrils. They wrap around my ankles as we pass, but they don't hold on. It's cold as ice sliding over my skin, but at the same time it feels lovely, like a painful pleasure.

Lian and I run along the path to the park. Greg and Callie stay close. Others follow, but I don't know who. I hear more screams and glance over my shoulder. A flock of crows swoops in loops and dives, joining into a mass before breaking apart.

The mist has gone.

I stop, and Lian's hand comes free from mine.

"Look at all the birds." She takes a few gulping breaths.

The crows rise into the air, forming a mass of feathers, then they dive at a maddening pace, heading straight for us.

"Run," Greg cries.

I grab Lian but when I turn, I trip and sprawl onto my stomach. She stumbles over me and runs a few steps, then comes back to help me up. I make it to my knees, then a crow hits Lian in the chest and she falls backwards, landing hard. More crows descend on her and she flails her arms to fight them off. I crawl to her, swatting and punching birds to get them away. Greg drops to his knees and grabs at the crows, throwing them off Lian. Other people run past, but none of them stop to help.

"Get them off her," Callie screams.

Sirens wail in the distance, and the noise adds to the screams, the cawing, and the rustling of feathers. Lian is lying on the ground covered in crows, and no matter how many Greg and I get off her, more take their place. It's like they're rematerializing and multiplying at the same time.

Someone grabs my shoulders and pulls me back, but I fight them off because I have to get Lian out from under the crows.

"Stop," Jack yells in my ear. "Toni is helping."

I struggle for a few seconds more, then I fall onto my arse and look around. Toni is standing under one of the lights, propped up on her crutches, the grimoire clutched to her chest. Her lips are moving, and she's staring at Lian, but I can't make out what she's saying.

"Greg, stop," I say.

He looks up, then stops grabbing at the mass of feathers, crawling away from Lian. His hands are covered in smears of blood.

Some of the crows fly towards Toni but drop at her feet as if they've hit an invisible wall in front of her. Others fly into the air and disappear against the dark sky. The remaining birds turn to mist, covering Lian like a veil before rolling into a mass and slipping across the ground.

Crows fall from the sky in a downward spiral, joining with the ones at Toni's feet. They flop away from her, and combine with the black mass before it seeps into the shadows and disappears.

I crawl to Lian and help her sit up. "You okay?"

"My chest hurts." She puts her hand up.

"Don't touch it."

I hold her hand and stop her from touching her wounds because I don't want her to spread blood everywhere. I quickly look her over from head to toe, but the only place she's injured is on her upper chest and around her collarbones. Blood drips into the neckline of her top, and I pull a hanky from my pocket to stop the flow.

"Man, that was some crazy shit." Greg is sitting on the ground with his arms draped over his knees.

"Why were they attacking her neck?" Jack asks. "Are they vampire crows?"

I ignore him and run a hand through my hair, taking a deep breath.

Toni crutches over to us. "That bitch has already tried to get the book. This time, she wanted the pendant."

I look up at her. We have one more item that belongs to the witch.

"She'll go for the athame next," I say.

"You know what, Harvey?" Toni says. "I think you're absolutely right."

13

I help Lian to her feet and we walk towards the road, through the park. It's almost empty now, with most of the kids having fled the scene. A few have stayed behind, and I figure they're the ones who actually care about Noah and Madison. Jack stays at Toni's side, and I glance at them, offering him a small smile.

Two police officers get out of their car when we reach the mouth of the path that leads from the park to the street. The car's lights flash, bathing the houses that line the opposite side of the road in a red and blue glow. An ambulance pulls up behind the police car, and two paramedics join us.

"We received a disturbing call," a police officer says. "You know anything about that?" He stares at me. His partner flashes her torch into the trees and along the path.

I don't know why he's singled me out. Maybe it's because

I'm the one holding the girl with the blood all over her chest.

One of the paramedics comes over to Lian. "What happened here?" she asks.

"Crows," I say before I can stop myself.

The paramedic looks at me sideways. "Crows?"

"A flock of them attacked me," Lian says.

"The call we received said someone was hurt at the lookout?" The female police officer shines her light along the path again.

"Our friends ..." Callie says. "They fell over the edge."

"What? Show us." The police officer runs down the path. The male paramedic follows. The officer puts his radio to his mouth, but by the time he starts talking he's too far away for me to hear what he says. Callie and Greg go after them.

"Okay. How about we sit over here?" The female paramedic leads Lian to a park bench on the side of the path, and I follow. Toni and Jack hang at the street. Toni adjusts her crutches while Jack fidgets with the sleeve of his jumper.

"Maybe it's not as bad as it looks?" I say.

The paramedic smiles. "Let's see." She opens a kit she brought with her and snaps on some latex gloves. "What's your name, sweetheart?"

"Lian. This is Harvey." Lian points to me.

"Nice to meet you. My name is Cindy." She bends down to inspect Lian's neck and chest. "Can I take your necklace off?"

Lian's hand goes to her throat. "I don't want to lose it."

"I'll get it." I go around behind the bench, hesitating before I move Lian's hair to the side to get to the clasp. I've never touched a girl's hair before. It's soft and smooth.

I pinch the clasp between my fingers and unhook it, taking the pendant off and dropping it into the palm of my hand.

"Don't—"

"Lian, I won't lose it." I stuff it into my pocket.

Cindy pulls a swab from her kit and wipes some of Lian's blood away. "It doesn't look too bad. A few minor lacerations." She wipes at the wounds a bit more. "Those kids, down at the lookout. They your friends?"

Lian nods, a tear dropping from the corner of her eye. "We didn't see what happened." She looks up at me.

"Okay. We're going to have to take you to the hospital," Cindy says. "You might need some antibiotics and a tetanus shot. And I'd like someone to check you over just to be sure you don't need stitches."

"Hospital," I say. "Great. Because we *love* that place."

"You kids look very familiar," Cindy says as she wipes Lian's skin. "Do I know you?"

"We were on the news a week or so ago," I say. "I'd be surprised if you didn't recognise us."

"Ah. The kids who fell in the hole."

I don't reply.

"Do I have to go in the ambulance?" Lian says. "I feel fine."

"Yes, you have to." Cindy packs up her case. "Is Harvey coming with you?" She doesn't look at me when she asks the question.

I glance over my shoulder at Toni and Jack, waiting at the road by the ambulance. "I need to get my friends home. They don't have a car. But I'll come and see you right after I drop them off." I look at Lian, and she stares at me with a weak smile.

"It's okay. She's in good hands," Cindy says. "We'll call her parents on the way."

Greg and Callie come back with the police and the other paramedic.

"We need to cordon the place off," one officer says. "Fire and rescue will be here in a minute."

Callie wraps her arms around her middle and sniffles, staring at the ground.

"I'll take you home," Greg says to her, putting a hand on her arm.

"We may need statements about what happened," the female officer says. "But it can wait until tomorrow. You should all go home and get some sleep." She looks at each of us in turn, then glances at Toni and Jack.

"They weren't there when it happened," I say.

"I was the only one there," Callie says, her eyes still downcast.

"Well, I'll take your number and we can talk about it tomorrow with your parents present." The officer pulls a notepad from her top pocket.

Cindy leads Lian to the ambulance and I join Toni and Jack, looking back over my shoulder at Callie and Greg. He gives me a nod before walking to his car with Callie. I don't want to stick around any longer. I say goodbye to Lian, making sure she's okay in the back of the ambulance, and Toni and Jack follow me to my car. We get in without saying anything, and we're silent on the drive to Jack's place.

"I guess I'll see you?" Jack says, his door open and his leg out of the car.

"Sure," I say. "I'll call you." I wait until Jack is inside

his house before pulling out of his driveway.

Toni rests the grimoire on her lap, her fingers gripping the edges. I want to ask her what she did to make the birds go away, but she's staring out the window, chewing her bottom lip, so I wait.

When we reach her house, I pull up to the gutter and kill the engine. We sit for a minute before either of us speaks. I wait for Toni to go first, jiggling my knee up and down as the silence gets to me.

"What were you saying back there?" I finally ask.

"Protection spell," she says without looking at me. "I wasn't sure if it would work again."

"Well … Lian's not dead."

"Yeah, so I guess it did." She falls silent, chewing her lip.

"What the hell have we gotten ourselves into?" I turn in my seat to face Toni, and she finally looks at me. Her eyes are wide and glassy, and I'm frightened because Toni hardly ever cries. She's really rattled by this.

"We should never have taken anything from that cavern, Harvey. We're in this too deep. We have to figure out how to stop it. Before she kills again."

"How do we do that?"

Toni looks down at the book she's holding. "We study this thing until we know absolutely everything there is to know about N."

"Which isn't much," I say. "And you've tried reading that book. It doesn't make enough sense for us to know or understand what it says."

"I think … maybe I can cast a spell that will help us."

"More spells?" I ask. "I don't like the sound of that."

"Can you think of a better idea?"

153

I shake my head and open my door. Grabbing Toni's crutches from the back seat, I go around to her side and help her out of the car.

"Thanks." She smiles, and we walk to her door in silence.

"Are you going to the hospital?" Toni asks, grabbing the doorknob.

I nod, stuffing my hands in my pockets. My fingers brush against something metal. The necklace. I'd forgotten about it. I pull my hand out, and the pendant dangles from the end of the chain.

"Think you'll be safe having this and the book?" I hold the pendant up.

"Sure." Toni takes it from me. "You won't be long anyway, will you?"

"I'll go and make sure she's okay. Then I'll come back. We have a lot of reading to do."

"Maybe you should get the athame as well."

I study Toni for a moment. "You sure you want all these things in your house?"

"One target that way." Toni shrugs. "I'll tell Mum you're staying."

I'm not sure how to reply, so I don't. I look back at Toni twice as I walk to my car, and she doesn't move from her position on the veranda until I'm sitting in the driver's seat. I take a deep breath and pull away from the kerb to head towards the hospital. I don't really want to leave Toni alone with the grimoire and the pendant, but I want to make sure Lian is all right. She told me to come, but on the drive there I find myself wondering if they will let me in this late. I'm pretty sure visiting hours finished a while ago.

I find a park on the street and walk in through emergency.

Not much time has passed since I left the lookout, so if she's gone through triage it shouldn't have been that long ago. I ask for Lian Lin at the desk, and they tell me she's just gone through.

"Can I see her?" I say.

"Are you family?"

"Um … yes. I'm her … brother."

I'm pretty sure the nurse doesn't believe me, but she presses a button under the desk and the door to my right clicks. The nurse meets me at the door and leads me along a wide hallway into the emergency department. We turn left and there are several bed bays with the curtains closed. The nurse peers around the last curtain before pulling it aside.

"Press the call button if you need me," she says to Lian before heading back to the front desk.

Lian is lying on the bed, her chest covered with a bandage patch. A drip on the left of the bed leads to her arm.

"Hey, Harvey." She smiles and fidgets with the pulse monitor on her finger.

I go to the edge of the bed. "You okay?"

"Sore, but they say I'll live."

"I'm glad." I return her smile, and then I don't know what else to say so I don't say anything. Lian reaches for my hand, and I let her take it. "Have they called your parents?" I finally ask.

"Yeah. They're getting coffee. Looks like you arrived at the right time."

I frown. *Does she not want me to meet her parents?*

She squeezes my hand. "I only mean because we can talk without them listening."

"Oh," I say.

"Do you have my pendant?"

I sit on the edge of the bed, still holding Lian's hand. "It's with Toni. I thought it would be safe with her."

"What if the witch attacks her?"

"I'm going back to her place. I wanted to make sure you were all right first."

"Shouldn't you go home and get some sleep?"

"I'm … staying at Toni's," I say, knowing it will hurt her but not wanting to lie. Lian presses her lips together and smiles with her mouth closed. "She's my best friend." I squeeze her hand. "You don't need to worry. We're going to work on figuring out how to stop what's happening."

Lian nods and stares at our hands. "The doctor said I can go home once the drip has finished."

We both look at the bag hanging from the frame beside the bed. I have no idea how long it takes for a drip to feed. As far as I know, it could be an hour or a day.

"Okay," is all I can manage.

She squeezes my hand back, and this time her smile is a bit brighter. I don't know what's happening between us, or what's happening *to* us, but I sometimes think that Lian liking me has absolutely nothing to do with Lian actually liking me. Too much weird shit has happened lately for me to be able to believe that anything good can come of it. I'm confused, and tired, and I want to go, but I feel like I can't leave yet.

"Will you come see me tomorrow?" Lian asks, breaking the silence.

I nod. "I have to help Dad with a few things in the morning, but I can come over after lunch."

My phone vibrates in my pocket and I use my free hand to fish it out.

Toni: Where r u???

"Who's that?" Lian asks.

"Just Toni." I slip my phone back into my pocket.

Lian nods and stares at our hands again. She adjusts her grip, and I give her fingers another gentle squeeze. I want to kiss her goodbye, but she isn't looking at me. I wait to see if she'll raise her head, but the moment stretches on forever. I'm about to pull my hand from hers when she finally looks up.

I smile and lean down, kissing her on the forehead because I chicken out.

"I'll see you tomorrow," I say, and then I have to go because if I don't I'll never leave, and Toni will keep messaging me until I reply.

I say thank you to the nurse on the way out, then text Toni a reply as I walk to my car. The streets are quiet since it's close to midnight, and I get every green light on the way home. I smile and thank the universe for giving me a small break for once. The drive takes less than twenty minutes, and for that time I lose myself in thoughts about Lian. What is she doing to me? Since when do I think about girls outside of characters in TV shows?

I quickly stop at home, parking my car a couple of houses away, then sneaking in the back door and up to my room to grab the athame. I stuff it into my backpack, and I'm in and out in a few minutes without Mum and Dad hearing me. If they did, I'd have no chance of going out again. I really should call Mum to tell her I won't be home tonight, but I don't want to have that conversation.

I send a text to Dad's phone instead to let him know I'll be staying at Toni's and that I'll be back in time to help him in the morning. He replies pretty much straight away.

Dad: Mum isn't 2 happy. Call her nxt time.

I tense a little as I cross the street to my car. My palms sweat, and I quicken my pace to get through the darkness. When I'm inside the car and the engine is running I feel safer, and I can focus on driving to Toni's place.

A few hundred metres down the street, a black shadow darts across in front of me. I jump in my seat and brake hard, but can't see anything outside. When I press my foot to the accelerator again, something hits the windscreen with a loud *crack*, and I cry out, swerving before slamming on the brakes and stopping at an angle in the gutter.

My chest heaves with heavy breaths as I stare at the crow that just committed suicide on my car. I grip the steering wheel, gathering the courage to get out and pull it off when its head moves, swivelling around until its beak taps the glass. Its beady eye stares at me, then it moves its wings. The rustling sound makes my skin crawl, sending an army of ants up my arms. The crow's wings flap, swatting the glass until the bird pulls itself free from the bloody smear on the windscreen. It flaps once more and flops onto the bonnet.

It shouldn't be alive.

I check my window is wound up and then step on the accelerator, swerving a few times down the street to try and shake the horrible bird off. It stays put until I turn the corner into Toni's street. The crow hits the asphalt with a wet *smack*.

I park outside Toni's place and hightail it out of the

car. A light on the second floor illuminates her bedroom. I run around to the back door and let myself in with the spare key that's hidden under a loose paver. Toni is standing at the top of the stairs. I have to take a deep breath to calm myself before creeping up quietly, avoiding the seventh step so I don't wake her mum and dad. Toni ushers me into her bedroom and shuts the door.

"You look terrified," Toni says. "What happened?"

I go to her window and look down at my car, then along the street. No crows in sight.

"More creepy birds … I'm okay. Don't like crows but." I take a seat on the bed. "Did you tell your folks I was coming back?"

"Of course." Toni rests her crutches against the wall and hops over to her desk chair. "They said you can stay in the spare room. Sure you're all right?""

I nod and pull the athame from my backpack, handing it to Toni. She stares at me for a few seconds, then swivels in her chair to grab the grimoire and the pendant. She rolls closer to the bed, handing me the book.

"I've been staring at that thing, flipping through it the whole time you've been gone, and I can't decipher anything more than what we already have," Toni says. "And Nona's Book of Shadows hasn't been helpful yet."

"What do you want me to do?"

"Just … look at it and see if you can see anything I can't."

I turn the grimoire over in my hands a few times and stare at the pentacle on the cover, running my finger around the circle. The string that held the book closed when Lian first found it is embedded into the leather, stiff with age. I run my fingers over the cover before opening it and sitting it in my lap.

The inside of the grimoire hasn't changed since the last time I looked at it, and I don't know what Toni is expecting. I turn a few of the yellowed pages and try to read the words, but I can only make out one in every ten.

"These are all spells?" I ask.

"I think most of them are, but there's also stuff in there about the Moonlight Coven and their members. There were thirteen of them all together, but most of what I do know I've found online and in Nona's book. Someone back in Italy has done a little research on them, but it's not all that helpful. No one *really* knows what happened to them."

"And you think if we can read this we'll find out?"

"Yes, I want to be able to read *all* of it. Maybe there's a vital piece of information we're missing because at the moment it's mumbo-jumbo." Toni stares at me. "I want to cast a spell to see if it helps."

"I'm not sure we should mess with it, Toni. We're not witches," I say.

"We don't have to be witches to cast a spell." Toni hands me a piece of paper. "We just need to know what we're doing."

"I have no idea what I'm doing." I look at the paper in my hand and read the words Toni has scrawled on the lines.

Powers of magic, I invoke thee.
Open my mind so I may see.
Reveal the meaning of these words to me.

"Where did you get this?" I ask. "Will it work?"

"I wrote it ... with guidance from Nona's notes. And I

have no idea."

"You wrote this?" I hand the paper back to her.

"It's not that hard. You just need to make it rhyme." Toni gets up from her chair and hops over to the bed. "And we need to use something to channel the magic."

"Huh?"

"Candles, Harvey. We need candles."

I stare at her and blink a few times.

She swats me on the arm. "Get with the program. Can you go downstairs to the top drawer in the hallstand? There're candles in there. I'd go myself, but we wouldn't be able to get started for another half an hour."

I take a breath and stand up. Before I make it to the door, my phone rings.

"It's Jack." I stare at the screen.

"Don't answer it," Toni says. "We can't get him involved. It's too dangerous."

"He probably wants to make sure we're okay."

"Just ... leave him out of it, okay?"

I press my lips together and nod, hitting the red phone icon on my screen. I creep downstairs as quietly as I can.

A couple of minutes later, I'm back in Toni's room and she's sitting on a cushion on the floor with her moon-booted leg sticking out to one side. She has the wooden box, book, athame, and pendant beside her, and a box of matches in her hand.

I pass the box of household candles to her, and Toni tips them onto the timber floor. There are six but she picks up five and puts one aside. I'm curious to see what she does, but at the same time I'm not sure I really want to be doing this.

"We need to set the candles in a circle," Toni says.

"How are they going to stand up?" I ask.

Toni lights a match and holds it to the bottom of one of the candles, dripping wax onto the floorboards. She then sticks the candle to the wood. Somehow, I don't think her parents are going to be too happy with this. Toni continues until she's made a circle large enough for the grimoire to sit in the middle. She sets the book in position then takes a glass bottle and small blue stone from the wooden box.

"What are those?" I ask.

"Lapis lazuli. For truth." Toni holds up the stone. "And salt. For protection and purification." She pulls the little cork from the bottle.

"Okay then. Why five candles? Why didn't you use them all?"

"Because a pentagram has five points, not six." Toni lights each candle. She picks up the athame and passes the tip through each of the flames, then holds the knife over the book. Next, she takes the blue stone and sets it on top of the book, then sprinkles a pinch of salt onto the knife blade. She raises her head and looks at me. "You ready?"

"No."

"Harvey, say the spell with me. Three times, okay?"

I nod, and together we say, "Powers of magic I invoke thee. Open my mind so I may see. Reveal the meaning of these words to me."

We repeat the spell twice more. Toni tips the athame so the salt falls onto the book before blowing the candles out one by one.

I don't feel as if anything has happened, but who am I to make a call like that? We stare at the grimoire. Toni sets the athame aside and reaches into the circle. She removes the blue stone, picks up the book and brushes the salt off. She opens the book carefully and hunches over it. Her eyes narrow, and then they widen as she turns the pages.

"What?" I say. "Did it work?"

Toni looks up. "I think it did."

163

14

It was late, so I left Toni hunched over the grimoire and flaked in the spare room. Now, I'm lying here, staring at the crack of sunlight on the edge of the blind and thinking I should get up because I need to get home.

I go to the bathroom and wash my face, then use my finger to brush my teeth. It's early, so I tiptoe to Toni's room and peek in. She's lying on her side, the blankets tangled around her bandaged leg. The book is open on the floor, her hand dangling over the side of the bed above it.

I'm curious whether I can read the pages now that we've cast the spell, but I need to get home before the wrath of my mother rains down on me in a fiery storm.

I grab my keys off Toni's desk as quietly as I can and leave the house via the back door. On the way to the car I send Toni a quick text.

Me: Tell me if u found anything. Call u later.

The sound of my crappy Commodore roaring to life is loud in the early morning, and I hope I haven't woken Toni or her parents.

Five minutes later, I'm pulling into my driveway. I turn the engine off and take a deep breath to calm myself before facing the onslaught I know will come when I open the front door.

Mum must be up, because the door is open to let the morning air in. I unlock the screen and try to be quiet as I enter, but it's impossible, and the metal door closes with a loud click.

Mum emerges from the kitchen before I'm able to get my shoes off.

"I'm not happy with you, Harvey Anderson." She stands in the doorway with her hands on her hips, a tea towel dangling from her fingers.

"You're up early, Mum." I put my Converse on the bottom shelf of the shoe rack.

"Where were you last night?"

"At Toni's," I say. "I sent Dad a message."

Mum's eyes well up, and she blinks. "Were you at that party?"

I don't answer right away. My first instinct is to say yes, and then I remember I'd told her I was going to Jack's house for pizza. "Um—"

"I saw the news. I'm mad at you. What if it was you who'd fallen over the edge? How do you think ..." Mum's lower lip quivers. "Your friends are dead."

I move past her into the kitchen and I can't figure out if she's really mad at me or sad that more people I know are dead.

"They weren't my friends," I say.

"So you *were* there? Did you … see what happened?"

I take a breath and tell her the truth. "Yes, I was there. And no, I didn't see what happened."

"Are you okay?"

"Lian was hurt and she had to go to hospital, but other than that, I'm fine. She was the girl I got … the one with Toni and me on camp."

"Oh honey, I'm sorry." Mum gives me a hug. I pat her on the back and she pulls away. "Do you want to talk about it?"

This is the most disorienting thing about my mother. One minute she's so mad at you the world is about to end, then a snap second later, she's upset and feels bad and is asking if everything is all right. Sometimes, her moods give me whiplash.

"There's nothing to talk about," I say. "And I'm sorry I didn't tell you I was going to the party. It was a last-minute decision."

"Okay, but next time, call me. I was worried."

I want to remind her that I'd texted Dad, so they knew I was alive. But I bite my tongue. "Where's Dad?"

"Out the back. Have you had breakfast?"

I grab an apple from the fruit bowl and head for the back door. "I'm good."

Dad is in the yard. He's already gotten the mower and the whipper snipper out. I glance at my watch, which reads seven-thirty a.m. I take a bite of my apple and go over to Dad.

"Hey," I say. "Lawn or edges?"

"You can do the grass." He tips some fuel into the

mower from the jerry can before looking up. "You talk to your mother?"

"Yes." I take another bite of my apple. "She okay? She seems more twitchy than usual."

"She worries about you, that's all."

"Well, I'm fine. I can take care of myself."

"If I had a dollar for every teenager who said that, I'd be a multi-billionaire." Dad smiles. "You're a good kid, Harvey. Stay that way."

I chew my apple. I'm not exactly sure where this has come from. "What did she say to you?"

Dad straightens up. "Honestly, she's worried. These deaths have rattled her, and she doesn't know what to think. Nothing like this has ever happened so close to home."

"She doesn't need to worry. I'm fine."

Dad regards me for a moment. "Then get on with it. The grass won't cut itself."

I walk over to the shed and toss my apple core on the compost heap. The mower starts for me first pull, and I work quickly because I promised Lian I'd go and see her today.

A few weeks ago, Lian Lin scared me half to death, so I'd never entertained any thoughts to do with her or her friends. I flew under the radar as much as I could. But recently, I can't stop wondering if she's okay. I'm not looking forward to telling Mum I'm going out for the afternoon. She'll either be fine about it, or will lose it and wrap me up in bubble wrap and send me to my room. It could go either way.

I help Dad pack up the last of the garden tools, then

head for the shower. I haven't had one since yesterday morning, and after working in the yard for the past few hours, I feel pretty disgusting. The hot water prickles my skin, and I find my thoughts drifting to Lian again. What the hell is wrong with me? I've never been this interested in a girl before, but I'm looking forward to seeing her.

After throwing on a clean T-shirt and some jeans, I go downstairs. Mum is in the kitchen again, and I swear it's her favourite room in the house. She has food out for lunch and is chopping up salad. I grab a bread roll and rip it open, then fill it with ham and a bit of everything she's cut up.

"You're not going to wait and eat with your dad and me?" Mum asks.

I look at the clock again. Half past eleven. "I want to go out this afternoon."

Mum stops chopping and puts the knife down, which is probably a good thing. I take a bite of my roll.

"Where are you going?"

For a second, I think I might lie and say Toni's place, but I don't want to get into trouble again. "I'm going over to Lian's. I want to see if she's all right."

Mum takes a deep breath, and I brace myself for a fight. "Will you be home for dinner?"

"Sure, Mum. I'll be here."

"Okay. Be careful." She goes back to chopping the lettuce.

I take my roll with me, eating it on the way to the car. I'd told Lian after lunch, so I hope being a bit early won't be a problem. Even though I know where her street is, I Google Maps her address before I start the car, just to double check.

THE Lovely DARK

When I get to her place, I park on the opposite side of the street with my car facing the direction I'd come. Before I get out of the car, I sit for a couple of minutes. I contemplate leaving and not going in to see her, but then I tell myself to get a grip. It's not like she's going to bite, but I'm not sure why I feel uneasy. I put it down to all the weird and horrible stuff that's been happening, and I get out of the car.

Lian opens the door on the second knock. "Come in." She smiles, stepping to the side to let me past. Her house is big.

"You home by yourself?" I ask. "It's … quiet."

"Dad has taken my brother to soccer, and Mum is with my sister at netball." Lian smiles. "I stopped playing weekend sport. Too much study to do."

"I don't do sport either," I say. My reasons are entirely different, mainly to do with my lack of coordination and strength, but I don't say that out loud.

"You want something to eat?" Lian asks.

"I'm good. I've had lunch."

We stand in the foyer and look at each other. She's wearing a low top and the bandage on her chest pokes out. Heat rises into my cheeks because I'm looking at her boobs. I try looking at her shoulder but that probably seems like I'm still looking at her boobs. I have no idea what to do in this situation. I've never been alone with a girl other than Toni. We have the place to ourselves, and I'm thinking about boobs.

"Want to see my room?" Lian says.

Crap. "Um … sure." I can't exactly say no.

Lian goes down the stairs to our left, and I follow her

to the bottom level of the house. Her room is the middle one of three along the hallway. It's a lot smaller than my room, but it's neat with everything in its place. She sits on the bed and I stand in the doorway, my hands in my pockets, unsure of where I'm meant to sit because there is nowhere else other than on the bed beside her.

"It's, nice," I say, and I cringe at myself. "How are you feeling?"

"I'm a bit sore." Lian's hand goes to her chest where she has the bandage on. "But nothing major. They let me come home not long after you left. I have to take antibiotics for the next week so I don't get an infection. But otherwise, I'm good."

"Were you … scared?" I stare at my shoes.

"Come sit down, Harvey."

I look up and our eyes meet. I want to go and sit, but I don't know what's going to happen when I do, and that scares me. I think that's why I shut so many things out and spend so much time in my room. If I don't acknowledge something, then I won't think about it and it can't hurt me.

Supposedly.

I want to explain all of this to Lian, but I don't have the words. And I don't want to look like an idiot, so I go and sit next to her.

We're quiet for a few minutes, then Lian says, "Did you go and see Toni?" She hasn't answered my question, but I answer hers anyway. I'm not going to push her to talk about something if she doesn't want to.

"Yeah, I stayed there last night … in the spare room." I don't know why I say that last part. Lian knows Toni is my best friend. "We cast a spell."

Lian raises her eyebrows. "A spell?"

"Toni's been having trouble trying to figure out what the book says. A lot of it is written in the witches' alphabet, and she can read some of the words, but then a lot of the sentences weren't making sense."

"Maybe there's a spell on the book," Lian says. "To stop people from reading it. Did your spell work?"

"Yeah, I think so. I had to get home this morning, so I've left it with her. She'll call if she finds anything interesting."

"That whole book is interesting."

I glance at her. "Were you able to make anything of it?"

Lian shakes her head. "I tried. But it's like the letters kept moving, and I could never pinpoint any particular words."

"The letters moved for you?"

"I'm dyslexic, so yeah."

"Oh … I didn't know."

"It's fine. I have my ways of coping, and I do pretty well at school. I study hard so I can pass my subjects. Sometimes I hate having to work harder than everyone else, but it's nice when I know I've achieved something myself without special help."

I pause for a few seconds. "Do your friends know?"

"Violette does … did … but you're the only one I've ever talked to openly about it. I'm sure other people know. I just don't make a big deal out of it." She shrugs. "I don't want to be different."

"But being different is what makes us who we are."

Lian looks into my eyes, and my stomach churns. My palms are sweaty, and I rub them on my jeans and stare at my shoes. It was easier with Lian last night, because

I couldn't see her as well, and I think it's the first time being in the dark has helped me instead of hindered me.

She reaches over and takes my hand. "I'm not going to bite."

I finally look at her, and she smiles. "I know. I'm just … nervous."

"Don't be. And to answer your question from before, yes. Of course I was scared last night."

I laugh. "Yeah, it was a stupid question."

"It's okay. It shows you care." She puts her hand on my chest and my heart spasms. "You're kind and caring, and that's why I like you so much."

I'm not prepared for how this girl is making me feel, and I freeze. What am I supposed to say back to her? I like you, too? You make me feel things I've never felt before? How the hell do guys do this with girls all the time?

Lian moves her hand up to my shoulder, then around to the back of my neck, and pulls my face towards her.

Our mouths meet, and we're straight into the movie kiss. No messing around with brushing lips—it's just straight-out tongue and spit swapping. Lian swings her leg over me and moves so she's sitting in my lap. Her fingers twist into my hair. She presses her body against me, and I hope she doesn't think the phone in my pocket is something else.

My hands are on her hips because I don't know where else to put them. Lian pulls back and tilts her head to the other side, and then she's kissing me again. I hope I don't taste like my lunch.

Something buzzes, and Lian stops. She sits back onto my legs and looks down. My phone is vibrating in my pocket and she giggles. Heat rises up my neck.

"Want to get that?" Lian asks.

She hops off my lap and I stand up, fishing my phone from my pocket and staring at the screen. I swipe my finger across it and answer the call, not making eye contact with Lian.

"Toni, this better be good." From the corner of my eye, I see Lian fold her arms over her chest.

"Hello to you, too," Toni says.

I close my eyes and pinch the bridge of my nose. "I'm sorry. What's up?"

"You have to get over here. I know more about why the witch is killing people."

"You mean apart from sucking souls to become corporeal? You can't tell me over the phone?"

"This is pretty big, Harvey. And I really want you to see the grimoire. We're running out of time."

I sigh. "All right. I'm at Lian's. I'll be there soon."

"Bring her with you. She's part of this, too."

I look at Lian. She has her arms crossed and she's frowning. "Okay. I'll ask her if she wants to come."

"Just ... get over here." Toni ends the call.

Lian and I stand in the middle of her room in silence. She seems upset, and I don't want her to be. I don't even understand why she would be. I've never gone through anything like this before, and I have no idea what I'm supposed to do or say to make her face not look like it does right now.

"Will you come to Toni's with me?" I finally ask, putting my phone back in my pocket. "She's found something in the book."

"You want me to come with you?" Lian looks at the floor.

And then I think maybe I know why she's upset. I step towards her, and before I can lose my nerve, I lift her chin with my finger and I kiss her like she kissed me. She grips my arms, digging her fingers into my skin, and I hold her waist, pulling her hips against mine.

Lian pulls away, gasping, and she stares into my eyes.

I smile. "Of course I want you to come."

15

Toni has the house to herself, with her parents out and her sister with friends. I let Lian and myself in through the back door and take Lian's hand, leading her up the stairs to Toni's room.

We find Toni sitting at her desk. Her laptop is open on the bed, and everything else that was on her desk is now on the floor. The surface of the desk has the grimoire open in the middle of it, and there are Post-It notes all over the place. Toni hunches over and scribbles in a notebook.

I sit on the bed and move the laptop over so Lian can sit as well.

"Toni," I say, because she hasn't looked up yet.

"Hang on," she says through the pencil she's chewing on. She scribbles something else down, then swivels in her chair to face us.

I raise my eyebrows. "What've you found?"

Toni picks up the book and passes it to me.

"I think I found out how we released the witch. Look at the first page."

I open the book, the Post-It notes rustling, and read what it says about the witch.

> *Within these pages we inscribe,*
> *A life, a death, a soul's demise.*
> *With blood if thrice her name repeat,*
> *Then death thy soul cannot defeat.*
> *Death will come in turn for thee,*
> *At the mighty power of three.*
> *Rising from the pit of hate,*
> *Nine and three her soul will take.*
> *Beware, the Lovely Dark when free,*
> *By moonlight's glow, so shall it be.*

Beneath that is her name, *Nerezza*, in the same swirly script I saw the first time I'd looked at this page. I'm amazed I can read the other words now when before they were a jumbled mess of letters and symbols. I don't want to say any of the words out loud though. I think I get what the verse is saying, but I'm not sure I want to acknowledge it.

"Twelve souls," Toni says, making me look up. "She needs twelve souls to become corporeal."

Beside me, Lian wraps her arms around herself. "I should've left it where it was."

"You think?" I say, then wish I hadn't. "Sorry. How many are dead so far?"

"Five in the clearing. Violette. Two at the hospital, and Noah and Madison at the lookout." Toni stands up and balances on her good leg, reaching over to take the grimoire from me. "That makes ten. But we can't be sure she *actually* took their souls. We didn't see her suck face with all of them."

"How do we stop her?" I ask, because I know it's what the three of us are thinking.

"Is it even possible?" Lian rubs her arms as if she's cold. "To stop her?"

"We have to try," Toni says. "We don't know who will be next. *Death will come in turn for thee, at the mighty power of three.* It might be someone else we love. Lian has lost three of her friends. We've been lucky so far, Harvey. She hasn't come for our loved ones."

"Maybe she thinks Violette and the others are our friends. Or maybe the people who rescued us count somehow," I say. "Maybe she doesn't discriminate."

"Whatever it is, we made this mess so we need to fix it." Toni looks at me, then at Lian.

"I agree." I stand up. "But *how* do we fix it?"

Toni leafs through the grimoire. I kind of want to know what else is in there, but there are a lot of Post-It notes, and I'm probably better off relying on Toni to tell me the important stuff.

She stops at a page and runs her finger down it. "There are all sorts of spells in here for a million different things. From what I've read so far, the Moonlight Coven was very powerful. You were heading in the right direction, Harvey, when you mentioned a binding spell, but a simple one isn't going to cut it. We have to find one that's powerful enough to get rid of N, but we have to be able to pull it off. So far I haven't had much luck." Toni looks up.

I run a hand through my hair and put my hands on my hips. "Didn't it take twelve *real* witches to bind her the first time? How the hell are *we* going to do that?"

"I don't know." Toni glares at me. "But we have to try."

"This isn't going to be easy," Lian says.

I take the book from Toni again and flip through it. She's right about the spells. There are so many. Towards the back of the grimoire, I find a section about the Moonlight Coven. There are thirteen pages, one for each of the witches. The pages have details about them, and are accompanied by an illustrated portrait. The thirteenth witch, and the last page in the book, is Nerezza.

"This is her." I hold the book up.

The portrait of Nerezza shows her with her chin slightly raised, as if in contempt of everyone around her. Her eyes are hooded, and she appears sexy and dangerous all at once. Her dark hair flows in waves around her shoulders, and her black lips are slightly parted.

"Quite the looker, isn't she?" Toni says.

"What do her looks have to do with anything?" Lian stands and takes the book from me, staring at the last page. She holds it for a few minutes, and her eyebrows knit together. I'm about to ask her what she's thinking when she says, "There's something odd ..."

I move to her side and peer over her shoulder. "What's odd?"

"The back cover ... something's different about it."

Lian runs her hand over the paper that covers the inside back of the grimoire. I look more closely, then take the book from her and use my fingernail to get under one of the corners. It comes away easily, and I look at Toni.

"I think there's something under here." I move so I'm standing beside Toni's chair.

She takes the book from me and carefully peels the lining paper back towards the spine. Tucked underneath are some smaller sheets of paper.

"What's that?" I ask, and then I think how stupid my question is because they are obviously sheets of paper. "I mean, what do they say?"

Toni picks the sheets up and closes the grimoire, setting it aside on the desk. She scans the words, shuffling from one page to the other.

"I think we've found our binding spell," Toni says.

"That's great." I step back and smile at her.

Toni presses her lips together. "It's not going to be *that* easy."

"What do you mean?" Lian comes to my side and leans into me.

"We need some of the witch's belongings in order to cast the spell."

I frown. "We have some of those."

Toni stands up and hops over to the bed. I drop down beside her, and Lian stands in front of us. Toni stares at the pieces of paper in her hands.

"We have the pendant, and the athame. But we need one more item," she says.

"We have the book." Lian picks it up from the desk. "Will it do?"

Toni shakes her head. "The third belonging is her wand. Did you see anything that looks like this while we were underground?"

I take the piece of paper and stare at the small ink illustration of Nerezza's wand. It's a stick with a stone bound to the end with some sort of twine.

Lian and I look at each other. "Did you see anything?" I ask.

She shakes her head. "I only saw candles."

"Logic says, if all her other witchy stuff was in the cavern, her wand would be there, too," Toni says. "We need to get that wand."

"And how the hell are we going to do that?" I ask.

The girls stare at me. None of us speak, because we all know the answer. I want to scrunch the piece of paper into a ball, but instead I run a hand through my hair and grip it, pulling until it hurts. I want to go home, turn the TV on and watch Netflix.

The real world sucks.

"I'm not going back to that place." I let the piece of paper fall from my fingers. Then I walk out of Toni's room, and don't look back.

16

Toni tried to call me about a million times between the time I left her place and now. Lian tried a few times as well, but I switched my phone off, half regretting giving her my number. I don't want to talk to either of them. I don't want to deal with any of this. If they want to go back to that place then they can, but I want to be left out of it.

The last thing I want to do today is go to school, but Mum would never believe me if I told her I was sick.

I pick Jack up like normal, and we head to school.

"What's up with you?" he asks as he climbs into the front seat. "You didn't answer any of my calls."

"I don't want to talk about it." *I want it to all just go away.*

He doesn't push the issue.

I park where I usually do and get out, walking up the school driveway without saying anything to Jack. He has to jog to catch up.

"What's wrong with you this morning?" Jack pants beside me and adjusts the strap of his backpack on his shoulder.

"I said I don't want to talk about it."

There are a lot of things I don't want to do today.

I don't want to meet Toni at her locker.

I don't want to talk to Toni.

I don't want to go to class.

I don't even want to see or talk to Lian.

I don't want to talk to anyone.

It seems I'm not going to get what I want though, because Jack won't leave my side, and as soon as I enter the hallway to head to homeroom, I pass Lian. She turns to look at me, but I don't stop.

"Harvey," she says.

I keep walking, and I know it's mean and rude, but I don't care.

The next second, Lian is beside me.

"He's in a bit of a mood this morning," Jack says.

"Harvey, stop." Lian grabs my arm, and I turn to face her in the middle of the hall.

I'm not sure what she expects me to say. She slips her hand into mine and steps closer, and I can sense Jack's eyes widening because she's touching me. At school. In public. Where people can see. We're not at a party in the dark.

"Did I miss something?" Jack asks.

I close my eyes for a second and wish I had superpowers, because right now is when I would fly away, or disappear in a cloud of smoke. Then I imagine a black cloud of mist like the witch and I open my eyes again. Lian has come closer, and her face is near enough for me to kiss her.

I want to.

But I don't.

"Why are you doing this?" Lian's voice is almost a whisper. "Don't shut me out. Don't shut Toni out."

"I told you, I don't want to go back." I pull my hand from hers and walk away. I'm getting good at walking away.

I don't owe Lian anything anyway. It's not like we've been friends for years and I'm really hurting her. We had a thing, and now we don't have a thing. Simple. But then I think of Toni and how long we've been friends, and I probably do owe her something. It's good I haven't seen her today, because I'm not looking forward to what will probably come out of her mouth when I do.

Jack follows me down the hall, and we take our seats in homeroom. Our names are called, then we listen to the morning announcements. I'm glad because I don't want to explain anything to him. I don't have any classes with Jack this morning, and when the bell goes I get up to head for the door.

"I'll see you later," I say without turning around.

"Harvey," Jack calls after me, but I keep walking.

I spend the entire morning with my head down, ignoring pretty much everyone. I'm thankful I don't have classes with Toni, either, until after lunch. I don't even know if she's at school today because I didn't go to her locker like I usually do. I find myself wondering if she's okay, and I feel guilty for a moment, then I snap out of it and think about what I'll do when I get home instead, to take my mind off everything.

I'm stuck in my own thoughts, on autopilot, before I

even realise that I've made my way to where I always sit with Toni and Jack. They're already there, and it's too late to turn around because they've seen me. Somehow, I don't think I'll get away with walking away from Toni as easily as I did with Lian.

Lian and Greg walk over, and I stare at the ground, willing the universe for once to help me out.

No cracks.

Never any cracks in the ground when I actually need them.

"We're staging an intervention," Toni says. "Sit."

"An intervention." I stare at the four of them.

"You can't walk away from this." Toni stands and stumbles a bit. She looks awkward, more so than usual.

"When did you lose the crutches?" I frown.

"This morning at my check-up," Toni says. "But you're changing the subject. Sit down."

"No. You're not the boss of me."

"That's really mature," Toni says.

The four of them look at me. Toni scowls. Greg has his arm around Lian's shoulders, but I'm too annoyed already to be upset about it. Jack opens his mouth to say something, and then Lian steps forward, raises her hand, and slaps me.

The sting spreads across my cheek.

Lian's eyes widen, and her hand flies to her mouth. "Harvey, I'm so sorry. I ... don't know why I did that."

I glare at her. Then I turn around and I walk.

Screw this.

Screw today.

Screw them.

I reach my car, reef the door open and throw my bag in. The engine roars to life when I turn the key, and I back out of my parking space, heading for the road. I look in my rear-view mirror and Lian is standing in the middle of the school driveway, her face wet with tears.

I smack the steering wheel and yell. Then I pull over and turn the car off. I'm only a few hundred metres from school, and I could go back. I should go back and apologise. But she slapped me.

My phone buzzes in my pocket, and I take it out. 'Jack' flashes on the screen. For a second I don't think I'm going to answer it. Then I do.

"Hey," I say.

The other end of the phone is silent. Then Jack's voice comes through. "Want me to come with?"

I take a deep breath but I can't answer. I'm not sure if having him around will help or not. I'd rather be alone.

"We can take off and see a movie?" Jack says. "You don't have to talk to me. But maybe you could use the time out. Toni and the others filled me in on what happened after the party."

I still don't know what to say.

"Come on, man. This is heavy stuff. We could chill out for a bit." There's a tap on my window and Jack is standing there, his phone to his ear.

I hang up and nod. He goes around the front of the car and gets in the passenger side. I start the car again and drive us towards the shopping centre on the other side of the train line. A movie might be exactly what I need to take my mind off everything for a while. We'll probably get into trouble for ditching school, but at this point, I don't really care.

We walk from the car into the shops and take the travellator to the top level. There's ten minutes before the next session, and I don't even look to see what movie is showing. Jack buys the tickets and we go upstairs to the cinema. I make sure I sit as close to the exit as possible so I can get out if I have a panic attack. I'm usually okay at the movies, but I like to be prepared, so we take the last seats in the back row on the aisle.

The movie playing on the screen doesn't register, and I sit with blurry eyes and a heavy feeling inside my chest. I wish I was sitting with Lian so I could reach over and take her hand. Something tells me Jack wouldn't be too keen to hold mine.

There are only three other people in the cinema, so we pretty much have the place to ourselves, but Jack's idea of it taking my mind off things isn't really working. I slouch in my seat and close my eyes, trying to focus on the noise coming from the speakers. But my mind keeps drifting to everything that's happened, and I can't turn it off.

Something explodes, and my eyes fly open. I wasn't expecting such a loud noise, and I turn to look at Jack. His eyes are fixed intently on the screen, and he raises his hand to his mouth to stuff popcorn into it.

I see something move at the end of our row of seats, but it's dark, and I can't make out any sort of shape. There's no one else sitting in our row. The other people are a few rows in front of us. I put it down to being jumpy, and then I see something move again.

Black mist rolls onto the last seat in our row, and I

freeze. The familiar rustling sound echoes in my ears. My skin crawls and I go cold. In seconds, the mist is halfway along the row of seats. It rises into the air in a cloud full of snaking tendrils, and I grab Jack's arm. He drops his popcorn and it spills into his lap and onto the floor.

Jack looks at me then follows my gaze through the darkened cinema. He jumps in his seat, his back pressing into the armrest between us.

The movie plays on, the images on the screen cast flashes of light and colour around the cinema. Through one flash, I see a face in the mist, and then everything goes dark again as the image on the screen changes.

I want to scream but my voice is stuck in my throat.

The black cloud blends with the shadows, rising higher until it's above us. It's so thick it partially blocks out the movie. Jack leans back, trying to get away through his seat. The movie screen flashes again and the light fills out the features of a face that forms and hovers over us, surrounded by floating dark hair.

It's the first time I've seen Nerezza as anything other than black mist or crows.

The cloud spreads out around her, flowing and rolling and twisting, forming the shape of her body, then becoming smoky again. She changes shape as she morphs from mist, to a human form, and back. All the while her eyes are trained on me. Her face is pale and translucent. Her lips are black.

She's beautiful.

I can't move. My mind is telling me to run, but my body won't listen.

Jack has stopped scrambling, as if the witch has us both in a trance. I want to tell him to fight, to get up and run, but we sink into the seats beneath us.

Nerezza smiles, and I see an evil in her eyes so fierce I think she may kill me with just that look. She edges closer, and all I can do is wait for what will come next because I can't move.

I open my mouth, and her smile widens.

A desire to touch her fills my chest.

She's … lovely.

Jack moans.

My fingers dig into the armrests of my seat, and I try to turn my head to look at him, but I can't take my eyes off Nerezza.

She moves.

So fast it takes a second for my brain to catch up.

I open my mouth wider. I want her mist inside me, and I wait to feel her but I don't.

Jack jolts beside me, his chest thrusting forward, and I finally manage to turn and look at him. His mouth opens, and black mist pours into him so fast he gags. His eyes widen, and his body convulses as he makes a choking sound. When all the mist is gone, he slumps forward, his head lolling to the side.

Finally, I'm able to move. I lunge and grab his shoulders to stop him from falling out of his seat, and then his mouth opens again and he spews black mist into my face. It's cold, and I shudder at its touch.

The mist pours over me, and I squeeze my eyes closed. Now that it's touching me I can't believe I ever wanted Nerezza. She rolls away, coiling tendrils of darkness over the seats. She stops at the end of the row and her face appears again, less translucent this time.

She smiles, and instead of lust I feel an all-consuming hatred for her.

She melts away into the shadows, and I'm left holding my dead best friend.

17

J ack is heavy. I don't know what to do. I don't want to leave him, but I have to go and get someone, or call someone, or do something. The other people in the cinema are oblivious, watching the movie.

I let go of Jack and stand, running my hands through my hair. He slumps forward, and I catch him to stop him from falling out of his seat. I pat his face in the hope that he'll wake up.

"Jack … Jack?" I shake his shoulders.

"Hey, be quiet," someone says.

I ignore them and press my fingers to Jack's neck, waiting to feel his pulse.

"Jack?" I yell, patting his face harder this time.

Nothing.

"What's happening?" A guy has hopped over the seats into the row in front of us.

"My friend. He's not breathing." I let go of Jack's shoulders and put my hand over my mouth. My eyes are hot. Air puffs from my mouth in short bursts.

The guy near me is on his phone but I don't register what he's saying. Then he's over the seat and pressing his fingers to Jack's neck. My eyes blur, and I can't see in the dark cinema. My chest tightens. My palms are clammy. It's hard to breathe, and I'm dizzy.

"Help me get him out so we can lie him down," the guy says.

I blink and stumble because I don't feel well, falling onto the back of the seat in front of me. The other two people who were watching the movie have come over, and one of them helps me to my feet, leading me out of the row and to the vestibule at the back of the cinema.

The other two carry Jack and lay him on the floor near me. The guy who'd used his phone checks Jack's airway, then rolls him onto his back and starts pumping his chest, breathing into his mouth at regular intervals. At first, I count the compressions, but then I look away, hanging my head between my knees and closing my eyes.

I want to vomit.

The door bursts open and two paramedics come in. The guy doing CPR moves away and the paramedics crouch beside Jack. They also attempt CPR, and after what feels like an hour but is probably no more than a few minutes, they stop.

I want to yell at them to keep going.

Jack can't be dead.

"Can you tell us who this boy is?" One of the paramedics puts her hand on my arm.

I lift my head. "He's my best friend … Jack Marshall."

"How about we go out to the hall?" The female paramedic tugs my arm to help me to my feet. "Is there someone you'd like me to call for you?" She pushes the swinging doors open.

I shake my head, *no*. My stomach rolls, and I can't settle it anymore. I lurch forward and dry retch into a display flowerpot. My stomach acid is bitter in my mouth, and I realise I haven't eaten since breakfast so I don't have anything to throw up. Still, my stomach rolls again.

The other people from the cinema are still here, and I'm so disoriented I don't know if they have been in with Jack or out here in the hall the whole time. The paramedic sits me down against the wall and asks them to stay with me. She goes back through the swinging doors.

Two police officers arrive, and they go into the cinema. One comes back out with the female paramedic, and they talk to the moviegoers before coming over and crouching in front of me.

"Hi … I'm Officer Newell." The female officer smiles with her lips closed. "This nice lady here is Kate. What's your name?"

"Harvey," I manage to say.

"Can you tell me what happened to Jack?" she asks.

I'm sitting with my legs apart and my knees up, one elbow pressing into my thigh. I grip my hair, pulling so I have a sensation to focus on that's not the urge to vomit again. "I don't know … He … We were watching." I swallow a sob. "Eating popcorn … He stopped breathing."

"It appears your friend has choked on something," Kate says.

"I didn't see." I pull my hair harder. "I was watching the movie."

It's not like I can say he's had his soul sucked by a thousand-year-old witch. They'd probably strap me to a gurney as well.

"Okay, are you able to give me a number for Jack's parents?" Officer Newell says.

I look up at the police officer, and she smiles with her lips closed again. I'm not sure I can talk anymore, even though I know Jack's numbers by heart, so I pull my phone from my pocket. I'm wondering when she's going to ask why we're not in school, but maybe it's not so important right now. I press my home button and enter my password, then go to my favourites and press the 'i' next to Jack's name. I hold the phone so Officer Newell can write down his home number.

The male paramedic who has been in with Jack comes over to talk to Officer Newell. "The transfer crew is on its way."

I don't even want to know what that means.

Officer Newell nods. "Harvey, you don't have to talk to me, but I'd like to know what happened," she says. The other police officer comes out of the cinema and stands behind her.

I nod, but I don't get up. My stomach rolls again as I think about Jack. His parents are going to be gutted. How will I face them? How will I face Toni and Lian? My parents?

This is all my fault.

If I'd just agreed to go back to the cavern instead of walking away, maybe Jack would still be alive.

The guy from the movie who made the phone call is there, and he helps me to my feet. I thank him for sticking around. He and his friends chat to the other police officer before leaving.

"What ..." I clench my jaw and squeeze my eyes closed. "What's going to happen to Jack?"

"We'll assess the scene ... Don't worry, he'll be well looked after." Office Newell pats my arm.

A few people are milling around. I hadn't noticed them until now, and I figure they're being nosy and watching the drama. I want to scream at them that someone has died—have some respect. But all I can do is stuff my hands in my pockets.

"Can I take your number as well?" Officer Newell asks. "I might need to talk to you and your parents." I give her my number because what's the point in protesting? "Can you get home on your own?"

I nod and turn away, suddenly wanting to get out of there.

On my way to the car, I call Mum. Before she picks up, I imagine myself being calm and collected, but when I hear her voice, I lose it.

"Harvey? Are you crying? What's the matter?" Mum says. "What happened?"

"It's Jack," I say through my tears. "He's ... he died, Mum."

At first, there's no response at the other end of the phone. I put my head in my hand and keep walking through the shopping centre towards the car park.

Mum takes a sharp breath. "Oh, honey. I'm so sorry."

"I'm on my way home."

"Okay, I'll see you soon."

After I hang up, I stare at the screen of my phone and lean against my car. Toni is in my favourites, and I hover my finger over her name. I don't want to tell her what's happened. She's so mad at me already, and I'm scared telling her will make it worse. Then I snap out of it because Jack is dead, and I need to stop being a dick and thinking about myself.

Toni answers on the second ring. "Harvey. Finally you—"

"Jack's dead," I say before I can chicken out.

Like Mum, she's silent at the end of the line. "Okay," she finally says.

Toni doesn't say anything else, but I heard the quaver in her voice with that one word.

"I'm going home," I say before hanging up.

I grip my phone hard enough for my knuckles to turn white. Tears sting my eyes, making them burn. I get into my car but I don't start the engine straight away. Instead, I sit and stare at Jack's bag sitting in the footwell of the passenger seat, wondering what the hell went wrong and what he ever did to deserve something like this happening. Jack never hurt anyone. Why had the witch picked him?

When I get home, Toni is sitting on my couch, chewing on the edge of her thumb. I want to say something, but I don't know what. 'I'm sorry' doesn't seem to cut it.

I half expect her to launch into a rant at any second, scolding me and telling me she told me so. But she doesn't. Maybe she's in shock. Or maybe she knows I wouldn't be able to handle it right now. What are you supposed to say to your best friend when your other best friend has died?

"Are you going to tell me what happened?" she finally asks.

"The witch happened."

"But Jack ..."

"Lian has lost three of her friends. Maybe it's my turn." I take a deep breath and look at her across my lounge room.

We don't say anything for a while, because we both know what Nerezza is capable of. And some things are just too damn hard to explain.

18

I don't go to school for two days, and Mum and Dad step around me as if they're walking on hot coals. The police called, but Dad said unless I was a suspect, I'd been traumatised enough and wouldn't be making a statement. They assured him I would be questioned as a witness, and if I felt up to it to please let them know. Apparently they already have statements from the other people who were there, and I haven't been implicated in any way.

The subject of Jack's death hangs over us like a black cloud. My parents don't know what to say to me, and in some ways, I'm grateful because I don't know what to tell them either. So we don't really talk. We just … exist in the same house.

And that's what it feels like. Existing. Not really living. Just existing.

Lian tries to call me a few times in the two days I'm

away, but I don't answer any calls or texts. She'll have questions, and I don't want to answer them right now.

Toni has tried calling, too, and I feel a little bit bad about not wanting to talk to her because she's hurting just as much as me. Still, this is something I have to do by myself. No one could ever understand the guilt and the pain I feel.

I could have done something to stop it.

But I didn't.

I remember Lian after Violette died, how she wanted to bring her back, raise the dead. I think exactly the same thing about Jack, even though I know it's not possible. It shouldn't be possible. Still, I spend a lot of the time while I'm alone in my room trawling the web to see if there's a spell I could use. I find the simplest one I can and write it down, but I'm too scared to try it. It seems too easy, and knowing my luck I'd stuff it up somehow. I've seen *Pet Cemetery*; I don't want Jack to end up like Gage.

These thoughts have been running through my head for two days, and I think maybe I'll go crazy soon. I haven't left my room except to pee. I haven't even showered because I can't bring myself to do anything that will make me feel good.

Mum has been bringing food for me, but I don't eat much when she does because I have a constant sick feeling in my stomach that won't go away.

There's a knock at my door. Three light taps.

I don't move from the bed to answer it. I never do. Mum usually comes in anyway. This time the door doesn't open, and I turn my head to the side to stare at it.

THE Lovely DARK

The three knocks come again, followed by Toni's voice. "Harvey? Can I come in?"

I blink a few times and keep staring at the door. The handle turns, and it opens slowly. I haven't wanted to see anyone since Jack died on Monday afternoon, but when I look at Toni all I want to do is hug her.

But I'm numb. My arms and legs don't have the strength to move an inch let alone push me up off the bed. She hobbles in on her moonboot and closes the door. She's getting better at walking without her crutches.

Toni stands in the middle of my room. With her hands on her hips, she stares down at me. Her face has this look on it like she wants to yell at me and hug me all at the same time. I know exactly how she feels.

"I'm not going to ask if you're okay," she says. "Because I know you're not."

"And I know you're not either." My voice is croaky, and it feels like I haven't spoken in months.

Toni comes over to the bed and sits on the edge, putting her elbows on her knees and her face in her hands. Her shoulders shake, and I reach up to put a hand on her back. She lies down next to me on her side, her back facing me, and I roll so I can hug her.

We cry together for I don't know how long. All I know is it feels good to share the pain with someone, even if the hurt seems unbearable.

Toni sniffles and wipes her nose with her sleeve. "We have to go back. You know that, right?"

I bury my face into her curly hair and nod, hugging her tighter. Toni slips her hand over mine and squeezes before moving to sit up, but I don't know if I have the strength to be upright. I rub my face and take a deep breath.

"I'm sorry I walked away," I say. "None of this would've happened if—"

"You can't say that. You don't know. The same thing could've happened, Harvey."

"We need a plan." I push myself up and swing my legs over the side of the bed. Everything aches. "We have to stop her before she kills anyone else."

Toni gets to her feet and takes her phone from the back pocket of her jeans. "We need to call Lian. The three of us have to be in this together."

I want to ask why but Toni already has the phone to her ear, so I wait until she speaks to Lian, asking her to come to my house before hanging up.

"Is there any way we can leave her out of this?" I say. "I don't … I don't want her getting hurt."

Toni raises her eyebrows. "But you're happy for me to go with you, broken foot and all?"

I laugh, and it feels good. But then I stop because it really isn't funny, and I don't deserve to feel anything but sadness right now. "I don't want you hurt either, but you seem to know what you're doing more than any of us."

"I was joking, Harvey." Toni smiles, but it doesn't reach her eyes.

"What do we do when we go back?" I ask.

"We cast the spell that the original twelve witches used to bind her."

"But doesn't Nerezza need to be there in order for us to do that?"

"She'll be there," Toni says. "We have what she wants. She's already tried to get the grimoire and the pendant.

Which means, she'll probably try for the athame next. Once we have the wand as well, she'll show up."

"How do we know she doesn't already have the wand?"

"We don't, but we need to try, Harvey." Toni picks at the edge of her phone case. "If we need to, we'll summon her and she'll have to come."

There's a knock at the door, and Mum says, "Harvey? You have a visitor."

"Come in." I run a hand through my hair.

Mum opens the door and Lian steps through. She smiles but doesn't come very far into the room.

"Door open, please." Mum raises her eyebrows and purses her lips.

"Sure, whatever." I stare at the floor as the heat rises up my neck. Mum has never told Toni and me we can't close the door.

"I'll make some snacks," Mum says before turning to leave.

"Thanks, Mrs Anderson." Lian twists her fingers together.

The three of us don't talk until we hear Mum downstairs in the kitchen.

"You don't have to stand in the doorway," I say to Lian.

Toni plonks herself in my desk chair, and I'm grateful because it means Lian can come and sit beside me on the bed. She doesn't move though, so I get up and take the two steps across the room to where she's standing.

The last time I saw Lian she slapped me, and there's a hint of guilt in the way her eyebrows are pinched and she's chewing her bottom lip. I've already forgiven her, but she doesn't know that so I slip my hand into hers and squeeze.

She squeezes back, and her lips curl into a small smile. I realise I don't even want her to apologise, because it should be me who's apologising to her.

Her lips part as if she's about to say something but I don't let her. I kiss her, in front of Toni, and I don't care. It's the best way I can think of to say sorry for walking away. She lets go of my hand and wraps her arms around my neck.

Toni clears her throat. "Can we focus here, please?"

I pull away from Lian and smile. "I guess we have some things to talk about."

I go to the bed, and Lian sits beside me. "We're going back, aren't we?" she asks.

"I think we need to bury this bitch where we found her," Toni says. "So yes. We're going back."

"When?" I ask.

Toni pulls the grimoire from her backpack. "According to the binding spell we found, the moon has to be full." She leans down again and takes a chart from her bag. "The only time we can do this is on Tuesday night. Otherwise we have to wait another full cycle, and by then I'm guessing she'll be completely corporeal and much harder to … kill."

"Harder than now?" I ask.

Toni scowls. "Tuesday night. That's when we have to do this."

I take a deep breath. "Okay, so put aside the fact that we have to do all this witchy mojo for a second. How the hell are we going to convince our parents that we should go back to the place where we fell into a giant hole?"

Toni shrugs. "We lie."

Lian is quiet, and I look at her. "Do you have an idea that won't involve us getting into more trouble than we can handle?"

"Lying is the best option," she says. "If we tell the truth, they'll think we're crazy and never let us go. 'Hey Mum, I need to bind a wicked witch, so I'm just going to go camping for the night under a full moon so I can cast a spell and get rid of her.'" Lian rolls her eyes.

I'm actually quite proud that some of my sarcasm has rubbed off on her, and for a moment, I don't even know how to respond.

"Lying it is then," I say. "What's the plan?"

"I could say I'm staying over at Nora's," Lian says. "You could say Ja ..." Lian stops and her hand flies to her mouth. "I'm so sorry."

I press my lips together. "It's okay. Toni and I will work something out."

"We could not say anything at all," Toni says. "Or you could say you'll be at my place, and I can say I'll be at yours?"

Lian stiffens beside me, and I'm annoyed with her reaction. Toni is my best friend, and if Lian can't cope with it then she isn't the girl for me. I reach over and take her hand. Maybe I need to show her what she means to me more.

"How about we cross that bridge when we come to it?" I say.

Toni nods. "We should make a list of what we'll need to take with us. Plenty of food and water this time, just in case."

"Do we know how we're going to get back out of the

hole?" Lian asks.

"I hadn't thought about that," I say, frowning.

"We can sort it out later." Toni takes a deep breath. "Maybe an idea will come to us."

"We'll need to take first aid supplies," Lian says.

"How are you going to get there?" I stare at Toni's leg.

"I've been walking in this thing fine for the past few days. I'll be okay."

"It's a long walk through the bush. And speaking of that, do we even know where we're going?"

Toni rifles through the grimoire. "Maybe we can cast a spell to help with that. The clearing is full of witch energy that played havoc with our compass and radio. If we can do something to balance that energy, we should be able to find the clearing using the map."

"Should be able to?" I say.

"I don't know what's going to happen, Harvey, until we actually try."

"And we have to try," Lian says. "I don't want anyone else to die."

I couldn't agree with her more. I wish no one had died at all, but we can't change the past. All we can do is try to fix the mess we've made so no one else loses their life.

We assign each other jobs to get done over the next few days. Lian is on food prep, I'm on safety, and Toni is on spells. I don't plan on going back to school this week because I don't want to deal with it right now, and I figure Mum and Dad will understand.

Mum comes to my door and Toni closes the grimoire in her lap, holding the top edge to hide the cover with her arms.

"I just got off the phone with Vivian." Mum puts a

plate of cookies on top of my speaker. "She said Jack's funeral is on Friday next week."

I stare at her blankly. Funeral. I don't like the word, and no one should be using it in the same sentence as my best friend's name.

"Okay," I say, because I don't think I can say anything else.

"I've told her you'll be there. Harvey?" Mum presses her lips together.

"Of course."

We look at each other for a few more moments. Toni and Lian stay quiet until Mum goes back downstairs.

"This sucks," Toni says.

I stand up and close my bedroom door. Screw Mum's open-door rule that's never been a rule before. There's a tennis ball on my desk, still new because I don't play tennis, and I grab it before sitting back down. I throw the ball at the door, and it bounces back to me. I keep doing it, getting into a rhythm and listening to the *thwack* sound on the wood. It helps me block everything out because right now, I don't want to think about crazy witches or dead best friends. All I want to do is feel numb, because when you're numb it doesn't hurt.

"Harvey!" Toni catches the ball mid-air. "Would you stop?"

I look up at her. "Sorry."

"Don't be." She goes back to the desk chair and sits.

Lian is quiet beside me, sitting straight with her hands on her knees. I take her hand again, and she squeezes. It makes me feel a little better.

"Tuesday is five days away. What the hell are we

supposed to do between now and then?" I say. "She could strike again. Someone else could die, and we won't be able to do anything."

"I'll see if I can find something in the book," Toni says. "Maybe there's a spell we can cast … to protect our families at least."

"Can't you use whatever it was you were mumbling when we were underground?" I ask. "You know, the first time she appeared all misty-like. Or whatever it was you said when the crows attacked Lian?"

"We can't use them. They were too specific, and only protected those within the immediate area." Toni bites the side of her thumb. "I need some time."

"How long?"

Toni shrugs. "A day or so. You'll be the first to know when I find something."

"If you find something."

"She will," Lian says.

"At this point we probably need prayers, not spells," I say.

"Maybe they're the same thing," Lian says, her voice quiet. "Prayers and spells I mean."

"Come to my place Saturday morning, both of you." Toni gets up and shoulders her backpack, limping to the door. "We'll have the place to ourselves. We can see if we can figure something out."

"We can get everything ready for Tuesday as well," Lian says.

The three of us stare at each other, and I take a deep breath. "Looks like we play the waiting game now. I guess praying doesn't seem like such a bad idea."

19

Friday was uneventful, thank God, although Lian found out that Violette's funeral is the same week as Jack's. They both had autopsies, but the bodies have been released. Noah and Madison's funerals haven't been scheduled. Something to do with the investigation into their deaths. I don't venture out anywhere, and neither do Toni or Lian. We're too scared to in case we draw the witch to a populated area.

But she won't stay away forever, and I'm nervous about what we need to do. Not because I could die, but because I have no idea what we've gotten ourselves into.

Although, dying would also suck.

I stand at Toni's front door, one hand stuffed in my jeans pocket. I don't want to do this. I don't want to go inside her house and talk about spells, and witches, and saving the world. I want to go home and watch TV. Maybe

invite Lian over so we can make out. I raise my other hand to knock

"Hey, Harvey," Lian says from beside me.

I don't jump even though she's crept up on me, but I shake my head to stop myself thinking about making out with her.

She frowns. "What's wrong? You have this funny look on your face."

I drop my hand towards the door and knock. "Nothing. I'm good. Just ... you know." I shrug.

"Yeah. This kinda blows."

The door opens before I can say anything in return. The doorway frames Toni's wild curly hair and she stares at us, her face blank.

"You okay?" I ask. "Nothing creepy happen since we saw you last?"

"If it did, you'd be the first to know." Toni steps aside to let us in.

I glance around the house, knowing full well we're alone because Toni's parents are out with her sister at gymnastics like they are every Saturday. Still, I want to make sure no one will hear what I say next.

"Did you find out anything else about the witch?"

Toni takes a deep breath. "Nothing I haven't already read in the grimoire. But it could be hiding stuff from us."

"Even after the spell we did?" I ask.

Toni shuts the door, and Lian and I follow her up to her room. "I'm surprised that spell, or any of our spells, even worked."

"Well, we better figure out how to make sure they do," Lian says. "Because if we don't get it right on Tuesday night, we're screwed."

I run a hand through my hair and sit on Toni's bed. There's so much I want to say but I don't know where to begin, or what question to ask first. I stare at the book that's lying on Toni's desk and silently curse it. Maybe I shouldn't have done that. I chuckle to myself.

"What's so funny?" Toni says.

"Nothing. I'm nervous."

"Aren't we all?" Lian sits next to me and pats my knee.

I want to swat her hand away, but I grab it instead and twist my fingers through hers.

Toni plops into her desk chair and picks up the grimoire, opening it in her lap. "I don't think there's anything else I can tell you that we didn't already go through the other day."

"The spell by the twelve witches," Lian says. "Will it work?"

"I'm not sure." Toni chews her thumb.

"You're not sure?" I ask. "We have to get this right."

"I know, Harvey," Toni says. "I'm doing my best."

"Okay, I'm sorry. I know you are. I'm just … I want to do this for Jack." I stare at the shiny floorboards and will my eyes not to start crying again.

"Why don't we make sure we have everything we need, and then work out how we're going to get into that stupid hole and back out again," Lian says.

I nod and get to my feet. "I'll go raid the garage for the camping stuff."

Lian stands to follow.

"Lian, can you help me with the maps?" Toni asks.

I hold my breath until I reach the top of the stairs,

wishing Toni had let Lian come with me. I take the steps two at a time and head for the garage door, grabbing an apple from the fruit bowl on the kitchen bench as I pass. In the garage, I open the cupboard where Toni's family camping supplies are kept. I find a couple of torches, a backpack, some rope, and a few other things I'm not sure we'll need. But I stuff it all into the backpack anyway and head back upstairs. We shouldn't take too much with us, because we're not planning to be out there longer than one night. *But look what happened last time.*

Toni and Lian are sitting on the floor with three maps spread out in front them. Both of the girls are hunkered over the pieces of paper and pointing to different sections.

"I think it's here," Lian says. "That bit there can't be it."

"But we walked this way." Toni runs her finger over one of the maps. "It has to be this green section here."

I flop onto the bed. *Great. We don't even know where we're going.* I had a feeling this might happen, so I pull my map from my backpack and unfold it on my knees without saying anything.

I trace the markings on it with my finger. "It's around here." I hold up my map and point to it. "This is the mark Greg made when he left us."

Toni gets up awkwardly and comes to sit beside me on the bed. She spreads out her own map and looks between the two of them.

"How did we end up so far away from camp?" she asks.

"Our compass wasn't working, remember? It's not hard to get lost in the bush when you have no idea what direction you're supposed to be going."

"I don't think it matters," Lian says. "What matters

is if we can get back."

"The compass is working," I say. "I've checked it."

"But do we have a backup plan?" Lian raises her eyebrows. "It might work now. Here. What if it fails like last time? How will we know where we're going?"

Toni folds her map. "Maybe we can worry about that when the time comes. There are other things we need to figure out first. Like how we're going to get in and out of the cave. We were stuck in there for over twenty-four hours. We go in again, and we probably won't be able to get out."

I stare at the girls. Toni is right. If we go in the way we fell in, then how will we get out again? We didn't find another exit while we were there.

"We might not have to worry about that," I say. "They've been investigating the localised earthquake and gas leaks. Hopefully there's something out there we can use."

"But we can't rely on that," Toni says. "We have to have a plan B."

"Yeah, because I'm so great with those."

"Okay, what else is there?" Lian says. "We should be making a list."

Toni gets up and hobbles to her desk. *How the hell is she going to get back out to the clearing in her moonboot?* She has to be in some sort of pain, but if she is, she doesn't show it. I decide to leave it alone for now.

"I have a list." Toni picks up a notebook from the desk and comes back to sit on the bed. I take it from her and thumb to the last page. She's written:

- Find location
- Get in and out of cave
- Retrieve wand

- Cast spell
- Take supplies

"This is ... comprehensive," I say.

Toni snatches the notebook. "I've been working more on how we can pull off the spell."

"So what's the problem with it?"

"There are three of us," Toni says, opening the grimoire. "There were twelve of them when they bound N. How are three of us going to be strong enough?"

"Can't we use the power of three and all that?" I smile.

"This isn't a joke, Harvey." Toni scowls. "When I cast the spell so we could see what was in the book, it made the text readable. But maybe it's not showing us everything. Maybe the spell wasn't strong enough to unlock all the information."

"Then cast another spell." I shrug.

Toni takes a breath and slips her fingers into her hair, gripping it. "It's not that easy. Spell-casting is delicate and can be dangerous. Maybe we've gotten in too deep. I don't know what to do."

Lian takes the book and opens it. "The first page has the warning about releasing the witch. We can pretty much guess what we did wrong there, and we've suffered for it." Lian turns pages and Toni's Post-It notes ruffle. "Then there are the sections with different kinds of spells and stuff. Then there's the information about the members of the Moonlight Coven. There's nothing else."

"Okay, maybe I need to step away for a moment," Toni says. "I'm going down to the garage. I think I have an idea for our backup plan if there's nothing in the clearing that will help us get into the cave."

"What is it?" Lian asks.

Toni limps to the door and stops with her hand on the jamb. "Just … look through the book. I'll be back in a minute."

She leaves me alone in her room with Lian. My palms sweat. I'm nervous when it's just us. I get all scared and confused.

"I don't know what to look for." Lian flips the pages. "Maybe we should think about casting that protection spell … just in case."

It's a good idea, and I'd forgotten to ask Toni if she'd come up with something. If Toni managed to protect us in the cave, I'm sure we can find something to protect our family and friends until we get Nerezza back into her book. And I can't help thinking that if we'd done it earlier, then Jack, and everyone else who died, might still be alive.

"Harvey?" Lian is staring at me.

"Huh? Did you say something?"

Lian holds the loose pieces of paper we found hidden in the back of the grimoire. "I think I have an idea." She looks back at the spell. "There are five verses, but only three of us. What if we alternate the verses somehow? If there were twelve witches originally, then maybe they said the spell in groups."

"Or maybe they just said it all together." I shrug.

Lian stares at the paper. "Maybe. But what if we say the first verse together, then each take a verse after that, then say the final verse together, will that invoke the power of three?"

I laugh. "I have absolutely no idea. Let's ask Toni when she gets back."

Lian slips the pieces of paper into the book and closes it, setting it on the bed beside her. She turns slightly to face me but stares at her hands. It's then that I realise she's just as nervous being alone with me as I am with her. This is all so new to me. I have no idea what to do, but the last thing I want is for her to feel uncomfortable. She's picking at her fingernails and I put a hand over hers not really to stop her, but to let her know she can relax. Then I worry my hand is sweaty, and I go to take it away, but Lian raises her head and looks at me.

"I'm scared, Harvey."

"Me too." I try to smile, but before I can Lian leans forward and kisses me.

Smiling is not what I want my lips to do right now anyway. Kissing is much better.

Lian presses against me. My hand is still over hers and she pulls them free, running her fingers over my shoulders and linking her arms around my neck. She lifts one leg and puts it over mine. I want to get closer to her still, so I hug her and hope I'm not being too awkward. She doesn't protest, and our lips move together. I think I'm finally getting the hang of this kissing thing.

"Um ... guys?" Toni says.

Lian flies off my lap and stands. A red glow creeps into her cheeks. "Sorry," she mutters, staring at the floor.

"Aren't you supposed to be looking in the book for ideas?" Toni takes a few steps into the room, smirking.

"We think we've figured something out, but first ... What is that?" I point to her hands. She's holding a mass of rope.

"This is Louisa's rope ladder," Toni says.

"Like the ones we have to climb in P.E.?" Lian asks.

Toni nods. "I figure it might be long enough to use to get in and out of the cave. And if it isn't, it can't be too far off. It's about five metres long."

Toni dumps it on the floor near the door.

"I shotgun not having to carry it," I say.

"You want the invalid with the broken foot to carry it?" Toni puts her hands on her hips.

"I was joking." *Sort of.* "How do we secure it?"

Toni puts her hand behind her back and pulls some tent pegs from her pocket. "Sand pegs. Or normal tent pegs. We'll take both and see what works best. They should hold. I hope."

"It looks pretty heavy," Lian says.

"It's not that heavy. We'll manage." Toni sits beside me on the bed and picks up the book. "What did you find?"

"Lian has a theory about the spell. She thinks we need to say different parts to get it to work. You know, recite some together and then other bits individually."

Toni picks up the loose pieces of paper and studies them. "I think we also need to physically bind her possessions as we each say our part." Toni looks up. "Three times three ... we might need to adjust the spell a bit though because there's only three of us and not twelve."

"And we're not witches," I say. "You keep forgetting that part."

Toni snaps the book shut. "Anyone can be a witch if they want to. You just have to believe the words you say and the actions you take."

"I think we should cast another protection spell." Lian

is still standing in the middle of the room. She tucks her hair behind her ears. "We have another three days before we can do this. A lot can happen in three days."

"You're right." Toni opens the grimoire again. "We need to protect our loved ones. But I'm not sure we can go beyond that."

"What happened to believing words and actions?" I raise my eyebrows.

Toni takes a deep breath. "I guess we have to hope it's enough."

She gets up and lays the grimoire open on her desk, then takes the candles we used the other day from her top drawer, along with the wooden box, a box of matches, and a small metal tray. Toni brings the grimoire, a notepad, and the other supplies to the floor, and sits with her right leg tucked underneath her and her left leg stretched to the side. She sets the candles in a triangle with the tray in the middle. Lian and I join her as she tears three pages from the notepad.

"Write the names of who you want protected," she says, handing us a sheet each.

Lian goes first. I don't see what names she writes down before she folds her paper in half. I write my parents' names on my piece of paper and hand the pen to Toni. She scribbles her names, then folds her paper twice and places it on the floor in front of one of the candles. She lights it, and the smell of the sulphur stings my nose.

"Come on," Toni says. "Light your candles."

Lian and I place our pieces of paper on the floor and use the matches to light a candle each. We wait patiently to see what Toni is going to do next.

She opens the wooden box and takes out a bundle of leaves tied together with twine. "Sage," she says before I can ask.

Toni puts the end of the sage to her flame and waits for it to light. It smoulders and she places it on the metal tray. Toni opens the grimoire in her lap. "Recite the words then burn your piece of paper and blow out your candle."

I raise my eyebrows. "It's that simple?"

"You have to *believe* what you're saying."

"How will we know if it works?" Lian says.

Toni shrugs. "I guess if none of our family die, then it worked. Ready?"

Lian and I nod, then Toni looks into the flame of her candle and says the spell.

"I use the power within me,
I use it three times three.
Protection for the ones I love,
by earth below and air above.
Keep them safe from evil and harm,
by charging this protection charm.
So mote it be."

She picks up her folded paper and holds the corner of it to the flame, dropping the fiery mass onto the tray before blowing out her candle. The top sash of Toni's window drops with a bang, and the force makes the curtain billow out into the room. Lian's hair flies around her face. A howl races around the room, stopping when the curtain settles. My skin prickles with goosebumps

We all look at each other with wide eyes.

"Your turn." Toni passes me the grimoire, her hand shaky.

With trembling fingers, I copy her exactly, and then it's Lian's turn. The wind and howling come both times, and I hope it's a good sign. At least there was no rustling, or crows cawing.

Once all three of our candles are out, we sit quietly. I feel like if I say something I'll break the spell, and I do *not* want to break this one. The paper burns out, leaving ash on the tray. Toni picks up the sage and snuffs it out.

A noise downstairs brings us back to the present, and Toni gets to her feet as quickly as she can with a broken foot. We help her put the candles and other stuff away and seconds later, there's a knock on her door.

"We're home," her mum says as the door swings open.

"Hey," Toni says, plonking down in her desk chair.

Lian and I smile, and Lian offers a tentative wave.

Toni's mum raises her eyebrows. "What have you kids been up to?"

Toni and I exchange a glance. "Not much," I say.

She eyes the rope ladder and frowns but doesn't say anything about it. "Your dad and I are heading out for the afternoon. Louisa is in the kitchen. Will you be home for dinner, Toni? Harvey and Lian are welcome to stay."

"Thanks, Mrs Garcia, but Mum is expecting me," I say.

"On a Saturday night, Harvey?" She smiles.

I return the smile but don't reply.

"Just me for dinner, Mum," Toni says.

"All right then." Mrs Garcia leaves us to it, and I let out a breath I didn't realise I'd been holding.

"What now?" I ask.

Toni shrugs. "There's not much more we can do before Tuesday. I'll keep reading the book. I've been working on understanding some basic spells that can be used with willpower and gesture. The single word kind that don't have to rhyme."

I blink a few times. "You've been practising witchcraft without us?"

"Is that a good idea?" Lian asks.

"I'm not evil." Toni stares at the two of us. "And I want to be prepared. It's quite interesting actually."

I fold my arms across my chest and sit on the edge of the bed. "Great. Now I feel left out and useless."

"Come on, Harvey. You're a great help," Toni says.

"Then tell me what Lian and I can actually do."

Toni shrugs. "The three of us need to make sure the spell works. Other than that, you guys can … I don't know. Stay alive? That's pretty important."

A crash from downstairs echoes through the house, and Lian jumps.

I get up and run out the door to peer over the banister. "Louisa? Are you okay?"

Toni brushes past me on her way to the stairs and hobbles down them.

"Louisa? So help me, God. Say something," she yells.

I run past Toni and take the steps two at a time with Lian in my wake. At the bottom of the stairs, I turn hard left towards the kitchen. Louisa is lying on the floor, broken pieces of plate scattered around her. A sandwich lies next to her foot. Blood trickles over her temple from a cut on her forehead.

Lian grabs a tea towel and presses it to Louisa's wound.

"What the hell happened?"

I kneel beside Louisa and check her up and down, then put my fingers under her nose and feel her warm breath. She's breathing. *Good.* There doesn't seem to be anything else wrong with her, but she can't tell me if there is because she's unconscious.

Toni bursts into the kitchen. "Louisa?"

"Oh no." Lian's eyes go wide, and she points towards Toni.

Black mist hovers in the doorway over Toni's head. I lunge and grab her, not caring if I hurt her injured foot. Better injured than dead. She stumbles into me and I manage to get between all three girls and the witch hovering in Toni's kitchen.

I'd like to have the athame in my hand right about now, but it's up in Toni's room.

"I don't think the spell worked," Lian says.

"It has to have worked," I say. "Otherwise Louisa would be dead, and her soul would be witch food." Although I'd be really grateful if she woke up.

The mist rolls over itself, tendrils of black snaking this way and that. Then a face forms in the centre of the mass, the tendrils becoming like hair around pale skin and black eyes. A crow caws in the yard, and the rustling sound is so close it's as if it's inside my head.

"You can protect people all you like, but you won't be able to defeat me," Nerezza says. "I'm too powerful."

It's the first time I've heard her speak, and I wonder how I can understand her. She's speaking Italian, but I know exactly what she's saying. Her voice is as smooth as silk, flowing over me like the tendrils of her mist. I stare into her eyes and her face gets closer, blocking out everything around me. Darkness seeps into my surroundings.

"Like hell you are," Toni says.

She's in front of me, and I don't remember her moving there, but her voice sounds far away. I want her to get out of the way because she's blocking the lovely darkness.

"Harvey?" Lian shakes my shoulder, and I shrug her off.

"*Tutelare ci,*" Toni yells, her arms stretched out in front of her.

Light explodes, shattering the dark, and when it fades the cloud of mist falls to the floor and disappears. I shake my head and look around. Toni and Lian are frowning at me. Louisa groans and stirs on the floor.

"What did you say to get rid of her?" I stare at my best friend, not sure if I'm angry because she made it go away or if I want to hug her for the same reason.

Toni shrugs. "I said *protect us* in Italian. It seemed to work."

Louisa groans again. I put my arm around her shoulders and help her to her feet, easing her onto one of the chairs at the kitchen counter. She leans on the bench with one elbow, her hand pressing the tea towel to her head.

"Can you tell us what happened?" Toni moves to her sister's side and sits in the chair next to her.

"I … don't know," Louisa says, pulling the tea towel away from her head and staring at the blood on it. "I was making a sandwich for lunch and then … I think I fainted."

I rub my face with my hands. It could have been a lot worse. Louisa could be dead and the witch one soul stronger, and I want to say all of that but I can't in front of her. She doesn't need to be pulled into this mess, even though what's happening affects everyone we love, whether we like it or not. We aren't *really* witches, but we need to cast the binding spell to get rid of this evil bitch.

Tuesday night can't come fast enough.

20

We spent Sunday sneaking our supplies into my car and fine tuning what we planned to do on Tuesday night. Toni wrote out the spell for me and Lian so we could memorise it. She wrapped the athame and the pendant in an old pillowcase and packed them at the bottom of her backpack, along with the box, book, and original sheets of paper that hold the binding spell.

Monday, I couldn't face school, not without Jack there, so I holed up in my room for most of the day. Mum made me fresh cookies, and I watched TV until my eyes were blurry.

Toni keeps assuring me we'll pull the spell off because it's all about faith in what we're saying. I don't want to tell her I think we've already lost, because seriously? How can we win against someone so powerful?

I throw my backpack into the car and try not to think

about the fact that today might be the last day I'll be alive. Maybe that's a bit dramatic, but without a miracle, the three of us are dead.

The drive to school is really hard, because it's the first time since I got my licence I've done this trip without Jack by my side. I look over at the empty passenger seat, and all I want to do is cry. But if I start now, I'll never stop, and I can't walk into school with red, puffy eyes.

Toni is at her locker as usual, and I know exactly what she's thinking when she turns to look at me. Her eyes are as sad as I feel, and I have to take a deep breath before I force a smile.

Today is going to be a hard day.

Who am I kidding? Lately, every day has been a hard day.

"Everything set?" Toni asks.

I nod. "I haven't taken stuff out of the car in the past day, if that's what you're referring to. We're fully equipped for some witch-arse kicking."

"Good," Lian says from beside me. "Because I saw the news yesterday, and it wasn't. Good, I mean."

"The news?" I look between Lian and Toni.

"You didn't hear?" Toni asks. "How could you not have seen the news report?"

"I … it's not exactly my favourite TV show." I cross my arms over my chest.

"There's been another death."

"We don't know if it's definitely *her*, but … it would bring the body count up to twelve." Lian bites her lip.

Nine and three her soul will take.

Twelve people dead.

Crap.

"Who was it?" I ask. "Anyone we know?"

Toni shakes her head. "At this point, who they are doesn't matter, but it means when we do see the witch again, she'll be at her strongest."

"She'll be corporeal," I say.

"And harder to kill." Toni's brow furrows.

"It's okay," Lian says, sucking her lip between her teeth again. "We can do this."

I smile at her and want to kiss her for being so optimistic, but I'm still not good with that when there are lots of people around. Jack is dead, and it's bad enough everyone is already staring at me without adding kiss-fuel to the fire.

"I guess we can't do anything until later then," Toni says. "I hate this." She stares at her moonboot.

"Yep," I say. "Waiting sucks."

Greg comes over. "Hey, guys. What's happening?"

I'm still not used to him being nice to us. "Not much."

"I'm sorry about ..." He play-punches me on the arm, and I wince. "You know ... Jack."

"Thanks." I stare at him. What else am I supposed to say?

The homeroom bell sounds, and Lian stands on her toes to kiss me on the cheek. "I'll see you at lunch."

She's walking down the hall before I can reply, so I mumble "sure" under my breath as the heat creeps into my face.

Greg raises his eyebrows. "You and Lian are together, together, now?"

"You're not going to kill me, are you?" I ask.

"Dude, your best friend just died—"

"Friends of yours died, too."

Greg frowns and presses his lips together, nodding. "Then I guess it's time we be nice to each other." He slaps me on the shoulder before walking off down the hall.

"What just happened?" I ask.

"The universe exploded. Come on," Toni says.

We walk towards our homerooms. A few people offer their condolences about Jack along the way, but I just nod. Toni navigates the hall with her moonboot, and I think about how we're going to get back to the clearing and the stone circle.

I want Toni to have to walk as short a distance as possible, so I've been studying maps for the past two days, and I think I have a way to get us closer to the site than we can if we go from the campground, but I don't own a four-wheel drive, and I'm not sure it's going to work. I have no idea what the track I discovered is like, because according to all the information I can find, it's been closed for years with emergency vehicle access only. We won't know until we get there, which is why I haven't said anything to the girls yet. I've stowed a pair of bolt cutters in my boot, just in case we need them.

Toni and I part ways at the door to my homeroom, and the longest day of my existence begins. The minutes drag on, and by the time we meet up at lunch I feel as if I've been at school for a week.

"I want to go now." I stare at the girls, who haven't even had a chance to sit down.

"Now?" Toni raises her eyebrows. "You want to ditch?"

"I want to ditch," I say. "I want to get this over with."

Lian dumps her bag on the ground and sits on the

metal seat that lines the wall. "Leaving now won't make tonight come any faster, Harvey."

I clench my jaw. "I know that, but we'll have more time to prepare. I want to get out there and make sure we do this right. And besides, she might not even follow us. We have to make sure we can somehow summon her."

Lian bites her lip. "I hadn't thought of that."

"Damn," Toni says. "We should go."

"So now *you* want to ditch?" I smile.

Toni swats me on the arm. "Come on."

Lian and I follow her to my car and we all get in. I haven't told Mum or Dad that I won't be home tonight. I kind of figured I could deal with that problem when I needed to, and as we turn out of the school driveway, I realise that I have to do something about it soon. I can't not go home without saying anything. I don't want them to worry, not after falling into that stupid hole in the first place and making them worry while we were lost.

I have to come up with something to tell them. Saying I'm staying at Toni's is a possibility, but what if our parents speak to each other? I might have to take the chance.

I slip my key into the ignition but I don't start the car. "I need to call my parents. I don't want them to worry."

"I do, too. But I haven't thought of an excuse yet," Toni says from the passenger seat beside me.

"I've already told mine I'm staying at Nora's," Lian says.

I look in the rear-view mirror at Lian, and she's biting her lip again. Her nerves are filling the car and making me uneasy. I pull my phone from my pocket and bring up my home number.

"What are you going to say?" Toni asks.

Instead of answering her I put my phone to my ear, because I don't actually know the answer to her question. Mum picks up on the second ring.

"Hey, Mum," I say. "I—"

"Harvey, what's wrong?" Mum asks.

I still don't know what to tell her, so I say the first thing that comes into my head. "I'm not coming home tonight."

The line is silent apart from Mum's deep breath.

"Mum? Did you hear me?" I stare at Toni and she frowns, because what sort of an explanation is that?

"Okay," Mum says, but her tone of voice says anything but *okay*. "Where are you going?"

I sigh, because I feel guilty, but the alternative is far worse. "I … need a break. I want to spend some time with Toni. It will be good for both of us."

"Will you be at Toni's?"

"Yes. I'll be fine. I'll call you tomorrow," I say before Mum can reply, and then I hang up.

Toni scowls at me, and I fear Lian's lip will start bleeding from her chewing on it.

"Great," Toni says. "Guess I'm staying at your place."

"What was I supposed to say? I'm not coming home because I'm going to slay a thousand-year-old witch?"

Toni shakes her head and gets her phone out of her bag. "I hope this doesn't come back and bite us in the arse."

"And I hope we don't die," I say.

She makes the call, then we drive towards the place that has made my life a living nightmare. None of us speak during the twenty minutes or so it takes us to get there. I pull into the carpark where the main campsite is and kill the engine. I open my door and get out. The reserve is quiet, for which I'm thankful. The last thing we need is a bunch of campers wondering what we're doing here on a school day.

I go to the boot of the car and pull out the clothes I'd packed in there on the weekend, quickly changing out of my school uniform while Lian and Toni are in the car.

Lian opens her door and comes to the back of the car. "I bet my parents find out I lied. And when they do, I'm going to be in big trouble if we get through this. I've always been good. Maybe I should have prepared them a bit better."

"What do you mean, if?" I say. "We're going to get through this."

Lian looks at me, her arms folded around her stomach as if she's trying to keep herself together. I hug her. She keeps her arms folded and presses her forehead into the crook of my neck. I rest my cheek on the side of her head, and rub her back.

After a few heartbeats, she pulls away and rummages through the boot of the car for her change of clothes. The moment is gone. I want to kiss her; lately, all I want to do is kiss her, but she has her mouth set into a thin line, so I walk around to the front of the car to give her some privacy.

I open Toni's door and lean in to see what she's doing. She's hunched over, studying one of my maps. It's marked with a few purple lines and two *Xs*.

"Purple was the only colour I could find," I say.

Toni raises her head and stares at me. "What are you up to, Harvey?"

"If we go this way ..." I point to one of the lines, "... we should be able to get the car closer to the clearing."

"But?" Toni raises her eyebrows.

"But ... I couldn't find anything that told me if the track was drivable or not. There are a lot of walking tracks, but it's a national park, emergency access only, which means there are probably gates. I brought bolt cutters for that."

"Did you look at Google Earth?" Toni asks.

"Of course I did," I say. "That's how I know we can't get any closer than here with the car." I point to a purple X on the map. "This other spot is where I think the clearing is."

"Okay then." Toni gets out of the car and hands me the maps before going around to the boot.

I wait until both girls are decent, and then we get back in so we can drive into the bush. I'm not sure if my car will be able to handle the rough track, but I guess we'll find out. We drive about five hundred metres before hitting a gate.

"Is it locked?" Toni asks, peering through the front windscreen.

"I'll have a look." I put the car in neutral, pull the handbrake on and jump out.

It's one of those hard-core steel-bar fire-trail gates that swing open from one side. There's a heavy chain and a padlock holding it firm to the post, and a warning sign saying emergency vehicles only.

"Doesn't look good," Lian says, and I jump. "Sorry." She smiles.

"S'okay. You crept up on me, that's all. We'll have to

cut the chain." I go back to the car and grab the bolt cutters from the boot.

Back at the gate, I put a link of the chain between the teeth of the bolt cutters and squeeze the handles together. It takes a little bit of effort before the chain breaks and falls against the post with a *clink*.

A breeze whips up along the trail and blows some leaves around. Lian hugs herself and stares into the bush. A crow caws and she jumps, searching for it, stepping closer to me. A black bird lands on a nearby tree branch. It opens its beak and caws again.

"Let's keep going." I pull the chain free and swing the gate open.

Lian rubs her arms, and we quickly get back in the car.

"I don't like crows much anymore," Toni says as I put the stick into first.

The track is slow-going in parts. Some sections are gravel and we have no trouble, but there are a couple of rocky places that my Commodore doesn't like. It doesn't have much clearance, and we get to a point where we can't go any farther. I don't want to risk damaging something under the car and then having no way, other than walking, to get out later.

I pull the car as far over to the side of the track as I can. We make sure it's locked before I pocket the keys and head to the boot. Each of us takes a backpack with the basics like food, water, and medical supplies. Toni has all the witchy stuff. We also have one other barrel bag between us which has the rope ladder inside, along with some camping mats, and our warm jumpers. The plan is to not be out here longer than a night, so I hope what we have will be enough.

I hope we actually make it back.

The last item I pull from the boot is a collapsible two-wheel luggage trolley I found in the back of my garage. I strap the barrel bag to it and we're ready to start walking.

"Compass?" I look at Toni.

She pulls it from the front pocket of her backpack, then shoulders her bag. "Let's hope it doesn't stop working."

"Lian, you want to take the map?" She nods and I pass it to her. "Okay then. Toni, can you point us north-east please?" I grab the handle of the trolley.

Toni rolls her eyes, but she flips the compass open and holds it out to get a reading. After a few moments, she starts walking.

"I guess we're going this way." Lian falls into step behind Toni.

I bring up the rear, lugging the trolley behind me. It's on wheels, but they're not exactly cut out for uneven ground. Still, it's better than having to try and carry the bag.

I stare at my feet as we walk so I have less chance of falling over. We trudge on in silence. I want to see if Lian is okay, but she's in front of me. If I could see her face, then maybe I'd be able to tell what degree of okay-ness she was at, but then I think I'd have no idea anyway.

"You girls all right?" I ask, not wanting to leave Toni out.

"Fine," she says.

"I'm good." Lian glances over her shoulder.

The trolley clunks along behind me, and I listen to the rhythmic sound it makes as the wheels turn. After fifteen minutes or so I have to swap hands because my palm is sweaty, and the right side of my body has started to ache from the angle I've been walking at. It's time to let the left side ache to even it up.

Toni stops and shakes the compass, and I think we're about to have problems, but then she grunts and keeps walking. Every now and then she looks up. I wonder how she hasn't fallen flat on her face. I laugh at my own thoughts, and Lian glances at me.

"Private joke?" she asks.

"Something like that," I say, because if I explain myself I'll sound like I'm crazy, which I'm starting to believe I probably am, since I'm trudging through the bush in search of a stone circle, armed with a spell to banish an evil witch.

Toni stops again, and this time I definitely know something is wrong because she doesn't keep walking. She shakes the compass, looks around, then shakes the compass again.

"The needle is going haywire," Toni says before I have the chance to ask what's wrong.

I set the trolley upright and make sure it won't fall over before wiping my sweaty hand on the leg of my jeans. "Let me guess. We're lost?"

Lian looks at the map. "Can you be lost if you kind of know where you are?"

I take a deep breath. "If we're trying to get somewhere and we can't get there, then yes. I think we're lost." I take the map from her and study my purple lines. "We've been walking long enough to have gotten to around here ... I think." I frown at the map and stare at the tip of my finger, which lingers near the green patch that should be the clearing. "We shouldn't have too far to go."

"And it probably explains the compass going nuts," Toni says. "If it's doing that again, then we're close."

"We did stumble into the clearing last time," I say. "Maybe if we keep going we'll get lucky and fall into it again."

"It's a pretty big clearing." Toni turns a circle and looks around. "I kind of like our chances of finding it if we keep going."

"But what if this time she doesn't want us to find it?" Lian asks. "She could do some witchy mojo thing to stop us. We could be out here walking in circles forever. Maybe we're on the wrong path entirely."

"Could we try and get higher and see where we are?" Toni looks at me.

Of course, I'm the one who has to find higher ground. I glance around, and there's an outcrop up ahead, so I grab my trolley handle and head in that direction without saying anything. At the base of the rock formation, I stop and assess the best way up. The climb better be worth it, because I'm tired and totally over it.

I pick myself a path, climbing over the bigger rocks, sending some small stones skittering off below. I don't stop until I reach the top. Toni and Lian are standing at the base, staring up at me with their eyes shaded.

"What can you see?" Toni yells, her hand cupped around her mouth.

I glance around at the bush below, and my gaze settles on the open space I'm searching for. I'm surprised to find the clearing is not in the direction I'd thought. *Of course it wouldn't be that easy.* Nothing about any of this has been easy.

I point where I think is west. "Over that way. It's not far."

I start to make my way down when one of the girls screams. The sound makes me lose my footing, and I send rocks rolling down the side of the slope. I search for the girls but can't find them. They were there a minute ago.

"Toni? Lian?" I yell. "Are you okay?"

No answer.

Another scream.

Then a black mass moves between the trees, twisting around the trunks and swirling over the ground. I clamber down the slope as fast as I can, catching my toes on several rocks and sliding most of the way.

At the bottom, I can't find the girls.

"Toni?" I yell again.

The mist is gone, but I know I saw it.

"Lian?" I scream into the trees.

Nothing.

A crow sits on a branch above me, tapping its beak against the wood.

"What have you done with them?" I yell at it, moving into the bush and searching for any sign of my friends.

Footsteps crunch leaves and snap twigs, and I turn to see the girls running towards me. A flock of crows flies above them, swooping and diving. Toni and Lian have their hands above their heads, fending them off. Toni falls behind, her moonboot slowing her down.

I race to meet them, punching out at the birds to try and stop their onslaught. Lian pulls up when I'm close to her.

"The athame," I say. "Toni has it."

I keep running until I reach my best friend, crows flying at me from all directions. I can hardly see through

the black mass. I slam into Toni, and we fall to the ground.

"Harvey." Toni grabs for me.

"Hold still." I claw at her backpack, reefing the zipper open and shoving my hand in to find the knife.

"There are too many," Lian screams.

I don't have time to reply. The athame is wrapped in the pillowcase and I shake it but the knife doesn't come free. I grab the handle and swing my arm in an arc over my head anyway, through the crows, praying I hit at least one of them.

They still come.

Feathers beat at my hand, rustling against my skin.

Toni grabs my arm, her head down and her eyes slitted. "The pillowcase is around the blade."

We frantically get the athame free, and I swing again, this time hitting a crow straight in its chest. The bird squawks and flops onto the ground, blood seeping into the dirt.

Laughter rings out through the bush.

Rustling fills my ears.

Then the crows are gone.

Air rushes in and out of my lungs, and I close my eyes for a second.

I look at Toni. "You okay?"

She nods but doesn't say anything, her eyes wide and her bottom lip clenched between her teeth. I pass Toni the athame, and she wraps it in the pillowcase that's lying next to her, dirty and crumpled. I scramble onto my knees, then help Toni to her feet. Lian moans, and I find her lying on the ground about ten metres away. She pushes to sit and puts a hand to her head. Blood trickles down her temple.

"You don't have much luck with your head," I say, crouching beside her.

She attempts a smile, then winces.

Toni hands me a swab from her backpack, and I clean up Lian's wound before helping her stand.

"It's only a small cut." I give Lian's arm a gentle squeeze before letting go.

"She's messing with us." Toni looks around, her eyes still wide.

Lian touches her temple again. "We can't stop now."

"We need to keep going," I say.

The three of us stare at each other, and I know in my heart that both girls are just as terrified as I am. I glance back to the top of the outcrop, trying to remember which way I was looking while I was up there.

I scan the trees. "There was a clearing that way ... I think."

"Shit. I lost the map." Lian searches the ground around us. "Where is it?"

I scan our surroundings, taking in the scuffed dirt and tracks we've left. Over amongst a thick section of trees I spot something white. I jog over and grab it.

"It's dirty and ripped, but still readable." I come back to the girls and hand the map to Lian. "I think we need to go straight ahead from this outcrop." I point into the bush.

Lian is looking at the map. "That's the wrong way, according to this."

"How do you know when the compass isn't working?" I ask. "Let's go that way. You okay to walk, Toni?"

She nods and starts off. Lian scowls but I have a

feeling it's because she didn't get her way, not because she's mad at me. I grab the trolley from where I left it and start pulling. It clunks along and Lian falls into step beside me.

"How the hell are we going to get back out of here?" Toni says, over her shoulder. "We should have dropped breadcrumbs, or stones, or something."

"Or used spray paint," Lian says.

"We're only thinking of this now, why?" I stare at her.

"We can't always think of everything when we need to, Harvey." Toni glances over her shoulder at me. "It's been quite a stressful ordeal, don't you think?"

Yep. *Totally.*

"Hopefully once the witch is gone everything will go back to normal," Lian says.

"It wasn't normal here before we woke her up," Toni says.

I adjust my grip on the trolley. "We'll think of something."

We walk a little farther through the bush, and I notice we're heading up. I have a feeling when we do find the clearing we won't be anywhere near where we entered it the first time. I look at my watch, and it's almost four o'clock. The time has gotten away.

"Are we there yet?" Toni says.

I ignore her and keep pulling the trolley. It's getting harder to roll it over the rocks, and I get snared on a tree root. My sweaty hand slips and the cart topples over. I throw my hands in the air and sit on a nearby rock, ready for a rest.

Toni sits beside me and takes out her water bottle. Lian struggles with the trolley to get it upright, and I help her stand it up before perching on my rock again.

238

She fiddles with it a bit more and is eventually happy with how it's sitting, so comes to stand beside me.

"We shouldn't stop too long," Lian says.

"We still have time," I say. Even though I'd just looked at my watch and had a sinking feeling that time was running out. If we don't get this right, there's another month until the next full moon.

"Come on." Toni gets up and starts walking again, looping her thumbs through her pack straps.

She's limping more than she has been. Her foot must be hurting her. But I know Toni well enough to know that she won't say anything. She hardly complained when she'd freshly broken it.

Lian follows Toni, and I bring up the rear again, tugging the trolley which now feels like it weighs ten times as much as it did when we left. I'm about to say I need to stop again because my hands are cramping from being curled around the handle for so long, when Toni yells out.

"Found it." She turns, and a smile spreads across her face.

I'm not sure I'm as happy as she is to be back at this place, but I'm happy we can stop and that I won't have to lug this stupid trolley much farther. I catch up to Toni and Lian, and we stand there and stare down at the clearing where we unleashed the Wicked Witch.

It's time for Nerezza to get what she deserves.

21

The girls and I make our way down into the clearing. The stone circle is visible from our vantage point on the side of the crater-like wall. There isn't much evidence left from our rescue or the investigation. But the section around the hole has blue and white police tape around it, tied to star pickets stuck into the ground. The tails of the tape flutter in the breeze and one section has come away, flapping around like one of those crazy air-puppet dolls they have outside used car yards.

The three of us walk over to the edge of the hole in the ground, and my stomach does a flip or two as I peer over the side. The last thing I want to do is go back in there.

"Well, I guess this is it," Toni says.

"No." I shake my head. "This is just the start of *it*. We can't say this is it until we actually cast the stupid spell."

I let go of the trolley handle, and it stands upright

with a thud. The elastic strap I used to fasten the bag on snaps back when I release it, hitting me on the arm. I wince at the sting of pain and grit my teeth, trying not to think about the darkness below. Toni unzips the bag and hauls the rope ladder out. I grab the rubber mallet and the tent pegs from the bag, then place the ladder at the edge of the hole entrance. Just to make sure, I use both the normal metal pegs and the sand pegs. I don't want to risk not being able to climb out again, and I hope it will be strong enough to hold.

"Make sure you put them in on an angle," Lian says.

"Since when did you become the camping equipment expert?" I ask, trying to make a joke. But when I look up, Lian's mouth is set into a thin line. She's worried. We all are. But she could have at least laughed.

I make sure the bag is closed, and I go and stash it away from the entrance so it's out of the way. Toni stands at the mouth of the hole, favouring her good leg. I'm worried about her and I want to ask if she's okay, but she'll say she's fine. Lian adjusts the ladder and then flips it over the edge so it rolls out and down the dirt wall. I take my torch from my backpack and shine it into the hole to check how far down the ladder has gone. It's roughly five metres long, and we were hoping it would be enough. I can't quite see where it ends so I guess the only way to find out is to go and look.

I don't want to.

It's almost dusk, and once the sun drops behind the trees it will get dark pretty quickly. I take a deep breath, loop my torch strap over my wrist, and swing one leg into the hole.

Rope ladders suck at the best of times, which is why I'm glad it's up against the dirt wall. I pick my way down slowly, the beam from my torch bouncing around in the darkness below as the torch swings from my wrist.

"Did it go far enough?" Toni calls down into the hole.

I grab my torch and shine it below me. When I look down I get a sudden wave of vertigo, and my grip on the ladder tightens. I take another shaky breath and blink a few times.

"Yeah, I think it will be all right." I move down a few more rungs, and I'm almost at the end of the ladder. "There's a bit of a jump at the bottom."

I've run out of ladder rungs so I dig my toes into the dirt wall and work my hands down the rope while shuffling my feet down as well until I'm holding the last rung. The drop to the ground isn't too far, but it's still farther than my height with my arms stretched above my head. I'm going to have to catch the girls when they get to the bottom since they're both shorter than me, especially Toni. Plus she has a broken foot.

"Come on, Toni. Your turn." I stare up at her and Lian. The light behind them is fading fast.

Toni swings her legs over and works her way down the ladder. She does it faster than I did, but she's not the one who's scared of the dark.

She looks down at me when she reaches the end. "You'll have to help me, Harvey. I can't jump and land on my foot without it hurting."

I laugh. "I might have to touch your arse."

"I'm okay with that if you are." She smiles.

"What are you doing?" Lian says. "Can I come down yet?"

I'm not sure if she heard the arse comment, but I feel the blush creeping into my neck. I'm actually looking forward to the possibility of touching Lian's arse, too.

"Almost," I say to Lian. "Just need to get Toni on the ground."

Toni is standing on the last rung. "How did you do this, Harvey?"

"Push your good toe into the dirt and then keep hold of the ladder. You'll probably slide a bit, but I'll catch you."

Toni does as I say and edges her way down the last part of the ladder until she's holding the bottom.

"Now what?" She looks over her shoulder at me.

I lower my voice and put my hands up. "Now I get to touch your arse."

"Don't be an idiot, Harvey."

"When you feel me, just let go and I'll hold your weight."

"Are you sure? You're not that strong."

I laugh. "You got another idea?"

"Okay then."

Toni lowers herself a bit farther until she's almost hanging from the ladder. I'm able to grab her just below her hips, and when I do she lets go of the rope. I thought I was prepared to take her weight, but she falls on top of me, and we hit the ground with a thud. The wind is knocked out of me as she lands with her arse on my stomach.

Toni rolls off, laughing.

"What's … so …" I cough. "Funny?" I take a deep breath, trying to dispel the squashed feeling in my lungs.

"Nothing." Toni grins. "You're no good at the hero stuff."

I get up and go back to the bottom of the ladder, ready to do it all again with Lian. If she falls on top of me I

probably won't mind so much.

"Your turn," I call up to her. "Take it slow."

"I've climbed a rope ladder before, Harvey," she says.

I don't reply, and wait for her to make her way down. She's faster than Toni was, but then, she doesn't have a moonboot strapped to her foot.

"I can probably do a safety drop from the end of the ladder," Lian says when she's all the way down.

"I can help," I say. "I'll catch you."

"Like you caught Toni?" She raises her eyebrows.

I laugh. "At least she didn't hurt her foot again."

"Okay, but I want to do this differently. I watched Toni from up there, and she came really close to hitting her face on the wall. It was a good thing she fell back into you."

Lian is half twisted around to face me, and I stare at her blankly.

"I'm going to turn around once I'm hanging from the ladder," Lian says. She slides her backpack off and drops it down to me.

"Okay." I stand under her and wait for her to push her feet into the wall and shimmy down until her arms are stretched above her head.

She adjusts her hands on the bottom rung until she's twisted around and facing me. I put my arms up ready so I can catch her around the waist. She drops, and this time I'm more prepared, and I manage to keep us upright. I grab her and her hands hit my shoulders before the rest of her presses against me. Lian slides down me, and her feet touch the ground. Her arms are still up with her hands on my shoulders.

"Good catch," she says.

244

THE Lovely DARK

I didn't get to touch her arse, but wow. My knees buckle at the way she's looking at me. For a moment, I forget we're underground in a dark cave. And then I remember. I squeeze her waist before letting go and looking around at Toni. The light outside is almost gone, and I can just make out her face in the gloom. My torchlight is aimed at the ground, so I grab the handle and shine it around the cave.

"Well, this place hasn't changed," I say.

Toni opens her backpack and has a drink from her water bottle. She takes out her head torch and straps it on. Lian does the same. The sun has completely left the sky, and I'm uneasy in the dim light of the cave. Even with our torches, there isn't enough light for my liking.

Lian goes around to the entrance of the tunnel that leads down into the bigger cavern below us. There are rocks piled over the opening, but some of them have been moved since we stacked them there. I'm guessing from the force of Nerezza coming out.

The girls pick their way through the rocks and debris and enter the tunnel. I take a deep breath, not wanting to go any farther, and then I follow. My heart rate quickens and my palms go clammy. At one point, I drop my torch and it hits me against the leg, swinging from the strap around my wrist. I have to put my other hand on the wall to anchor myself. It's too cramped and dark.

"Ouch!" Toni cries out. "Watch your head up here."

"Thanks. I'd forgotten about that." I shine my torch on her, and she squints.

"Not in my eyes, Harvey." Toni holds a hand up.

"I think it's just a bump," I say, wishing she'd hurry

up so we could get out of the dark. "There's no blood."

Toni drops her hand away from her face and looks at me, her head torch momentarily blinding me.

"You okay?" she asks. "You look—"

"I'm fine," I say, even though we both know I'm not.

When we emerge at the end of the tunnel I breathe a little easier, but my hands are shaking and my body is covered in a thin film of sweat. The glow worms are still here, and Toni stops to stare at the walls of the cavern.

"There are bats, too," Lian says. "Just thought I'd warn you." She picks a path down to the cavern floor.

"And spiders," I say. "Don't forget the spiders."

I follow Lian because I'm eager to get some space and air around me after being in the tunnel. Toni comes down behind me, and I stop a couple of times to make sure she can step over and around the rocks properly without falling.

"Where do we look?" Toni asks. "Where was it you found the grimoire?" She turns a full circle once she's on the cavern floor, the beam from her head torch illuminating the space.

"Over this way." Lian walks towards where we found the crevice. She crouches down and shines her torch inside. "There's a hole in the wall in here where I found the book and the box. Now that I'm a bit wiser about this stuff, I think it's an altar."

Toni goes over to stand beside Lian, who moves aside to let my best friend take a look.

"Do you think the wand is in there?" I ask.

"No idea," Lian says.

"There's no way Harvey will fit through this opening,"

Toni says. "And I'm not sure I can twist myself the right way with this thing on my leg."

"I got in there before." Lian shrugs. "I'll go in again."

"Why don't we see if we can find it with magic first?" I ask. "I can't believe I just said that."

"You're right." Toni straightens up and takes her backpack off. "We can use a locator spell now that we're here."

I raise my eyebrows, then realise she probably can't see me in the dark. "Of course we can."

"What's that supposed to mean?" Toni looks up, and her torch shines in my eyes.

"We've cast so many spells, and we have no idea what we're doing." I go and sit beside her. "What if we've messed something up somewhere and we don't know about it?"

Lian crouches down and looks into the crevice. "We can't go back now. We have to finish this."

I run a hand through my hair. "I know. I'm just ... sick of all this witchy mojo crap."

Lian twists her shoulder and ducks through the crevice, the same way she did the first time I came down here with her. I want to protest, but what would be the use? We need to find the wand, and the most obvious place for it to be is in the same place we found the book and the box.

I get up and go over to the crevice, shining my torch inside to see what Lian is doing. She has her hand in the hole in the wall, but when she pulls her arm out she hasn't found anything.

"No luck?" I ask.

Lian looks around the small room, her torchlight

bouncing off the walls and floor. "No. There's nothing else in here. And I can't see anything on the ground except these candles." She kicks one of them and it rolls along the dirt floor until it hits the wall.

"What colour are the candles?" Toni asks.

"What difference does it make?" I glance at Toni over my shoulder, still crouched in front of the crevice.

"I need a black candle." Toni looks up from the book. "I've found a spell. I have to change a couple of words, but hopefully it will work."

"Hopefully?" I straighten and move to her side to read the page over her shoulder.

"I think this one is black." Lian squeezes out of the crevice with a candle in her hand. "It's probably dirty. It's hard to see properly in torchlight."

She hands it to Toni who inspects it. "Should do."

Toni places the candle on the ground in front of her. Lian and I stand either side so we make a loose circle, or triangle. It's pretty hard to make a circle with only three people.

"What do we do?" Lian says.

Toni fishes in the front pocket of her backpack and takes out a lighter. "Look at the flame and think about finding the wand."

"That's it?" I ask.

Toni looks at me, and her head torch blinds me again. "Just do it, Harvey. I'll recite the spell and we'll pray that it works."

"It better," Lian says. "This is a big cavern."

Toni strikes the lighter and lights the candle. "Okay, torches out." She flicks hers off and Lian does the same.

"What?" I shine my torch at her, my palms already sweaty from the increased darkness. "You never said we had to turn our torches off."

"Well, I am now," Toni says. "You'll be fine. The flame will give some light. Face your fears, Harvey."

I hesitate a few more seconds. Face my fears. That's easier said than done. I take a deep breath and press the button on my torch, plunging us into darkness. The flame gives off hardly any light at all, and it's then that I notice the glow worms are pretty much out, too. I grip the handle of my torch, ready to turn it on again as soon as the spell is over.

"Look at the flame," Toni says. "Concentrate on the wand."

We're all silent for a few heartbeats, and Toni recites the spell.

"Great Goddess, help us find
a stone of black and the branch that binds.
Use your power, your guiding light,
to make a path through the night.
By earth, sea, wind, and fire,
show us that which we desire.
So mote it be."

The flame dances and flickers, as if it's been jostled by a breeze. Then it moves, and at first, I don't know what's happening, until I feel Toni stand beside me from the rock she's been sitting on. The flame rises into the darkness, hovering in front of Toni's face. It moves towards Lian, and then me. Then it floats out into the cavern.

"I guess we follow it?" I say, not really liking the idea of walking around in the dark.

Toni grabs my hand, and I'm grateful. I'm also glad she has a broken foot because it means she can't move very fast. I fumble for Lian where I think she's standing and find her hand after brushing something that I know is definitely *not* her hand. Heat creeps up my neck and into my cheeks, and I'm glad she can't see me.

The three of us follow the flame through the darkness. It leads us over to the right side of the cavern. At least I think it's the right, but it's too hard to see where we are exactly in the large space.

The flame stops, hovers for a moment, and then goes out.

I yelp because we're now in complete darkness. For a moment I panic, and then I manage to find the button on my torch and switch it on. The girls turn their head torches on at the same time. My heart slows a bit when I see their faces, but I'm swimming in a pool of my own sweat. I can't wait to get out of this place and back to the surface.

"I don't see the wand," Lian says.

The flame has led us to a far corner of the cavern. And Lian is right. There's no wand, and we're staring at solid rock in front of us.

Toni reaches out and touches the wall. She runs her hand along it, walking a few metres to the left. When she reaches what looks like a corner in the rock, she disappears.

"Toni?" I say.

She comes back into view before I've taken two steps. "Did you not find this the first time you were here?" Toni's

eyes are wide.

Lian and I go to where she's standing and look around the rock. There's an opening into another cave, and when I shine my torch inside I have no idea what to think.

The ground is littered with bones.

22

I shine my torch beam across the floor, then up the walls and back to the floor. An uneasy feeling settles into the pit of my stomach. I don't want to ask the question I'm about to ask, but I can't help myself.

"Are those human bones?"

Lian tenses beside me. "I hope not."

Toni takes a few steps into the cave, moving to the left and skirting around the wall. I follow, and Lian comes close behind. I feel her grab the back of my T-shirt. I don't mind the contact. I'm creeped out and glad I'm not down here by myself.

As we move farther into the cave, it becomes clear that something terrible has happened here. Toni stops, and the light from her head torch shines on a human skull. I jump and a funny noise comes out of my mouth. Black, gaping holes stare at us. A huge spider slowly

crawls out of one of the eye sockets, and an invisible finger traces my spine. Bile rises into my throat, and I suppress the urge to vomit.

Lian grips my arm and presses against me. We crowd in behind Toni, neither of us prepared to have any space between us. For some reason, I feel safer huddled together although it's probably not the best idea if we need to run away screaming.

"Yep. Definitely human," Toni says.

She runs her torch around again and more skulls shine white in the darkness. Some of them are still attached to skeletons, which are sitting on rocks with their backs against the wall, bits of clothing draped off them. Other skulls lie on the ground, detached and without bodies. I keep my torchlight on the spider. I do *not* want it creeping up on me in the dark.

"Who *are* they?" Lian asks.

"Something tells me we won't find a driver's licence in their pockets," I say.

"Can anyone see the wand?" Toni takes another step forward.

Lian and I shuffle with her, and I grab her arm with my free hand. The three of us search the cave with our torches, and my stomach rolls again. Our lights bounce around, and then I catch something that glimmers.

"There." I point and realise neither of the girls can see me because all our light is in front of us. "I think … oh God." I train my light where I saw the shiny thing. "It's … is that a hand?"

Finger bones curl around a stick with a stone at the end. The stone is black but shiny enough to reflect our torchlight. Twine binds the stone to the head of the wand in a twisted mass. It's not very pretty.

"I don't want it to be a hand," Lian says. "Shotgun not getting it."

Toni snorts. "Seriously?"

"What?" Lian says. "I said it first."

"You can recover quickly after a spider runs up your arm," I say, "but you can't pluck a stick from a dead person's fingers?"

"You do it then. I have no trouble admitting I don't want to touch dead people."

Toni hasn't offered to get it either, even after questioning Lian. She's as scared as us, which makes this a whole lot worse. Up until now, Toni has been the level-headed one. The one with all the answers. Now, her arm shakes beneath my hand.

I take a breath. "Get ready to … I don't know. Kill the dead people if they attack me."

I let go of Toni and take a step around her. Lian lets go of my arm, and fear rushes through me as I lose physical contact with both the girls. I take a few measured steps towards the hand holding the wand, careful not to step on any bones along the way.

Until now, I haven't considered that the hand might be attached to an arm, attached to a body. I shine my torch around and wish I hadn't. It *is* attached to someone, or at least, a skeleton that used to be someone. Strips of fabric fall in tatters around the form. With every step, I get more scared.

"They're all dead," I mumble under my breath. "They can't hurt me."

Only we're dealing with witches and magic here, and I don't actually know that these bones will leave me alone. Especially since I'm about to take something from them. I edge forward and stretch out my free hand, clutching my torch tightly with the other. I stop and lean forward, not wanting to get any closer, and use the length of my arm to get the wand.

My fingers brush the bones as I grab the stick and I yelp, pulling my hand back.

"What?" Toni asks. "What is it?"

"Nothing," I say.

I flex my fingers and try again, telling myself that it's no big deal, they're just bones. Finger bones, but just bones, nonetheless. I manage to grip the wand, and I pull to free it from the dead skeleton's grasp. At first it doesn't move, and then it comes away with a *snap*.

I jump back with the wand in my hand, the bony fingers still gripping to it.

"Oh my God," Toni says. "You broke the hand off!"

"I didn't mean to," I say.

Lian shines her torch on it. "That's gross."

I shine my torch on her face, and she grimaces. "Can one of you help, please?"

"Why? You've got plenty of hands," Toni says.

"Ha, funny." I cringe at the thing I'm holding. Now is *not* the best time for jokes. And making them in situations like this is usually my job.

"Shake it," Lian says. "Maybe it'll fall off."

I give the stick in my hand a good shake, but the bones don't come loose. Instead, they rattle, making a horrible clacking sound. Gritting my teeth, I poke them

with the torch, and they finally slide down the wand and land at my feet. I go back to the girls who are both looking at the wand, so all lights are on me.

Toni looks up, and her torch beam moves around the cave. "There are thirteen."

"Thirteen what?" I ask.

"Skulls," she says. "Thirteen skulls."

I drop my hand holding the wand to my side, and use the torch to look and see if she's right. The light bounces off each skull as I count, and a chill creeps up my spine. Thirteen dead people, and before I can voice my thoughts, Lian beats me to it.

"The Moonlight Coven." She moves closer to me. "Do you think …?"

I swallow, and stare at the clump of bones that I dropped into the dirt. "It's *her.*"

I look back to where the witch's hand was once connected to her body. I can't be completely sure, but it looks like she had been kneeling or sitting on the ground, her back pressed against the wall. What's left of her clothing is stuck to her bones or in tattered pieces on the floor around her skeleton.

"What the hell happened here?" Toni asks.

"I don't know, but whatever they did to her, it doesn't look like much fun," I say.

"Let's get out of here." Lian tugs on my arm.

The three of us shuffle back through the opening and into the cavern. I want to get out as fast as I can, but the glow worms are still out, and the only light we have is our torches. I have to stop myself from breaking into a run. We don't need another broken foot, and I have to make sure the girls are okay.

Lian clutches my arm, and my fingers are curled so tightly around the wand they start to ache. We reach the other side of the cavern and I wait for the girls to climb up first, shining my torch beam along the path for them to see, even though they have their own lights. I scramble up behind them, my heart thumping in my chest. I feel fear like I never have before, and I don't know if it's because of the darkness or being in the vicinity of thirteen dead witches in the darkness that's the problem.

We reach the top and Lian enters the tunnel first, followed by Toni then me.

A howl echoes around the cavern behind us. Feathers rustle, and the light in my torch pops. I jump with a yelp.

Toni grabs my hand. "Come on. We need to get back to the surface so we can regroup."

I clutch her hand tightly, not wanting to let go, because if I lose her I'll be alone in the dark.

Regrouping would be good.

Anything other than being underground with dead people would be good.

We burst into the chamber where the hole is, and Lian is at the wall, jumping to reach the rope ladder. She can't get to it. I don't hesitate, coming up behind her and grabbing her waist. The wand drops from my hand, but I leave it for now. I lift Lian, but she can't get high enough.

Another howl rips through the air and I go cold. I glance over my shoulder and see nothing in the darkness. My skin crawls.

"Hurry up," Toni says.

Lian slips back to the ground. "Use my hands," I say,

letting go of her and locking my fingers together. "I'll hoist you up."

Lian steps onto my palm, one hand on the wall, and I lift, grunting as I heave her upwards until she can grab the bottom rung of the ladder.

"Pull," I say. "You have to pull yourself up."

Lian's legs flail around as she dangles from the ladder. After a few moments, she stops panicking and digs her toes into the wall. They slip on the dirt but she tries again and manages to pull herself up a rung. Two more rungs and she has her feet on the rope ladder.

"Take a breath," Toni says, the light from her torch shining up towards Lian. "Then climb." Toni moves her torch beam and it lights up my hand. "Where's the wand, Harvey?"

"Crap. I dropped it helping Lian."

We both look around on the ground at our feet.

"Found it," Toni says. She takes off her backpack and shoves the piece of wood inside.

Now we have to figure out how to get Toni onto the ladder. She's shorter than Lian, and she has an injury. Boosting her with my hands isn't going to work.

"You might have to stand on my shoulders," I say when Lian is almost at the top.

Toni looks me up and down then laughs, adjusting the straps of her pack. "You're not strong enough. You suck at being a guy, remember?"

I stare at her blankly. I do remember the last time she said that. I was attempting to erect a tent with Jack. He got all flustered when Lian came to talk to us and ended up dropping his sleeping bag. Remembering is too much.

My palms sweat and I start to shake. I need to get out of the darkness. I need some fresh air.

"Just ... I'll crouch down and you put a foot on my shoulder. Then I'll boost you up so you can grab the ladder. You need to get it first go though, because you're right," I say. "I'm weak, and I suck at being a guy."

I get into position, my knees popping as I bend down, and brace myself with my hands on the wall.

"I'm out," Lian says. "Come on, guys."

Feathers rustle again and I resist the urge to look into the darkness. *No one is chasing us.* But I feel an urgency to get out of here. The hole in the ground is far creepier now I know there are dead witches below us. If I've learnt anything recently, it's that nothing should ever be underestimated, no matter how weird it is.

"Coming," I say. "Toni, you ready?"

She puts her hands on my shoulders from behind. "As ready as I'll ever be."

"Use your good foot to step on me. I don't want a moonboot imprint on my back."

Toni gets her leg up and into position. I get her to steady herself so she can move with me when I stand up, and then I do. She lets out a small yelp but at least she doesn't fall back. I can't see what she's doing above me but I know she has the ladder when her weight lessens.

"Now what?" Toni asks. She has both of her feet on my shoulders but only just.

"You have to pull yourself up," I say.

"Great." Toni grunts, and it takes a bit of effort, but it turns out her moonboot is actually quite good at gripping the dirt wall. She makes her way up the ladder a few rungs and I stare at her, wondering how on earth I'm going to get to the bottom rung.

And then I remember the footholds I dug when I was trying to get us out of the hole the first time. I want to smack my forehead, but no one can see me, so what's the point? Why didn't I think of it before? It would have saved a lot of trouble.

I go to the wall in search of my foot and hand holes. They aren't in the same line as the ladder, but I should be able to reach across to it once I'm high enough. I start up the wall, using the holes carefully so they don't give way and I don't slip. When I'm in line with the ladder, I press down on my left foot to anchor myself, then reach across with my right to snare the rope. It takes a few tries, but I eventually manage to hook my toe into it.

I pull the ladder towards me and grab hold. My arms and legs ache from clinging to the wall. When I have hold of the rope my legs give way, and I swing and twist, banging my shoulder into the hard dirt.

"Ouch!" I say, mumbling a few more choice words under my breath.

"Harvey, you okay?" Toni asks.

"Just fine." I grit my teeth and use my feet against the wall to stop swaying.

The climb up is much harder than the climb down had been, and it brings back horrible memories of climbing the rope ladder in P.E. class. I can't say it was one of my favourite things to do.

The girls are kneeling on the ground when I finally make it to the top, out of breath and panting. They grab me and help me out. I want to tell them I'm grateful, but

I can't talk from being so puffed out.

Instead, I roll onto the grass and stare at the night sky. A feeling of vast heaviness washes over me, and the inky darkness looks as if it could fall and smother me at any moment. Stars twinkle in the gaps between the clouds, and the full moon has risen. A knot forms in the pit of my stomach. The time to cast the spell is getting closer, which means it won't be long before we see Nerezza again, and my guess is that if she doesn't take our lives, she'll take our souls instead.

23

I roll my head to the side to look at Toni who is staring at me, her head torch still on.

"We should get ready," Toni says. "We don't know if … she'll turn up before …"

"Yeah, yeah." With a sigh, I get to my feet. "What if she's not here by the time we're ready?"

"Does she need to be here for us to bind her?" Lian asks, wringing her hands together.

"Unfortunately, yes," Toni says. "And if she's not, then we'll have to summon her."

"Great. That should be fun." I shine my torch into the hole, cursing under my breath, unable to fully believe that we've come back here. "Do we need a pentacle for the spell?"

"Yes. But I think we should estimate where the cavern is below us," Toni says, walking outside the stone circle. "The power will be strongest above it because that's where

we found ... you know." She looks around at the broken ground and the pile of rocks that is now less a pile and more a scattering.

"All the dead people," I say.

"Maybe over here." Lian walks away from the edge of the hole and around the right side of the rocks towards Toni. "If I remember, when we went down into the cavern it sloped to the left, so the ground here should be more solid. Is it close enough to where the cavern is?" She glances between Toni and me. "I do *not* want to fall in there again. It hurt."

"Yep." Toni limps over to where Lian is standing, her fingers curled around the strap of her backpack. I frown. Toni's foot is obviously hurting, but she hasn't said anything.

I join the girls and stand beside Toni. "You okay?"

"I'm fine, Harvey. Let's get this over with."

The trees on the edge of the clearing sway, and a howl rips through the night air. Black birds silhouette against the grey clouds which are lit from behind by the moonlight.

"I'm betting she's already here," I say. "She's just playing with us again."

"We should hurry then." Toni drops her bag on the ground, then crouches to unzip it. She pulls out the wooden box, three candles, and the grimoire, as well as the wand, pendant, and athame, wrapped in the now dirty pillowcase.

The moon tucks itself behind a cloud, and the clearing becomes littered with odd-shaped shadows. My watch reads almost ten-thirty p.m.

Lian hugs herself as a breeze picks up, tossing her dark hair around her face.

263

Toni sets the candles on the ground in a line—one for each object we're using to bind the witch. She looks around before opening the book and flipping through it.

"What can we draw a pentacle with?" I ask. "Can we scratch it into the ground?" I stare at the grass and try scuffing it with my shoe. It doesn't mark easily.

Toni shakes her head and snaps the grimoire shut. "No. We can use salt."

She bends down and shoves her hand into her pack, bringing out a large plastic clip-lock bag filled with white granules. There are at least two kilos of salt in it, and I wonder how heavy that would've felt by the time we made it to the clearing.

"There's another one of these in the bag on the trolley," Toni says. "Can you get it for me, Harvey?"

My mouth falls open. "No wonder it was so heavy. You never mentioned bringing four kilos of salt."

"It was a last-minute decision," Toni says. "Salt can be used for all sorts of things. Like drawing pentacles." She raises her eyebrows.

I take a breath and jog over to where we left the trolley, digging around inside the bag until I find the salt. The night air prickles my arms so I pull my jumper from the barrel bag and slip it on over my head. I grab Lian and Toni's jumpers, too, and they put them on.

Lian and I step back and let Toni do her thing. It takes her almost half an hour, and all of the salt, to draw a pentacle big enough for the three of us to stand in. Apparently, it will make the spell more powerful.

I'm good with more power.

Toni opens the wooden box and takes out the small

bottle filled with brown liquid. She splashes a little bit in each point of the star inside the pentacle before tipping the rest out in the middle.

"What's that stuff?" Lian asks.

Tony pushes the cork back into the bottle and tosses it on the grass. "Dandelion root elixir. It's for summoning spirits."

"Awesome," I say.

Toni adjusts the candles so there will be one each at our feet when we're ready to get into position. It's after eleven p.m. now, so we each take an object and place it next to our candle. Lian has the pendant, I have the athame, and Toni has the newly discovered wand. She opens the grimoire and places it in the centre of the pentacle.

I know it's not because we need to read from it. It's because that's where Nerezza will go once we bind her. My hands start to sweat as I run through my verse again in my head, glad Toni had written it down beforehand for me to memorise. What if I get it wrong? What if I say something that makes everything worse? I'm not cut out for this kind of stuff. I like watching it, not doing it.

"If she's not here by eleven-forty-five we should summon her," Toni says.

"It's not like we sent her an invitation," I say.

"We have her wand. That's a good enough invitation if you ask me."

Lian is quiet. She rubs her arms against the chill, and I want to hug her. The breeze flicks her hair around her face and she tames it by tucking it behind her ears. None of us speak, and the silence drags on for an eternity.

I want to say something, but I have nothing to say. Maybe I should say goodbye to Toni and Lian, but I don't want to believe that tonight will be the last night I ever see them, even though it's a very real possibility. I stare at the athame on the ground in front of me and wonder if I stab the witch with it, straight through her wicked heart, would it be enough to *really* hurt her?

Toni glances at her watch, and I reflexively do the same. It's almost time to think about getting Nerezza here if she doesn't turn up on her own. Toni goes to the book in the centre. She flips through the pages for a moment then stops, staring at it, her brow creasing. She walks back to her part of the pentacle.

"It's probably a good thing she hasn't shown up," Toni says.

"I don't disagree," I say.

"Why?" Lian asks, rubbing her arms again.

"Because if we summon her, we might also be able to contain her long enough to bind her," Toni says.

I run a hand through my hair. "Why didn't you think of this before?"

"Sorry." She scowls. "I was busy helping you rip a stick from the fingers of an ancient corpse."

"Okay, this isn't helping," Lian says. "Toni? I'm assuming we need a summoning spell?"

"I think this one will work, but we need to light the candles, and they need to stay lit in order for us to hold her."

I glance around at the swaying trees that surround the edge of the clearing. The breeze is light, but it's enough to blow out a candle or two.

"It doesn't look promising," I say.

"Then we have to work fast." Lian has stopped rubbing her arms but is now wringing her hands together. I want to go to her again and hold her. Tell her everything will be fine, even though I can't make a promise like that.

I take a deep breath. "Let's get this done."

Toni purses her lips and nods. She pulls the lighter from her pocket and hesitates, looking between Lian and me. "We have to be ready to do the binding spell and get rid of this bitch as soon as she shows up. We can't make any mistakes."

"Way to go with putting the pressure on," I say.

"Harvey … just say her name after I do. Each of us has to say it, okay?"

Lian and I nod, picking up our items. Toni steps around the pentacle and lights the three candles. I hold my breath as the flames flicker in the moonlight. There's more light in the clearing now with the cloud cover thinner than it was when we'd come out of the hole. It's as if the moon knows we need it.

Toni goes back to her place. "Ready?"

Lian and I nod, and I stare at my best friend and wait. She looks down at the grimoire and recites the spell.

> *"Powerful magic, black and white,*
> *Reach out across the night.*
> *Bring to us the soul we seek,*
> *Bring to us the name we speak.*
> *By this fire we summon her near,*
> *With these flames, we hold her here.*
> *Nerezza."*

267

At the end, Lian and I say the witch's name like Toni told us to. "Nerezza. Nerezza."

I hold my breath again, waiting for one of the candles to flicker out, but it doesn't. The wind whips up, and Toni's curls fly wildly around her head. Lian shields her eyes with her arm, and I blink against the grit stirred up from the ground. The flames stay alight.

The wind howls and blackness peels away from the sky, rolling towards us in misty waves. My heart pounds because I'm scared and angry all at the same time. This … *thing* … killed my best friend, and the thought of her taking Jack's soul is enough for the anger to come out on top.

The cloud explodes into a flock of crows that tumble into the centre of the pentacle, morphing back into a blur of blackness rolling over itself, writhing until it forms the shape of a woman. The curves of her hips flow in black waves, and for a second I feel the familiar loveliness, more intense by the time she has a face and penetrating eyes that stare at me. The edge of her mouth curls up, and it takes some strength for me to look away and focus on Lian. I will not let this witch get the better of me again. If I hadn't been so drawn to her at the cinema, maybe Jack would still be alive.

But I can't look away for long. The dark mist around the curves of the witch's body continues to roll and writhe. The shadows make crow-like shapes that drip from her form in a flowing gown. Then her transparent skin solidifies. Her black misty hair turns a bright auburn. And the darkness of her dress becomes midnight blue.

Nerezza is completely corporeal.

The flames wobble above the candles. My fingers ache

from gripping the athame, and I look to Toni.

"Now," she says. "We need to start now."

In unison, the three of us recite the first part of the spell.

"We stand beneath Full Moon's glow,
And call upon evil, to bestow,
The fate thy soul is due tonight,
We banish thee with all our might."

Toni holds out the witch's wand and says her part while wrapping a piece of twine around the handle from top to bottom.

"By the power of three I bind,
Thy magic until the end of time."

Nerezza screams, her face contorting into an ugly snarl. She lunges at Toni, but the flames hold her back with an invisible rope, tethering her to the centre of the pentacle. I go next with my part of the spell, wrapping my piece of twine around the athame so tightly I fear it might snap.

"By the power of three I bind,
Thy body until the end of time."

Nerezza baulks again, but she can't get to us. Lian ties twine around the pendant in her hand and says the words she needs to say.

"By the power of three I bind,
Thy soul until the end of time."

269

"You're not strong enough to defeat me," Nerezza says, and I'm amazed again that I can understand her perfectly. The three of us recite the last part of the spell.

"By earth and air, water and fire,
So be bound as we desire,
Stripped of all thy evil and power,
From now until Earth's last hour."

Nerezza laughs, and her shoulders shake. Her eyes shine brightly in the moonlight. I don't see what's so funny since she's about to be put back where she belongs, and if I were her I'd be fighting to break my bonds. But she hasn't tried to come at us again, and when she stops laughing, her mouth is curled into a smile that suggests she knows something that we don't.

Toni, Lian, and I say the last words, sealing the spell to send the witch back into the book.

"By the power of three times three
So mote it be."

But nothing happens.

For a heartbeat I stand frozen, holding my breath, wondering what the hell we did wrong. And then I look at my feet.

My candle has gone out.

Nerezza's laughter rings through the clearing. Toni stares with her mouth agape, the wand in her shaking hand. The witch draws back her arms and thrusts her hands in Toni's direction. Black shards fly from her fingertips like darts travelling on smoke.

Nerezza's magic hits Toni in the chest, and she falls backwards.

Lian screams.

"No," I yell, and race towards my best friend.

Nerezza reaches Toni before I can, travelling on her mist which floats around her like a thundercloud, rolling layers of black and dark blue. She hovers over my best friend who lies on the grass, her chest heaving, her eyes wide, clutching the wand in one hand.

Nerezza reaches down and yanks it from Toni's fingers. Toni doesn't fight, and I realise she can't.

What do I do? I don't know what to do.

I'm aware of an ache in my hand, and I look down. My knuckles are white from gripping the athame. I take two final steps towards the witch and lunge at her, plunging the blade towards her back.

She twists at the last moment, and all I succeed in doing is slicing the skin on the back of her pale arm. Blood trickles from the cut and she screeches, her mouth open so wide I can't help staring into the darkness. She screeches again and I stumble backwards, tripping over my own feet.

"Harvey?" Lian is at my side.

I want to ask if she's okay, but I'm unable look away from the witch's gaping mouth. Her cries make my ears ring, and I can't even lift my hands to cover them. The edges of my vision blacken, and my shoulders shake.

"Harvey, stop looking at her." Lian's face appears in front of me. "She's doing something to you."

The brown of Lian's eyes is almost black, replacing the void of the witch's mouth. I shake my head, but the screeching won't subside. My hand feels hot, and I stare at it. Blood covers the blade of the athame, and the metal splits open. Light beams out of it, and the handle grows so hot I have to drop it. It falls to the grass. I push my heels and hands into the ground to try and get away from it. Lian scrambles with me. I look to the witch, wondering why she hasn't killed us yet, but she's turned her attention back to Toni.

My best friend stares blankly up at Nerezza. I want to scream at Toni to move, but the words won't come out. Before I can get up and do something, the witch brings

her face close to Toni's and opens her mouth. Black tendrils flow out from between her lips and push Toni's mouth open. Toni's back arches, her fingers digging into the ground beneath her. All the while Nerezza is screeching, and the sound turns my blood to ice and buckles my knees.

Seconds later, Toni flops back to the grass. Her head rolls to the side, her eyes closed. I hold my breath, hoping she isn't dead, and crawl towards her. Lian tugs at my arm but I shrug her off and focus on Toni. *I can't lose her, too.*

I'm almost close enough to touch her hand when Toni's body convulses and she arches her back again. This time, the darkness flows from her mouth, and there's nothing I can do to save her.

The witch floats above Toni on her black cloud. The evil mist flows around her and attaches itself to her, shrouding her in inky darkness. It rustles like feathers and the sound makes me sick.

"No." The word puffs out with my breath, and I suck in another one, my throat tightening as if I can't breathe. "No," I yell this time. "You already have twelve souls."

Lian is beside me despite my effort to push her away before, and her shoulders shake against mine in time with her sobs. I dig my hands into the ground, the dirt caking under my fingernails.

What am I supposed to do?

The spell hasn't worked.

How can we defeat her now?

Toni would know what to do. But Toni is probably … dead.

I stare at her, willing her to open her eyes, to get up,

to move a finger. To give me one sign that she's still alive.

Defeat washes over me, and I hang my head until it almost touches the ground. Lian tugs at me again. She doesn't speak, and I don't blame her. I have no coherent words either.

Her hands are on my shoulders, pulling. "We can't give up. Harvey, get up."

She's right. We've come this far and survived, but giving up sounds so much easier.

Then Nerezza laughs again, and the sound stirs anger in my chest. Anger for every life she's taken and every soul she's stolen. I couldn't save Jack, or any of the others who have lost their lives, but maybe there's hope for Toni. If only I have hope, too.

I raise my head and stare at the witch, my jaw aching from clenching my teeth. *Get up!* I tell myself, because if I am going to die, I sure as hell am *not* going to do it on my knees.

"You bitch." I push myself up and to my feet. "We didn't come here to die."

Lian clutches my leg and I help her stand, pushing her behind me. She shoves something into my hand, and I feel the familiar grip of the athame's handle. It's warm.

"It hurt her," Lian says in my ear. "Maybe it will again."

I push the knife back at Lian. "You do it. I have another idea." Lian stares at me wide-eyed. "Hurry." I pull her in front of me so she's facing Nerezza.

Lian holds the ritual knife out in front of her. Nerezza scowls, but she doesn't back away. She floats to the ground, the mist around her legs writhing until it forms the skirt of her dress, layers of midnight blue that drape over her hips. The mist hangs around her like a faithful servant.

I need to work fast.

Scanning the ground, I grab one of the candles, but I don't have the lighter. I scramble towards Toni and shove my hands in her jeans pockets, fumbling the lighter out and onto the grass.

Lian lunges forward and screams. The tip of the athame slices through the fabric of the witch's dress and Nerezza whirls away, retreating outside the circle of the pentacle.

"Whatever you're doing, Harvey, hurry up," Lian yells.

I put the candle upright next to Toni and light the wick with trembling fingers, praying the wind doesn't blow it out. I need Toni so she can help me fix this. And I need her because she's Toni.

Hell, right now any help would do. There are twelve dead witches below us. Maybe one of them can help. I recite the spell I'd written down after Jack died. The one I wanted to use to raise the dead.

> *"Grimm Reaper, hear my plea,*
> *I call the darkness to summon thee.*
> *Bring back those she stole,*
> *Give life again and make them whole.*
> *Withdraw the dark to give them light,*
> *And banish her unto the night.*
> *So mote it be."*

I don't know if I've said it right, but the words are out before I can think about them too much.

We need Toni.

We need someone.

Lian and I can't do this on our own.

I stare at my lifeless friend and will her to wake up.

"It didn't work," I say.

What the hell do we do now?

"Harvey!" Lian screams.

I look up. Nerezza raises her wand and points it at Lian, a smile playing on her lips. The black stone in the tip sparks. Nerezza flicks the magic towards Lian, mumbling words that this time I don't understand. I stumble to my feet. If I can't save Toni, maybe I can get Lian out of the way and save her.

I'm on my feet a second before Lian screams. Black shards blur my vision, and pain explodes in my left shoulder, knocking me sideways. Lian lunges at the witch, burying the knife in folds of fabric. Nerezza waves her wand and Lian falls into me, her breath heaving. The witch rises and towers over both of us, floating. Her screech pierces my ears.

My vision blurs more and I drop to my knees, the strength going out of me.

"No," Lian says, tugging my arm. "Don't give up."

I want to give up.

Toni is gone.

Jack is gone.

I wait for Nerezza to take my soul, too, and I wonder if it will hurt as much as my shoulder does.

Hands grab me and the pain flares, making me cry out.

"Harvey?" Lian grips my arms. "Stay with me."

She pulls and I fall back into her. "Why hasn't she killed us?" I manage to ask.

"Look up." Lian touches my cheek.

I raise my head with effort. Light fills the clearing, and I wonder when the sun came up, but it's not the sun. Nerezza hovers above us, but she's suspended inside the light rays. Her arms fall at her sides, and her head lolls back as if she's staring at the moon.

Beyond the light, in the shadows around the entrance to the cave, is a figure. The longer I stare, the more I see, until I count twelve people standing in a half-circle around us. The figure in the centre has her arm raised, and the light is coming from the end of her hand. I blink a few times before I make out that she's holding a wand.

The figures come closer, their voices a low murmur, chanting words I don't understand.

"Who are they?" My brain is foggy.

"There's twelve of them." Lian clutches my arm. "You don't think …?"

"The Moonlight Coven?" I ask. "How?"

"Harvey, what did you do?" Lian helps me to my feet.

I blink sweat from my eyes, even though there's a chill in the air.

I don't know what to think. A month ago, I didn't believe in magic and witches outside TV and the movies. Now, I believe in everything that's unbelievable.

The coven continues their chant, and the grimoire slides across the grass until it reaches the feet of the centre witch. The athame pulls itself from Lian's grasp, and the pendant rises from the grass where Lian must have dropped it. They travel to the head witch and join the grimoire. Nerezza's arm swings in the air as the coven uses its power to take her wand. It floats to the ground and joins the other items at the head witch's feet. She twirls her free hand, and the ancient tome flips open.

"What are they doing?" Lian whispers.

I don't answer. I'm too afraid to move.

Nerezza stays trapped in the air. The witches continue to chant, and I open my mouth to ask what they're saying, because it sounds Italian, but the only Italian person here I know is Toni. She's on the ground at our feet and I glance at her to see if she's breathing, but it's too hard to tell with the bright light above us and the rest of the world in shadow. I pray that she is, because if I somehow managed to raise twelve witches from the dead, surely Toni is alive as well.

I panic for a moment before crouching down and pressing my fingers to her throat. The panic rises farther into my chest when I can't feel a pulse. Then the steady rhythm of Toni's heartbeat flutters under my fingertips. I stare at her chest for a few moments. It rises and falls in small, slow breaths.

"Shit." I let out a long breath and stand again.

The chanting gets to the point where I want to yell at them to stop, but I cover my ears instead. Lian pushes into my side as if she's trying to stick us together. I take one hand from my ear and lace my fingers through hers.

I'm about to move us around the floating witch when the first witch on the left end of the half-circle drops to the ground. A white line coils up from her body, like smoke, and rises towards the inky sky before darting into the blackness.

I tug Lian's hand, but before we can take more than two steps, the witch on the right end of the half-circle also drops to the ground. White smoke rises from her body and shoots into the night.

"What's happening?" I ask, not really expecting an answer.

Lian pushes me and we run until we're facing the centre witch. Her mouth moves, chanting monotonous words, and the next witch on the left falls.

"Harvey, they're stabbing themselves," Lian says.

"What?"

I look to the right, able to make out the faces and features of these mysterious women now that the brightest part of the light is behind us, trapping Nerezza. The next witch extends her arms, her hands clutching the hilt of a knife aimed at her heart. She plunges it into her chest and falls to the grass.

Lian and I watch as each witch drops around us, and with every sacrifice a trail of white smoke enters the sky, until the only witch left standing is the one in the middle with her wand raised.

The head witch lowers her arm, and I look over my shoulder to where Nerezza is slowly being lowered to the ground. The light fades, and the skirt of her dress pools around her in waves of fabric. Her head rolls to the side, and her open eyes stare at us. Their emptiness sends a shiver up my spine.

I turn back to the good witch. She collects Nerezza's wand from the ground at her feet. She hasn't said a word directly to us, but continues to chant, and I want to ask again what's happening. But all I can do is watch.

The witch twirls the fingers of her free hand, and Nerezza's athame rises to meet her grasp. She uses the tip of the knife to score a pentacle into the shiny surface of the stone in the end of the wand. The scratches crack, and yellow light glows along the lines. The witch places the wand at her feet, then aims the athame at her heart.

"Stop!" I run forward. I don't want her to kill herself. "Tell us what's happening."

The witch regards me with a neutral expression. She stops chanting and lowers the knife. Her vacant eyes focus on me as I move close enough to be within her striking distance, but I'm hoping she doesn't want to kill me.

"What are you doing?" Lian asks from my side.

The witch tilts her head and looks from me to Lian, blinking slowly. Each moment we stand here and stare at her feels longer than the last. I'm about to demand for her to tell us something when she finally speaks.

"You awoke the Lovely Dark."

I cringe. "Yeah. About that. Sorry?"

"She must sleep again," the witch says, raising the athame and taking aim.

"Please, wait." Lian steps forward, and I think she's about to grab the witch's hands.

The witch stares at us blankly and blinks a few times before speaking again. "We are the Moonlight Coven. We are the end of the curse. Nerezza must die. She will always die. We will send her back every time."

The witch raises her arms a little more before plunging Nerezza's athame into her chest. "The Lovely Dark will sleep again." Her knees buckle and she falls to the ground, a white trail of smoke rising from her chest and into the night sky. She instantly turns into a mass of old skin, bones, and fabric.

When I glance around, all the witches are in the same

state. It's as if the bones we found in the cavern are now strewn across the grass of the clearing.

Lian tugs my arm and points to Nerezza's body. It twists in on itself, fingers of darkness flicking out from a central mass. When the black shadows part, a tendril of white emerges and breaks away. The darkness writhes around it, and for a second it looks like it will be swallowed again, but the white smoke passes through part of the witch's essence, snagged for a moment on the evil presence before swirling like a whirlpool over Toni's body, the tip of its spiral aiming for her chest. In a flash it stabs into her, penetrating her body until it disappears.

The black mist tumbles towards the remains of the head witch. Light emanates from the pentacle she scratched onto the black stone of the wand. The golden rays reach out and grab Nerezza's essence, sucking it into the stone's darkness. The light fades.

My best friend opens her eyes, and I cry out with relief, tears making the backs of my eyes burn.

"Toni?" I run, stumble, and slide the last metre or so across the grass on my knees until I reach her side.

She rubs her forehead like she has a headache, then looks at me and blinks. "What happened?"

"We thought you were dead," Lian says.

I help Toni to a sitting position, and she glances around the clearing. "Where's the witch?"

Near us on the grass is a pile of rotting fabric.

"She's gone," I say. "The Moonlight Coven showed up."

"They sacrificed themselves and killed the witch," Lian says.

Toni raises her eyebrows. "What? How?"

"Harvey recited a raise-the-dead spell."

"You did what?" Toni's eyes go wide. "Necromancy is bad, Harvey."

"It's okay," I say. "I'm not sure it actually worked."

Toni shakes her head. "There's no way you could've brought back twelve witches. Do you know how much power you'd need to do that?"

"But you *did* wake up twelve witches," Lian says.

"I think they would've come anyway." I look from Toni to Lian. "Did you hear what she said? The last witch? They're the end of the curse. And they'll send her back every time."

"So you think they just showed up?" Toni asks. "And they've done this before?"

I squeeze Toni's arm. "I don't know what to think. I'm just happy you're alive."

Toni frowns. "It would've been good if they showed up earlier."

Lian presses her lips together. "I think those white things were souls, Harvey."

"Did she take my soul?" Toni rolls to the side so she can get to her feet. I stand to help her.

"You don't remember anything?" I ask.

Toni surveys the clearing again, and I study her face before following her line of sight. The remains of the witches appear grotesque and creepy under the lunar light. But piles of thousand-year-old dead people would look creepy on a bright summer day.

"I remember casting the spell, and the witch laughing … then nothing," Toni says. "We might have to do some more research on the Moonlight Coven."

"No!" Lian and I say at the same time.

Toni shakes her head again. "When we get home, you can fill me in on everything I missed." Toni takes a few steps then stops, her leg buckling at the knee. I catch her elbow, and the wince on her face.

"It's hurting, isn't it?"

"I think I might have done something to my foot again." Toni bites her lip. "I still can't believe you even attempted to raise the dead."

"We can talk about that later," Lian says. "How are we going to get out of here? You probably won't be able to walk far."

Toni shrugs and sucks her lip farther between her teeth.

"Maybe we should worry about what to do with ..." I gesture to the piles of dead people, unable to finish my sentence. I should feel relieved after everything we've been through, but until we're out of this place, I won't be able to stop and take a calm breath. At the moment, every breath is filled with fear and dread.

"Maybe we could use a spell to—"

"No!" Lian and I say at the same time again, staring at Toni as if she has two heads.

"I never want to cast another spell," I say. "Or even hear someone else cast a spell, ever again."

"I'm with Harvey," Lian says.

"We can't leave a bunch of dead people on the grass." Toni limps towards the witches. "What if someone goes for a bush walk one day and finds them?"

I sigh, because she's right. There's no way we can leave any evidence of what happened here. I'm not sure what the workers found when they came out to investigate the apparent localised earthquake, but I bet if they come back to piles of dead people, it won't go down too well.

Lian and I follow Toni to where the book is lying on the grass. She picks it up and flips through its pages. I notice Nerezza's wand on the ground at our feet. The pentacle is now a faint line on the onyx surface.

"I think she's in here." I pick up the wand, unsure what to do with it.

Toni takes it and turns the gnarled stick over a few times before putting it back on the ground next to the pendant. "Here," she says. She stabs a page of the book with her index finger. "It's like a clean-up spell. Grab me one of the candles." She doesn't look up from the book.

I take a breath and shake my head, but do as she asks, retrieving a candle from where it lay in our salt pentacle. Toni kneels on the ground in front of the head witch. I hand her the lighter and she lights the candle. She closes her eyes and says:

> *"Great Goddess, I invoke your power,*
> *Help us now at this dark hour.*
> *By fire and water, earth and air,*
> *Banish all that happened here.*
> *Take it back where it should go,*
> *Send it off, make it so."*

Toni leans forward and blows out the candle. The flame elongates and detaches itself from the wick, floating in the air and hovering over the pile of bones that was the head witch. Wind whips our faces, swirling around us and reducing the dead witches to ash. Lian clutches my arm, steadying herself against the force of the air element. The ash rises to join the twisting wind, enclosing us in a funnel before breaking away and diving into the hole leading to the cave.

Toni cries out as the book is torn from her hands. It tumbles to the grass, flipping over and landing beside the wand and pendant. The wooden box slides across the grass, and the athame moves towards the other items. They're all picked up by the wind, swirling together as though stuck in a small tornado before being tossed into the hole.

The sudden stillness makes Lian and I stumble and fall to the ground beside Toni. I hadn't realised how much I'd been resisting the force to keep myself upright.

Lian is breathing hard beside me, her fingers digging into my arm. Toni grips the grass in front of her. I look around at the now empty clearing. Even the salt pentacle is gone.

It's just the three of us in the middle of nowhere.

25

Getting out hadn't been easy, but we had done it, alternating between me piggybacking Toni, and her leaning on Lian and me so she could hop. We couldn't put her on the trolley because it had ended up with a flat tyre. By the time we got back to the car, the sun was up, and we were very tired—so tired we slept for a few hours before making our way out of the national park.

The doctor wasn't too happy with Toni, putting her into a cast and back onto crutches. She'd walked on it too much, and the fracture had worsened. This time it was crutches for another four weeks with absolutely no pressure on her foot. She isn't handling it well.

I glance over at Toni in the passenger seat of my Commodore. She's staring out the window, watching the world go by as we make our way to the local Catholic Church. I haven't asked how much trouble Toni and Lian

are in, but I've been grounded for two weeks. Mum and Dad were not impressed with me taking off and ditching school, even after everything I'd been through with Jack.

I park the car and jump out to go around to the passenger side. After grabbing Toni's crutches from the back seat, I help her out of the car. Her black dress falls to her knees, and she's wearing one sparkly black flat. The other foot is encased in thick plaster.

I told Lian we'd meet her at the church. I saw her yesterday at Violette's funeral. Toni and I figured we should go to support Lian and her friends, but I'll be surprised if Lian's parents ever allow her to talk to me, let alone see me, again.

The door slams when I close it, and Toni and I face the small crowd milling outside the church. I'm not sure if I can walk the short distance from the car park to the door. I still can't believe Jack is dead, but I'm glad Toni is here. I spot Greg standing on the edge of the crowd with Lian, his hands stuffed into his pockets.

Apparently, Jack had friends I didn't know about, because the turn-out to his funeral is more than I expected. Almost the whole eleventh grade is here. I wonder if it would've been the same for me.

Toni takes a swing on her crutches, heading towards the crowd, but I don't move away from the car.

"You coming?" She looks over her shoulder.

I stare at my feet. "I don't know if I can."

"Come on, Harvey." She regards me for a moment. "If I can do this, you can, too. Jack would want you to be here."

I don't disagree with her, but I'm seventeen. I shouldn't be saying goodbye to my dead best friend.

287

I take a deep breath and walk slowly with Toni to where everyone is standing at the back of the church. A few people nod and mumble their condolences. I search the crowd for Jack's family before I realise they must already be inside. Mum and Dad come over, and Mum squeezes my arm. We don't say anything. We've already said everything there is to say.

I'd expected Jack's funeral to be sooner, but they'd needed time to do the autopsy. According to the report, he'd died from asphyxiation. They'd put the cause down as popcorn, but I know what he really choked on.

Lian and Greg are a part of the main group but they're not talking to anyone, and I wonder why. All of us know everyone here, but none of the kids from school are making an effort to talk to Toni and me. I get the sad feeling they're here to get out of school.

Lian grabs Greg's arm and tugs him over to where Toni and I are standing a few paces away from the main crowd. They stop in front of us, and Lian offers me a weak smile.

"Hey." She twists her hands together.

I want to hug her, but I don't know if she wants to hug me, so I do nothing except try to smile back.

"Hey, Greg," Toni says, and I'm grateful for the change of attention.

He smiles with closed lips. "I'm really sorry, man. This sucks." He claps me on the arm.

"Yeah," I say. "It does."

Lian is still wringing her hands so I step forward and put my hand over hers. She slips her fingers into mine and squeezes. I don't need her to say anything. I know

she's feeling bad for me, and there's nothing she can say that will fix the pain. I also think I love her, because she knows no words she has will be enough. I gently pull her hand and she comes towards me until I can hug her. She buries her face into my neck and I bite my lip, closing my eyes. I can't start crying now. I haven't even gone inside the church.

"Has Lian filled you in?" Toni asks Greg.

I open my eyes to stare at them. Greg's brow furrows. Lian doesn't move, and I'm grateful for the warmth she's giving me.

"Most of it," Greg says. "Sounds like she was one mean bitch."

"You can say that again," I say.

The people outside the church filter in. Inside is the last place I want to go, because Jack is in there, and I'm not ready to say goodbye. Until now I've been distracted by a psycho witch and other stuff. Now everything is over and Nerezza is back where she belongs, I'm not sure what's better. Facing her, or facing the fact I will never see my best friend again.

Lian pulls away, and I have to remember I'm not the only one here who is hurting. Lian and Greg have lost people, too, and they may not have been friends with Jack, but the fact they're here says something. And Toni. She's as gutted as me. Jack was her best friend as well.

"We'll see you inside." Lian presses her lips together in a thin line. "Come on, Greg. Let Harvey and Toni have a moment."

It's the second time in as many minutes that I have thoughts about being in love with Lian, but I push them aside and turn to Toni.

"How you holding up?"

"I'm … I don't really know." She adjusts her crutches under her arms. "Nothing is ever going to be the same."

"No." I take a deep breath. "It isn't."

"You ready?" Toni looks up at me.

I want to tell her that I'll never be ready to do something like this. Not for Jack. Not for anyone. But instead, I nod and we walk together through the back door of the church.

Mum and Dad are seated up the front one row behind Jack's family. They're sitting with Toni's parents and her sister. Our three families have been close for a long time, and I know it's our rightful place to sit there, but I don't want to. I don't want to have all these people, who apparently care about Jack, staring at me. If they cared, why didn't they show it when he was alive?

When we reach my parents, I take Toni's crutches and help her sit in the pew. A few more people filter into the church, but I don't look to see who they are. I sit with my head bowed and my hands clenched on my thighs. This needs to be over now so I can get out. Being in this crowded church with all these people is almost as bad as being in the dark.

The service goes too long. After we made it back from the clearing, Jack's mum had asked me if I wanted to say anything today. Jack and I had been through so much together and she wanted me to honour my friend. But there was no way I could have stood up there and talked about how great Jack was. I wouldn't have been able to talk through the tears. And as the voices drone around me, all I can think is that the universe will never cut me a break.

But at least I'm alive.

I raise my head to look at Toni.

At least she's alive.

I turn and look at Lian sitting across the aisle. She smiles a tight-lipped smile.

At least she's alive, too.

Maybe the universe doesn't need to cut me some slack. Maybe I need to stop expecting it to.

It's time to say goodbye to my best friend, and I'm not sure I can. Jack's parents opted for an open casket, and I avoided coming into the church before the service to see him. I don't want to remember him this way. I want to remember the look on his face when we watched the very first episode of *Arrow*. Or the way he smiled when I mentioned a Netflix marathon. Even the way he looked when he was checking out girls in the most obvious ways.

But not this.

Not lying dead in a coffin.

I glance at Toni, and I realise she's struggling just as much as I am.

I slip my hand into hers and she gives me a startled look, as if she'd been off in another world and I scared her back into this one. I tug gently and tilt my head towards the coffin. The line is dwindling, and people are returning to their seats. As much as I don't want to say goodbye, I think we should.

Toni stands and I help her out of the pew. She crutches her way up the aisle in front of me, and I take a deep breath when we reach the open casket. I'm not sure what to expect, but when I stare down at my best friend, it's not as bad as I thought it would be. He looks peaceful. Jack's mum and dad chose to bury him in blue jeans and his favourite T-shirt—an old, scruffy superhero one we bought at Supanova one year. I have the same one, but I never wear it because I know it's his favourite. I might have to pull mine out and use it again, in honour of Jack, and the thought makes me smile.

I put one arm around Toni's shoulders, and she leans into me. She sniffles. I rest my cheek on the top of her head, closing my eyes, and that's when it all gets too much. Her shoulders shake as the tears roll down her cheeks and she turns into me, burying her face in my chest. I put my other arm around her and hug her. She grips a fist full of fabric from the back of my shirt, her sobs shaking through me. I cry with her, and for once, I don't care what everyone thinks, or if they're looking at us.

A hand touches my shoulder, and I open my eyes to see Jack's dad beside us. "You ready?"

I will never be ready, but I nod.

I help Toni back to her seat, not looking up into the crowd because right now, I can't meet anyone's eyes. And I don't want them to see the fear in mine. I'm scared I won't get through this, but I have to. For Jack.

My dad gets up and joins me, Jack's dad, and Toni's dad. The four of us wait as Mrs Marshall closes the lid of the coffin. We take our places and lift Jack until he rests on our shoulders. The casket is heavier than I expected, but this weight I will bear for him. If it meant he could come back, I would bear it a thousand times over.

We make our way out of the church. I pay no attention to what's going on around me. The people moving. The

voices murmuring. All I can concentrate on is making it to the hearse without falling and letting Jack down. When we reach the car, the four of us lower the casket, and slide it into the open back.

I step away, and Lian is at my side. I feel as if I need her to hold me up, and it takes all my strength to stop the tears. Everyone says to let it out, to grieve and cry and rant and scream, but I can't do that here. I won't. I realise now how strong Lian was at Violette's funeral yesterday. I'm glad I've been there for her, and I'm glad she's here with me now.

The driver closes the back of the hearse, and I jump at the reflection in the window. A pale, beautiful face surrounded by auburn wavy hair stares at me, translucent in the glass. My heart skips with a beat of fear at Nerezza's reflection. Her lips curl upwards, suggesting anything but happiness.

She can't be here. I saw the witches bind her again.

I turn and Toni is standing behind me. She crutches the last couple of steps to my side, and I look at the hearse again. Toni's sad face reflects back from where Nerezza's had been.

"What's the matter, Harvey?" Toni asks. "You look like you've seen a ghost."

"Maybe I have." I frown, and shove my hands deep into my pockets.

"What did you see?" Lian leans into me.

I shake my head. "Nothing. I thought I saw … It was … nothing."

But I don't think it was nothing. Now is not the time to be talking about crazy witches though. The hearse pulls slowly down the church drive leading to the street, and I stare at the darkened back window, waiting for her to appear again.

She doesn't.

Maybe it *was* nothing. Maybe I'm seeing things because I'm so stressed out. There are lots of maybes, and I have to stop myself from thinking up more.

"What now?" Lian rubs my arm.

"I don't know." I pull one hand from my pocket and put my arm around her.

The three of us stand in silence.

Toni rests on her crutches. The people around us slowly filter away towards their cars. Greg joins our small group and watches them with us, his mouth moving every now and then as if he has something to say but isn't sure how to say it.

"You okay, Harvey?" he finally asks.

I press my lips together, because I don't know if I am. "I guess. Maybe I will be. But I'm probably not ... now."

"You know what I think?" Toni says with fresh tears in her eyes. "I think the universe wouldn't have thrown all this crap at us if it didn't think we could handle it."

"Screw the universe," Lian says.

I pull her close and kiss her on the temple. I even manage a smile, because those three words are exactly what I need to hear.

ACKNOWLEDGEMENTS

They say it takes a village to raise a child—well, it takes a writers' group to raise a book. *The Lovely Dark* would never have been written without the support, brainstorming, and general awesomeness of the Story Queens. Selina, Serene, Rebecca, Lauren, Heather, Laura, Stacey, Bianca, and Ingrid. You are all amazing women, and I'm so privileged to be able to call you my writer family. Thank you. For all the things.

Special thanks to Selina, Serene, and Rebecca, for your time beta reading and your valuable feedback. You each brought something to *The Lovely Dark* that made it so much better.

Brendon, thank you for understanding how much I love writing, and giving me the space to live inside my head when I need to. My children, Emily and Jayden, I can't wait until you're old enough to read my books.

Thank you to my parents for your continued support and encouragement, and allowing me to take over the house with my make-shift office and boxes of books.

To my wonderful editor, Lauren Clarke, thank you, Lovely. Without you, my words are like dull rocks. You support and encourage me to polish them until they shine like diamonds.

Heather, thank you for your mad proofreading skills, I'm amazed at what you picked up after betas and edits. You're awesome!

Thank you, Cass, for your time and awesomeness. As always, your beta and proofreading are thorough, and thank you for making me LOL at your comments.

Lastly, dear reader, from the bottom of my heart I'm so grateful for you. Thank you for reading my books.

ABOUT THE AUTHOR

K. A. Last was born in Subiaco, Western Australia, and moved to Sydney when she was eight. Artistic and creative by nature, she studied Graphic Design and graduated with an Advanced Diploma. After marrying her high school sweetheart, she concentrated on her career before settling into family life. Blessed with a vivid imagination, K. A. Last began writing to let off creative steam, and fell in love with it. She has a Bachelor of Arts Degree from Charles Sturt University, with a major in English, and minors in Children's Literature, Art History, and Visual Culture. She now resides in the NSW countryside with her family and a menagerie of animals.

CONNECT WITH
K. A. LAST

Scan the code to subscribe to K. A. Last's newsletter.

Website www.kalastbooks.com.au
Facebook www.facebook.com/KALastBooks
Instagram www.instagram.com/kalastbooks
Pinterest www.pinterest.com/kalast
Goodreads www.goodreads.com/KALast
Twitter www.twitter.com/KALastBooks

Books by K. A. Last

YA Fantasy Fiction
Sacrifice – A Fall For Me Prequel
Fall For Me (The Tate Chronicles, #1)
Fight For Me (The Tate Chronicles, #2)
Die For Me (The Tate Chronicles, #3)
Immagica
The Lovely Dark
Ella and Ash (Happily Ever After, #1)
Chasing Neve (Happily Ever After, #2)
False Princess (Happily Ever After, #3)
Dance of Wishes (Happily Ever After, #4)
Winter Flame (Happily Ever After, #5)

YA Contemporary Fiction
Something (All the Things: part one)
Nothing (All the Things: part two)
Everything (All the Things: part three)
The Other Side of Me (All the Things: part four)

Non-fiction
A Novel Idea! Colouring Journal for Writers
A Novel Idea Workbook for Writers